Still Waters

Still Waters

Crime Stories
by
New England Writers

Edited by

Kate Flora

Ruth McCarty

Susan Oleksiw

LEVEL BEST BOOKS
PRIDES CROSSING, MASSACHUSETTS 01965

Level Best Books
P.O. Box 161
Prides Crossing, Massachusetts 01965
www.levelbestbooks.com

text composition/design by Susan Oleksiw
Printed in the USA

ISBN 978-0-9700984-4-3

Library of Congress Catalog Card Data available.
First Edition
10 9 8 7 6 5 4 3 2 1

Still Waters

Contents

Introduction

It is hard to believe that we have produced, and you are beginning to read, our fifth Level Best Books crime story anthology, *Still Waters*. When we began in 2002, the crime anthology was going to be a one-time thing—a single collection taking our long-desired snapshot of the New England crime scene through the eyes of the region's own writers. We talked at length over lunch about how important it was to give new writers and little-known writers a better chance at finding a readership. All we thought about was that one collection.

It was our writers who seduced us into doing a second book. We found ourselves fascinated by the stories they had to tell and by the impressive quality of their writing. There were so many good stories that needed to be shared, so many good writers who needed to be introduced to readers. Through their exciting fiction, we discover our contributors' unique voices as we are taken into their world, following their compelling characters through the cities, towns, and back roads of New England and beyond, into the hard patches and the moments of decision that will resonate throughout their lives.

As editors, we are genuinely honored that so many writers are willing to share their fine work with us. There is true excitement in that moment when we each get our packet of stories and begin to read, an excitement that doesn't abate despite the dozens of stories. There is always a fresh voice, an intriguing character, a surprising situation, an ending that leaves us breathless with surprise or stunned by truth or tragedy. There is the pleasure of seeing another fine story from a writer we've published before. The gem from an unpublished author who can be our discovery. The rejected story that comes back rewritten and irresistible. The delight all writers take in seeing a colleague's writing grow stronger and better.

As writers ourselves, we agree that one of our greatest pleasures is being able to offer our authors a group signing event at the New England Crime Bake, the annual mystery conference at which our yearly anthologies are introduced. Signings are a rare thing for short story authors. Signings with a line of twenty or thirty readers waiting eagerly for a story are almost unheard of. Watching their faces as they hold the books, sign the books, and accept the congratulations of fellow authors, we feel a little like proud parents. Here the proud parents of more than twenty adult children.

Which is another reason we keep publishing our anthologies: we believe in writers. These collections allow us to publish good writers and help them find an audience. In a world of ever-shrinking publishing opportunities, we have published ninety-nine stories that readers otherwise would not have had a chance to enjoy. We have published stories by award-winning authors, by authors who have published over five hundred stories, and by authors who have never before submitted a story. Our stories have been nominated for and received awards.

In this collection, you will find a story by Margaret Press offering another view of the murder in "Feral," which appeared in a previous collection. Kevin Carey, whose first story we had the pleasure of publishing, leads a crazy romp through Provincetown with a most unusual detective. Leslie Woods captures the anguish of a man trying to be true to himself, and Louy Castonguay records the delicate change in character of a self-satisfied woman confronted with a very different sort. Rosemary Harris's protagonist grows in other ways. Leslie Wheeler explores subtle ethical questions, and Leslie Schultz presents an ethical dilemma that will linger in the reader's mind for many days.

Janice Law once again takes us into a dark mind, and Stephen Liskow introduces us to a young couple struggling to adjust to a new stage in their marriage. The reader looking for humor wry or hilarious will find plenty in the stories by Glenda Baker, Ang Pompano, Mike Wiecek, and Mo Walsh.

Almost everyone will feel a certain satisfaction at the ending of Jim Shannon's story, and a guilty wish that life might be like this.

We have more great stories by Level Best regulars S.A. Daynard, Judith Green, and Stephen Rogers, and a stunning debut by Mark Ammons and this year's Al Blanchard award-winning story. Join us for another journey through the writing minds of New England.

Kate Flora
Ruth McCarty
Susan Oleksiw

Mercy 101

Pat Remick

The space beside him was cold. He rolled over and flicked on the light.

The clock read 3:30 A.M. He strained to hear the sound of the television coming from downstairs. Just the quiet ticking of the grandfather clock. Not even the cat was stirring. Jenny was away at college. Jack lived in New York with his new wife.

He was alone.

He turned off the bedside lamp and lay rigid in the dark, listening to the silence. It gave him no peace. It was that way in the daylight, too—dark and silent. And without peace.

But he knew where she had gone. The same place she went every night. Driving endless miles along New Hampshire Route 101. Her destination was a place where pain could not reach.

It had been this way for three months, two weeks, and three nights. It would be this way again tomorrow. She would return after daybreak. The tires would crawl across the gravel driveway at exactly 7:25 A.M.

The sound woke him. He was surprised that he had actually slept for a few hours. Most nights he just lay in the dark, thinking, worrying, waiting for her return.

He dressed and went downstairs. She was sitting at the scarred wooden kitchen table. Staring out the window, seeing nothing.

Steam coming from the red coffee cup in front of her, traces of wet sand on her battered sneakers.

He walked into their once cheery kitchen. "How are you?"

"Fine." She did not look at him.

"Did you stop at the beach?" He moved past her to the coffee pot.

"Yes."

He poured hot coffee into his cracked World's Greatest Dad mug. "See anyone last night?"

"Kristin." She picked up her cup and took a sip.

He sat down across from her. "Working?"

"On break. I stopped for coffee." She gazed out the window again.

"What did she have to say?"

"Not much. She got called out right away. A couple of guys off the road, probably drunk or high."

"Dead?"

"Maybe. Mass plates."

"She say anything else?"

"She misses him."

"Me, too." He looked away.

She stood and walked to the sink, filled with dirty dishes. She found an opening in the jumble of plates and glasses, and emptied her cup.

"I need to sleep."

"Of course." He said it automatically, without emotion, without judgment.

He watched her climb the stairs. She would stay there until late afternoon, sometimes sleeping but mostly tossing and turning. When she'd come back down, she'd move silently through the house in her socks and a well-worn sweatsuit, her partially gray hair tied back. The woman who had been his vibrant and impeccably dressed wife had been replaced by an empty shell. Eventually she would slide into her favorite armchair and stare at the television for hours.

Sometimes it was even turned on.

He would make supper. They ate in silence in front of the nightly news. Then he moved to the living room to read. But she preferred to remain surrounded by the sitcom laughter and commercials. At ten, she'd go upstairs again, change into a sweatshirt and blue jeans and lie down in bed, eyes closed. He'd kiss her goodnight when he came to bed after the eleven o'clock news. She never responded. But it was the only time she let him touch her.

Then the cycle resumed. He would fall asleep, then wake up to find her gone. He didn't worry anymore about her driving alone. But winter would soon be here and the weather could complicate her nightly journeys. Tomorrow he would try to persuade her to stop.

The next morning, he found her in the kitchen again. She was looking out the bay window into the backyard, a cup of coffee in her hand and a slight smile on her face. The morning newspaper was on the table.

He wondered if she was reliving a happy memory. She turned and for the first time in three months spoke first. "Good morning."

"You look happy. Good night?" He moved toward her. She stiffened, then raised her cup as if to shield herself.

"Not really."

He sat down and picked up the newspaper. He could make out the word "Gangstas" on the Massachusetts license plate of the mangled Dodge Intrepid. The headline over the photograph read "Teens Killed, Speed Suspected."

"Isn't this the wreck Kristin got called out on the other night? Looks like her in the corner of the picture."

She moved closer to the table. "I didn't notice." She bent to read the story. "They were from Lowell. Probably drug dealers if they were on 101 that time of night. Not exactly a big loss to society." She moved to refill her cup.

He was surprised by how cavalier she seemed. "They had mothers and fathers, too, you know," he said quietly.

Her face turned red and her eyes flashed with anger. She opened her mouth but quickly closed it.

"Say it, Janice. For God's sake, just say it."

She gulped, shook her head and rushed by him toward the stairs. It was the most emotion she had shown in months. He wanted it to continue. He wished she would yell, scream, even hit him.

Again, nothing.

He wasn't sure how much longer this could go on before he was the one doing the yelling, or leaving. He grabbed his book and sweater, and marched onto the screened porch. Maybe fresh air would help. His home had become a mausoleum and the air was stifling. He needed space, to breathe. But he was afraid to leave her alone for very long.

He put down the book and gazed into the backyard. It hurt to look. Too many memories. He could see them laughing, sweaty and dirty as they tumbled over each other like puppies. His three beautiful children had grown up well. Made him proud. As young adults, their playfulness moved from the yard onto the porch, where they shared stories and their new lives.

With his firstborn, Jimmy, that meant drinking coffee together after he ravished the hot breakfast his mother had waiting precisely at 7:25 A.M. She poured his juice when she heard his tires roll across the gravel. His arrival each morning was reassurance that his shift had ended safely. Breakfast together also helped Jimmy decompress before heading to his new apartment to sleep.

But the morning ritual ended when Trooper James Gardner, Jr., was killed as he returned to his patrol car after a routine traffic stop on Route 101. The investigators concluded it was a hit-and-run accident.

There had been no comfort in hearing that Jimmy died in the line of duty, doing what he loved. The pomp and circumstance of his funeral didn't help. Nor could the nearly one thousand somber law enforcement personnel who came from across New England to pay their respects, or the heartfelt remarks of the governor, remotely ease their pain.

Jimmy's death devastated them all, but in different ways. Jenny returned to college, her youthful optimism gone. At first, she came home on weekends, seeking comfort and a place to talk about her brother. She didn't find it. It soon became clear that her mother couldn't look at a living child without thinking of her dead one. It was easier for everyone if Jenny stayed at school. She called frequently but spoke only to him. Janice hadn't touched a telephone since Jimmy's death.

Jack used email to stay in contact from New York. There was little substance in the daily messages, but their youngest son ached, too. Janice also wouldn't use the computer, so he printed out Jack's emails and left them on the kitchen table. He would find them later in the trash, ripped into tiny fragments.

It seemed as though he had lost not only his son, but all of his children. He also had lost the woman who had been his wife. Anguish had turned the two of them into little more than shadows moving between light and dark, day and night. He prayed every day for an end to the cycle of sorrow. He knew his only hope for survival was accepting that a terrible accident had taken his son's life.

In the old days, he would have found comfort in a glass. But Jimmy's death had made him vow never to drink again. Still, each night he took the bottle of bourbon down from the cupboard and stared at it in the dark until he found the strength to put it back.

Mercy was his only way out of this hell. But he knew Janice could never forgive the driver who killed their son. She sought solace on Route 101. He wondered if she drove only the portion Jimmy patrolled or the entire ninety-five miles stretching from western New Hampshire through Manchester, the state's largest city, all the way to the ocean at Hampton Beach.

In the days after Jimmy died, Kristin and the other troopers contacted him whenever they spotted her Taurus sedan in the early morning hours. It was difficult to miss the "JJJJJ-G" license plate, or forget that now there was one less Gardner with a first name beginning with J. The troopers were concerned. Not that she drove alone along deserted stretches of highway, but that she might believe it could bring her closer to Jimmy.

They had no reason to stop her. She drove the speed limit. She wasn't intoxicated. She had the right to drive anywhere she wanted. So they simply flashed their headlights in greeting. They knew she would eventually find her way to Al's Diner, as Jimmy always had, and they would try to take their breaks with her if things were quiet. Kristin had told him it was heartbreaking to see Janice sitting alone at the counter as if she were waiting for Jimmy. Her face would light up when she saw a trooper's forest green and khaki knife-creased uniform, but sadness too quickly returned.

Kristin said the troopers would tell Janice about the shift or a funny story about Jimmy. Tears ran down her cheeks while the trooper pretended not to notice. Although she never asked, they knew she wanted to hear that the driver had been found. They were relieved they didn't have to tell her the investigation had gone cold.

Sometimes a trooper spent an entire break with Janice. But all too often, the trooper's radio crackled with news of an accident or erratic driving to investigate. Early on, the troopers tried to hug her goodbye. But it made her so uncomfortable that now they gently patted her arm or didn't touch her at all.

No one could keep so much grief inside forever. He wondered if she would ever break—or just continue to shrivel until she faded away.

Their brief exchanges and routines of grief had resumed. She seemed to have forgotten her anger over his comment about the dead teenagers having parents. The next morning he would broach his concerns about the unpredictable weather that would follow winter's arrival.

It was after eight when she got home. He could see through the bay window that there was a hint of buoyancy in her step as she moved toward the house. He even thought he heard humming as she unlocked the door. She looked startled to see him already at the table. "Oh, you're up," she said.

"How was your night?"

"Fine." She moved toward the coffee pot.

"Anything happen?" He watched her slowly fill her cup. Grief had deepened the lines on her face.

"Actually, yes." She opened the refrigerator and pulled out the cream. "A Nissan Maxima went off the road into Miller's Creek. I saw it in the rearview mirror after they honked at me."

"What did you do?"

She poured the cream into her cup. "I drove to Troop A to tell them. They called in the dive team but it was too late."

"How many?"

"Three guys in their twenties. Car had New Hampshire plates, registered in Milford." She stirred her coffee.

"That's the second fatal in two weeks in Troop A's district. Headquarters won't be happy." He looked past her into the backyard. The trees were losing their leaves.

"Everyone speeds on 101. They were probably drunk the way they were driving." She sipped her coffee.

"That's why I don't like you out there all night. And I'm worried about winter coming."

She got up and put two slices of bread into the toaster. "I had to give a statement."

"Who took it?"

"The rookie, Sousa. Had the nerve to ask me how I knew it was a Maxima in the dark."

"What did you say?"

"I told him that if everyone in law enforcement can learn to identify headlights in the dark, so can the mothers who help them practice. He knew I was upset so he changed the subject. Said if you wanted to sell the Wrangler, he'd buy it."

"Maybe I should."

There it was again: anger, almost outrage. She shook her head vigorously. Her eyes welled up. She rushed toward the stairs. "I need sleep."

"Of course."

He heard the bedroom door slam. Maybe she wasn't dead after all.

The Wrangler was stored in an old shed on the edge of his neighbor's farm. Jimmy had found the beat-up and rusted 1989 Jeep at an estate sale five years earlier and persuaded his father it would be a great retirement project to restore the junker together.

It became far more expensive and time-consuming than they'd anticipated. But he never regretted a single dollar or hour. The night he finished repainting it, he'd wanted to celebrate and surprise Jimmy. Now, he wasn't sure he could look at it again.

The evening news briefly mentioned a 101 accident had killed three unidentified men in their twenties. He suspected the story might have been longer if a news crew had videotaped the divers removing the bodies.

The newspaper account the next morning was more detailed. Fingerprints proved the victims were ex-cons. The story said an unnamed motorist had alerted State Police to the accident, and speed and alcohol were likely involved.

He was grateful Troop A hadn't revealed Janice's name. It might destroy her to be identified as "the mother of Trooper James

Gardner, who died in a tragic, unsolved hit-and-run accident in the same deserted area."

Jenny was coming home for the long Columbus Day weekend. He looked forward to having a conversation that was more than a few words long. God knows he had tried to reach Janice. But she pushed everyone away. He had suggested counseling or a support group, but she refused. He didn't know how much longer he could wait.

He felt so alone. Their friends no longer called or came by. Acquaintances acted as though their loss was contagious or pretended nothing had happened. He wasn't sure which was worse. Only the troopers stayed in touch.

But hadn't Janice seemed a little better lately? At least she was showing anger. And wasn't she humming that morning? Things might continue to improve with Jenny home.

But nothing changed. Janice still disappeared at night, slept through the day and seemed to sleepwalk through the evening. Jenny tried to make conversation, but Janice responded with one-word answers.

"Dad, what are we going to do?" Jenny pleaded after Janice went upstairs at 10:00 P.M. "Is she still going out every night?"

"She leaves after I fall asleep, I'd guess around midnight. She comes home at 7:25, just like your brother used to."

"Where does she go? 101 is less than a hundred miles long. Even if she drives from one end to the other and back, there's no traffic. It can't take more than four hours, tops."

"She stops at Al's. The troopers see her there. I think she also walks on the beach. I've seen sand on her shoes."

"Don't you ask?"

"Of course I ask, Jenny. She won't talk to me. But the doctor says as long as she's not hurting herself, or anyone else, we have to let her work it out."

"Maybe we should follow her to see where she goes."

"I know where she goes. I think it makes her feel closer to Jimmy to be on 101." He put his arm around Jenny's thin shoulders, trying to comfort her as much as himself.

"I want my mother back," Jenny sobbed.

"So do I, honey. But this is going to take time, lots of time."

They were waiting at the kitchen table when Janice returned the next morning. "Hi, Mom. Where were you?"

Janice stared at her, then moved to the coffee pot. "Driving," she said, her back to them.

"But where did you drive, Mom?"

"Nowhere. I saw Kristin at Al's. She says hi."

"I'd like to see her. Can I come with you tonight?"

"No." She put down her coffee cup and stomped out of the kitchen and up the stairs.

Jenny's lower lip quivered. "Dad, I'm sorry. I can't do this. I need to get back to school so I can focus."

With Jenny gone, the house turned desolate again. He had to get out. Maybe do some grocery shopping, although Janice barely ate. He would put gas in her car. It was the least he could do. Most gas stations were closed during the hours she traveled 101.

As the gas flowed into the tank, he moved around the car to wash the windows. There was something on the front bumper. It looked like blue paint and a small dent. He scraped the color off with his fingernails. Strange, she hadn't mentioned hitting anything.

During supper, he asked her about it.

"Maybe someone hit me when I was at Al's or parked at the beach." She continued eating.

"What do you do at the beach anyway?"

She took a drink of water. "Sometimes I walk. Sometimes I sleep in the car. Is that a problem?" She turned back to the evening news.

"No. I was just worried that you might have hit something."

The next morning she burst into the kitchen. Her agitation unnerved him.

She also looked directly at him for the first time in weeks. "A Ford Escort tailgated me for miles, flashing the high beams. They flipped me off and threw beer cans at the car when they finally passed me. Bunch of teenagers in a beater car."

He had forgotten how beautiful her eyes were. "Did they hit you?"

"I swerved." She sat down and rubbed her temples. "Remember how Jimmy always said that people who couldn't take care of their cars rarely took care of their lives? He could, but now he's gone. But a bunch of low-life dropouts can be out there terrorizing people. It's just not fair."

It was the most she had said in months. Maybe she was getting better. He reached for her hand. "But life isn't fair. We already know that."

She pulled away and stood. He thought she might cry, but she turned away. "I need sleep."

"Of course."

According to the noon news, a 1992 red Ford Escort carrying three teenaged boys and two girls from Manchester had slammed into a bank of trees near Epping around 4:00 A.M. Troop A Commander Bill Edwards reported that none of the victims was wearing seatbelts and beer cans were found in the wreckage. He suggested speed and alcohol were to blame, but asked the public to call with any information.

The news video also showed grieving young people with multiple tattoos and piercings leaving remembrances at the crash site. "We was partying, man, and they wanted to see the sun rise at the beach." A girl with black lipstick and spiked hair sniffled into the camera.

He believed the investigating officers would want to know that

Janice had encountered the Escort before it crashed. She lay on her side facing the wall of their darkened bedroom, snoring lightly. He gently shook her shoulder.

"Janice, wake up. Those kids in the Escort, they're dead. Commander Edwards is asking for the public's help. You have to tell them what you saw."

"I didn't see anything," she mumbled.

"You saw them before the wreck. Maybe you can help the investigation." She was groggy but he persisted. "You must have driven right by the accident. Didn't you see anything?"

"No. Please, let me sleep."

He went downstairs and stared at the telephone. He didn't want to upset Janice, but Jimmy would have told them to call. He punched in the number for dispatch.

An hour later, the phone rang. He told Patrolman Sousa about Janice's road rage encounter with the Escort. "She'll be mad that I called. But I knew you'd want to know."

"We're getting a lot of heat from the public about all the accidents on 101 so I hope we can wrap this up quickly," Sousa said. "We got a report from a trucker who says they harassed him, too, and he saw them tailgating a mini-Cooper and maybe a Jeep. We're hoping those drivers will come forward."

"Janice was pretty upset when she got home this morning."

"I didn't realize she was out last night. Hey, Mr. Gardner, speaking of Jeeps, I told Mrs. Gardner a couple of weeks ago that if you want to sell the Wrangler, I'd love to buy it. I know it's in pristine condition."

"I wouldn't even know how much to ask."

"Tell you what, I'll give you Blue Book value, okay?"

It wouldn't hurt to see what it was worth. But he needed to know the exact mileage in order to get an accurate estimate from the Blue Book web site. He decided to drive her car so he could fill it with gas on the way. But to his surprise, the tank was still three-quarters full so he drove directly to the shed. His hands trembled as he unlocked the peeling wood door.

He took a deep breath. The door opened with a creak as always, but it still made him jump. He felt his knees weaken when he saw the Jeep. The memory of the last time he saw Jimmy alive seared his brain. He felt sick.

He didn't bother to turn on the light. He slid into the front seat and turned the key. It purred to life. They had done good work. He was surprised that the mileage read 78,714. He thought it was lower, but so much had happened that he was unsure of anything anymore.

He turned off the ignition and opened the door. The car light flashed on just long enough for him to notice the clumps of something almost white on the floor. He reached down.

It was beach sand.

Someone had been in their Wrangler. He opened the glove compartment and unfolded the bill of sale. It showed the mileage as 77,659. He and Jimmy had probably added another forty miles or so. Who had driven the other thousand miles?

The shed was locked. Only he and Jimmy had keys. All of Jimmy's keys had been given to them after the accident. That meant someone had taken a key to the shed from the house.

It had to be Janice. But why? Was the Wrangler another place where she felt closer to Jimmy?

He backed the Jeep out of the shed into the daylight. He wasn't sure what he was looking for, but then he saw the dented front bumper. It was streaked with traces of red.

He sank to his knees. This couldn't be happening. Janice had barely shown any emotion for months. Surely she was too grief-stricken to find enough rage to force the red Escort off the road for tailgating. She had been upset when she came home, but upset enough to kill someone?

Maybe she had hit something again and not realized it. His mind raced. There had been three fatal accidents during the time she was driving on 101. Ten people were dead. But people drove too fast on that highway. There were lots of wrecks that weren't fatal, especially recently. Still, the governor had demanded increased patrols.

Even if Janice was responsible for the ten deaths, each victim probably would have come to a bad end eventually. And they might have hurt innocent people along the way.

Maybe Janice, or someone else, had done the world a favor.

Even if the investigators found out about the paint and dents on the fenders, they would never suspect a grief-stricken mother. If they did, she could plead temporary insanity from her beloved son's death.

He had to know if sorrow truly had stolen her sanity.

First, he had to stop her from using the Jeep. He would say he replaced the lock because it looked like someone had tried to break into the shed and he wanted to keep the Jeep safe while he decided what to do with it. He would hide the key from her.

He needed a rental car so he could follow her. She recognized headlights too well for his truck to remain undetected. He would sleep on the couch while she spent the day upstairs in bed, and she would never suspect that he, too, had been on 101 all night.

For the next two weeks, he pretended to sleep when she left at night. He sprinted down the block to the elementary school where the rental car was out of sight in a rear lot. Within minutes, he also was driving east on 101.

The most difficult part was not catching up to her. She drove the speed limit, but he tended to push it by ten miles per hour, or more, which might close the gap.

When she stopped at Al's, he drove to the all-night gas station at the next exit to watch for her car to go by en route to Hampton Beach. He followed until she parked at the beach. Then he rushed home to change clothes and pretend to be rested when she returned at 7:25.

He was beginning to think he was the one who was crazy. If nothing unusual happened tonight, he would stop following her.

Traffic was light as he steered the rental car onto 101, cranked up the radio and cracked open a window to stay awake. The route was tedious. He didn't understand how Janice could drive it the same way every night.

They were on their way back from Keene and had just rolled through Manchester when he realized he was gaining too quickly on her Taurus. He slowed and moved into the lane behind her. Fifteen minutes and a mind-numbing radio commentary later, he realized he had lost sight of her. He sped up but there was no sign of the Taurus ahead of him, or broken down along the shoulder.

When he neared the exit for Al's, he decided to risk detection and check the parking lot for her car. It wasn't there. He quickly turned around and headed back onto 101. Maybe she had decided to forego Al's to head directly to the beach. He sped up. He had almost reached the bridge before the Exeter exit when he was nearly blinded by the headlights looming in his rearview mirror. A vehicle was approaching quickly.

He hit the accelerator and switched lanes. The headlights followed, becoming brighter by the second. He swerved back into the right lane and pumped his brakes, trying to get the vehicle to back off. It didn't. He sped up again. The vehicle followed. They were going at least eighty. He desperately hoped someone would stop them for speeding—and soon.

He kept changing lanes, but the vehicle followed. It made no attempt to pass him. He felt a thud, and then another. The vehicle was hitting his car on purpose. He panicked. Maybe the same vehicle had pushed Janice off the highway earlier.

He jerked the steering wheel to the right, bounced off the

guardrail and then steered to the left. The vehicle hit him again, only harder. He heard metal crumple as he pulled the car back into the right lane. Miller's Creek was ahead. He might be forced off the road into the water unless he reached the bridge first. He accelerated again and heard a roar as the other vehicle pulled beside him. He looked over.

It was Janice.

The bridge lights provided just enough illumination to see the shock on her face before she accelerated and pulled into the lane in front of him. It happened too quickly for him to avoid slamming into the Taurus. He watched helplessly as his wife's car seemed to gather speed seconds before it flew through the guardrail and plunged into the creek.

He screeched to a stop. She had driven into the creek on purpose. If she had not died on impact, she would drown before he could reach her.

Her anguish was over. But his torment would continue.

The rental car would raise suspicions. Troopers would wonder why he was stalking his own wife along deserted portions of 101. They would know he hit the Taurus.

Eventually they would find the Jeep and match the paint on the bumper to the Escort. He might be charged with killing the five teenagers. That could be enough to reopen the investigations into the other accidents, as well. He could be charged in five more deaths. The accusations might not stop there.

He couldn't bear it if they learned the truth.

There had been enough blame. He would end it now. He backed up the rental car, shifted into drive, jammed his foot into the gas pedal and drove straight through the gap in the guardrail into the creek.

He wasn't afraid. His nightmare would end. No one would ever have to know he was drunk when the Jeep struck and killed his son.

The Catch

Mark Ammons

Michael Sean Figgis—"Fig," as in "go figure," to all who knew him—cursed his uniformly bad luck the moment he spotted them deep in the gloomy half-light below. Who were they and what the hell were they doing in his sewer?

As a duly appointed agent of the MWRA—officially the Massachusetts Water Resource Authority, unofficially the "Male Workers Relaxation Association" to all who knew it—Fig was suddenly faced with the unique task of actually having to do something. And on a Friday afternoon, no less.

Fig choked down the wad of coconut cruller he'd been worshiping and hooted a "Hey you!" to the dim figures in the chamber beneath him. He got nothing back. Yanking a monkey wrench from his belt, he raked the tool across the steel grid at his feet and hallooed again. And again, he received zip for his effort. But it wasn't all bad news.

At least whoever was down there didn't scurry for cover. That probably ruled out terrorists unless they were some new extrasneakily nonsneaky variety. With a heave of disgust, Fig popped the lock on the heavy security grate and began his long descent into the catch basin.

As he dropped off the ladder and turned to roust the interlopers,

Fig stopped in his tracks. His hand leapt to his chest and squared his holographically festooned ID badge as though that small symbol of authority might restore some semblance of order to the situation. Neither dog nor dead man seemed impressed.

The mutt was a mess. Like some mutant growth, a sea of mange werewolfed across his tattered ears and down the ridge of his scrawny neck until it reached haunches that were no more than skin and bones. But it was the gawky brute's eyes that nailed Fig. One unmoving orb superglued everything in its path—Fig included—while the other pinballed wildly as if following a mixed-triples Chinese Ping-Pong match.

No question about it, this four-legged train wreck was a stone-cold starving disaster. But not as stone cold as the dead man stretched out beside him on a cheap plastic pool lounger.

The homeless guy was the picture of perfect repose. Easily in his eighties, he reclined there in frayed trousers and a tattered Hawaiian shirt with feet casually crossed, a newspaper folded in his lap, and a pen still poised above it in his gnarled fingers. His dead but wide-open eyes gazed upward in seeming search of an elusive thought.

"Shit," Fig muttered. He already had enough problems and did-n't need one more. Besides, he had fifty bucks riding on that night's Red Sox-Yankees game and, as befitted the unholy ring of all things superstitious surrounding baseball, Fig never-ever-ever won on a game if he failed to make it home to his TV for the first pitch. Excluding the usual flotilla of drowned rats, the biggest corpse Fig had stumbled on in all his thirty years of sewer work had been a pizza-sized pancaked skunk. So it didn't take an Einstein to know this unfortunate turn of events would mean lots of questions and endless forms to fill out. The regulations were clear—any hint of a criminal act required reporting. It was a sure bet a full-sized dead body fit that bill. He could kiss his fifty goodbye and probably the whole three-game weekend series for that matter.

"Shit-shit-SHI-I-I-T!" This time Fig didn't mutter. His voice caromed around the vast chamber. But, at a full forty feet beneath Boston's massive Big Dig tunnel, and with an additional fifty feet and sixteen billion dollars of sloppily poured concrete between Fig and the streets above, only his echo could hear him.

His echo and the mutt, that is. For his part, the mutt loyally held his post beside the man, not even flinching at Fig's bellow. Instead, his orbiting eyeball steadied for a long moment as he seemed to give Fig a mournful shrug of agreement. Shit, indeed.

"You got it, pal," Fig confirmed as he flipped over a plastic bucket left behind by the last construction crew passing through. His fluorescent orange hip-waders squeaked loudly as he plopped down on the bucket and faced his new companions. "Any of you guys terrorists?" Fig inquired, "'Cuz if you are, you gotta leave."

Getting no reply, Fig continued for his own benefit, almost enjoying the singing-in-the-shower resonance the huge cement vault gave his reedy voice. "I knew that Homeland Security jerk would be a pain the minute he waddled through the door and zeroed in on me."

Talking to himself was one of the better fringe benefits of sewer work. There was nothing to stop him from doing it at home, either. Not now. So he talked. A lot.

He talked to his TV. He talked to his dripping toilet that he'd never been able to fix. When the spirit moved him, he even talked to his food. But, then, didn't everybody?

"Homeland Security, my ass. Whiny little runt. You should've heard him, 'Check the catch basins, a sleeper cell could be hiding there.' Oooooooo! Be afraid, very afraid. Yeah, well, if Osama is down here he's the one who should be afraid—afraid this whole goddamned gazillion dollar joke will cave in on him if someone slams a door too hard."

The dog peered curiously at Fig. Fig shifted on his bucket. Maybe talking to himself in the presence of strangers wasn't such a hot idea. Avoiding the mutt's gaze, Fig rocked back and surveyed the towering gray walls of the concrete chamber bathed in the even grayer work lights beyond the high grid above.

It really was one amazing catch basin. Big enough to play full-court basketball. You could almost drive a Winnebago down its gargantuan inlet pipe alone. Not like those dinky street-level basins designed to capture litter and junk before sending rainwater off to the cold Atlantic.

Same idea, though—an inlet pipe, a deep vat with a grated ceiling capping it to catch any floating debris and keep it in the chamber as the water rose, then an outlet pipe directly above the grate to carry off the screened overflow.

Fig gestured to the ominous space and once more addressed his companions, this time with the gusto of that guy he'd always hear in the movie previews. "Biggest public works project in history. Miles of superhighway shoved under a crumbling city. Some said it couldn't be done. They should've said it'd never be finished. But hey, job security!" Fig was warming to the moment. "But fancy as it is, this dump still needs a garbage disposal. Behold the lint filter of the Big Dig, my friends, capable of holding hundreds of thousands of gallons. Which it'll probably have to do if those damn slurry walls up there keep springing leaks."

Fig lit a cigarette. So what if the dog's eyeball had started randomly ponging again, it was good to have someone to talk to.

"So, how'd you guys get in here?" But Fig had a bad feeling he already knew. A life spent underground had taught him long ago that any unoccupied dry spots beneath a city—unused subway spurs, utility tunnels, abandoned subbasements, you name it—were fair game for the homeless. They always found a way to slip in, dragging their meager households behind.

These guys were a perfect example. Besides the usual rag bag of provisions, now fully spent, the geezer had managed to lug in his poor man's La-Z-Boy, a milk crate as a side table, a tall pile of old newspapers, which he'd stacked upon it, and a case of Alpo scrounged from somewhere. He'd even brought in a shiny stainless steel doggie bowl.

This unlucky pair was also a perfect example of what could go wrong. The danger in going underground was if things suddenly changed—if the building over your subbasement abode went under a wrecking ball at dawn, if a switch failed and a train made a wrong turn down your sleeping spur. This duo had probably cruised merrily down the mammoth inlet pipe from one of the many temporary construction entries dotting the streets above only to become trapped when the hatches were welded shut. They might have tried to get out by climbing the forty-foot service ladder through the hinged grate Fig had entered by. But the grate had been padlocked. Fig knew, because he'd unlocked it on his way in.

So, there you had it. Trapped for who knew how long, starvation had taken the old guy with the mutt not far behind. While Fig couldn't say for sure, from the way the empty tins were stacked neatly beside the doggie bowl against the far wall, it looked like all the Alpo had gone to the dog, maybe long after the old guy's own grub had run out. Whatever had happened, one thing was certain—all that was keeping the mutt going now was the trickle of seepage from somewhere high above pooling near the center of the chamber.

Not that anything would have made a bit of difference for either of them if Fig hadn't come along. In less than twenty-four hours this whole shebang was scheduled to come on line; the lights would go out and sluices would be opened. With the first summer storm, a wall of water was on its way. They'd have been goners anyway.

Fig stubbed out his cigarette and considered his predicament. So what if he'd figured out what had happened, nobody was going to give him a commendation for playing Sherlock of the sewers. They'd still merrily fry his butt if he didn't call it in right away.

Fig pulled out his walkie-talkie and turned it on. An eerie crackle filled the space. Cheap piece of crap. Good enough for govern-
ment work they'd told him, meaning good enough for someone like
him. Fig took a deep breath and fidgeted with the send button.
Suddenly, the crackle became a lethal hiss all too much like the static he'd sometimes hear late at night deep in his brain. Fig thrust the
unit aside.

Screw it. He owed it to himself to at least snatch at a few straws.
Maybe he'd jumped to conclusions. Maybe the mutt was naturally a
bag of bones. Maybe the geezer wasn't really dead. Maybe he was
just catatonic or cataleptic or catalytic or one of those other bizarro
things he'd seen on the Discovery Channel. Right, and maybe the
Sox would win another World Series in his lifetime.

Nonetheless, he'd take his best shot. Fig rose and approached
the old man. The mutt somberly maintained his sentry at his master's
right hand without a hint of threat.

Adopting a similar posture at the codger's other elbow, Fig and
the mutt stood there a second like mismatched temple dogs. Fig took
a cautionary sniff. No odor. A good sign. Fig leaned close to the old
man's ear. "Hey, Buddy, you okay?" As if on command, the mutt
leaned into his master's other ear and offered a soft, moaning howl.
Neither got a response. No blink of the old guy's open, questioning
eyes, no quiver, nothing. Another "Hey, Buddy," another howl . . .
another empty echo.

Fig knew what he had to do next, not that he was looking forward to it. He'd touched death in Vietnam—come to think of it,
maybe that was when he'd started talking to himself—but somehow
this was different, gentler, scarier.

He sucked it up. "What's the big deal? You've handled lots of
weird stuff in these cesspools." As it often had, the sound of his own
voice summoned courage. He reached out, grasped the man's shoulder, and shook. Nothing stirred except for the codger's pen, which

tumbled from his fingers and rolled across the floor.

Fig retreated to his bucket and slumped, head in hands. He was back at "Go." Every rule in the book required him to report this. If he didn't and got caught, he'd lose his job for sure. "Hell, if that psycho turd from Homeland has his way I'll end up in Guantanamo singing 'Danny Boy' in Farsi."

But if he did report it, more than his lousy fifty bucks was at stake. The boys in blue would swoop in with the white coats hot on their tails. By the next morning some snot-nosed junior coroner jockeying for extra credit would flop the coot on a slab. He'd whip out his bone saw to practice his swing on every nook and cranny of the poor bastard then dump what was left in the incinerator. Three days later, with no one to claim the mutt either, Animal Control would do pretty much the same to just one more abandoned pooch. Fig knew, because Fig could all too easily imagine the ultimate end of his own tunnel.

Something nudged Fig's leg. He jerked upright. The emaciated mutt sat at his knee with the old man's pen in his mouth. His good eye pleaded.

Fig sighed. "Great, let's play fetch. That'll fix everything." Plucking the pen from the big lunk's teeth, Fig sailed it across the chamber. With an unsteady gait the mutt tracked down the pen, seized it in his yellow maw and immediately shambled back to Fig. "One more time, Tiger?" Fig reached for the pen. But this time the mutt held onto it, firmly but without menace. Fig gave another small tug. The dog tugged back with what had to be the final shreds of his waning vigor as though trying to drag Fig up off the bucket.

"What? What?" Now the dog's orbiting eye also steadied and pleaded as well. Hanging onto one end of the pen, Fig rose and followed as the mutt led him over to the old man. When they arrived, the dog released the pen to Fig then poked his wet nose into the newspaper in his master's lap.

Fig peered down at it. The paper was folded open to the *Boston Globe* crossword. Every inch of the puzzle was filled except for one final square—two four-letter words, "MAR_" and "E_IT" with a single empty box connecting them. The first clue read "Sartre's *No* ____," the second "Groucho or Karl"

The mutt nuzzled Fig's pen hand. It took a second, then Fig understood. Leaning over the geezer's shoulder, Fig carefully added in the final *X*. It was probably an illusion, but at that moment Fig could swear he glimpsed the veil of elusive thought vanish from the old man's unseeing eyes. Fig reached out and quietly slid their lids shut.

What now? Stroking the dog's withered head, Fig stared at the dead man as if waiting for an answer. That's when he saw the faded tattoo on the old guy's forearm: a Navy Seabees insignia encircled by the motto "You Blow It, We Build It. Guam ~ Iwo ~ Guadalcanal."

For the first time, Fig smiled. If this old salt had built tunnels and bridges in war zones, maybe he'd actually chosen this tomb deep in the bowels of the Big Dig because he could truly appreciate the audacity of the feat surrounding him. Maybe he'd even chosen it for what he'd known would be his last mission.

Fig also smiled because he now knew what to do. Was there a crime here? Sure, there was—a big one, bigger even than all the gangs and gore, mayhem and madness on the streets above. Yeah, this was the real thing. But as far as Fig could see, the crime here was whatever this hard-hearted, mean-assed world had done to the poor soul to bring him to this desolate end. And there was the catch: where do you report that?

Fig snatched the walkie-talkie and punched it off. The crackle ceased, and with it his dreaded static. In the silence, Fig caught himself plucking at the suspenders on his floppy waders as an unfamiliar wave washed over him. Pride? Power? Sheer stupidity?

Whatever it was, it felt good. He'd already gone from clog buster to crime buster. The next leap would be easy. He'd render his verdict. Removing the completed crossword from the man's lap, Fig selected a fresh one from the pile of *Globe*'s on the makeshift side table. Fig slipped the pen back into the old man's still poised hand and tenderly placed the new crossword beneath it.

Fig turned to the teetering dog. Now the mutt seemed to be smiling too, in that droolingly odd way only dogs can.

In one swift move, Fig swept the pooch onto his shoulders and started up the service ladder. As they passed through the broad hinged grate, Fig left it wide open. To make sure it stayed that way, he plucked the padlock off its hasp and clattered it to the floor far below. When the floods came, as surely they would, the old salt would float right through the open hatch on his way to a proper burial at sea.

Fig cast his gaze upward to the thin halo of daylight glimmering around the manhole cover at the top of a second service ladder. As they ascended the final rungs, Fig knew he would no longer need to talk to himself. Turning his head to the mutt's, Michael Sean Figgis began what he hoped would be a long conversation. "You like baseball?"

After all, in a time of terror with new skyscrapers and old neighborhoods alike collapsing in ruin, dead bodies are a dime a dozen. But a good dog is hard to find.

The Boy Scout Sheriff

Leslie Woods

Sheriff Tom Mitchell drove his cruiser down the snow-covered dirt road and backed into a landing. The January storms had smoothed over the ruts and only his tracks marked the entrance to acreage that hadn't been logged in years. Every few weeks he parked between Cassie Fletcher's house and the main road where, in this northern Maine hamlet, any action would reasonably take place. He cut his lights and engine, then sat for a moment. Shaking his head, he questioned again what he was doing.

His feeble response was that a man needed some place to eat. Tom matched his watch to the cruiser's clock and wrote the time in his logbook even though he was technically off duty. As the county sheriff, he shoveled a pile of paperwork each day and seldom hit the road. He opened his window and ate, wondering if the scent of dark-roast coffee floated through the cold night to Cassie. Tom closed the window, recapped his thermos and made another notation in his log. He stepped out to brush any breadcrumbs off his uniform and held still to listen. What had he heard? Banging doors? Shouts? He strode onto the road.

In the starlight he spotted a flash of movement. He heard snow slide off tree boughs and strained as though he could make his ears bigger. A patter of running steps alerted him before he recognized a person. Faint and ghostly, the pale form flickered past the trees. As the white figure drew nearer, he heard a moan.

Tom rushed back to the cruiser and yanked a blanket from the trunk. By the time he returned to the road, she had reached the landing. He flung open the blanket and she stopped so quickly she sprawled backward onto the snow. Tom looked down at the dark place between her legs and then at her face.

She flung up one arm. "No. No." The words were muffled snorts. Her nose appeared black with what must be blood, and more dark smears seemed to create holes in her face.

"Cassie, it's me. It's Tom. I've got you." He grasped her arms, but she screamed and he pulled back. He lifted her by the one arm she raised to him and then put his hand on her naked back. "Damn it, Cassie."

She stepped up onto his boots and clung to him. After a moment, he bent away from her and almost fell over as he reached for the blanket. He wrapped her and held her as she stood on his boot tops. He felt naked in his soul while she was merely undressed. He said, "Your arm's broken?"

"Yeah."

"I have to take you to the hospital this time."

She pressed her face against his shoulder and squeezed him harder with her good arm. "Hold me."

In a few moments she began shivering, so he carried her to the cruiser. He located a box of tissues and handed it to her. She blew blood from her nose and flung the wad out the door. He wanted to punish her for leaving him, but he also burned with guilt.

He couldn't keep the scorn from his voice. "What do we call it this time? Hard to break your arm walking into a door."

"Stop it, Tom. Nobody here knew Jake before he came to town. You're just as responsible."

Tom knew what she meant. He had told her he didn't want to get married until he joined the state troopers because sheriff's deputies didn't earn much. Yet he liked being a deputy. He was the last Mitchell in town and he loved walking patrol in his crisp uniform and being recognized. He loved his code book, the black and white of law, the principles of behavior. Every day he pressed the pants of the stiff uniform that held him together and apart from his father.

Customers of Bill Mitchell's garage soon learned that the replacement parts were cheap imports or the oil was too thin. The county collection of rotten cars crawled onto Bill's lot for an inspection sticker and he barely held onto his license. The kitchen table, the doorknobs, the TV all passed on the grease from Bill's hands or sleeves. The apartment floors showed every step he took although Sandy Mitchell scrubbed them each morning. Bill had opened a garage in many towns, but happened to die in Barkerville, so that's where Tom stayed.

Each year Cassie lived with him, Tom said, "Wait a little longer." Then Jake Fletcher arrived on a wild wind and swept Cassie away. She was right. Nobody had known Jake then.

Tom walked back down the snowy road to retrieve the robe that had slipped off Cassie. She needed it to dodge questions at the hospital. He helped her put it on then flipped open his logbook. "Okay, Cassie, what happened tonight?" He felt slimy waiting for her to lie again.

"I fell in the tub."

A week later Sheriff Tom Mitchell backed his cruiser beneath the pines and parked at an angle to the convenience store. He chose the spot so his lights couldn't pick up a reflection and his tires made little noise over the crushed snow. Stores in the three surrounding towns had been hit over the past month including the other Stevens' Variety. Although most stores closed at ten, the Stevens brothers stayed open until midnight and advertised heavily to suck up the late traffic. Larry's place was ripe for a hit and he called the sheriff's office after his brother's store was robbed. "The state cops are cruising around, but we can't get our own sheriff's department to protect us. You doing anything to catch these guys?"

Tom was just as frustrated, but the state troopers patrolled the main roads and covered most of the stores. Everybody searched for a rusty black Chevy pickup, but when it wasn't being used for a holdup, the truck could be parked in a barn or next to junk farm machinery and disappear in plain sight. Tom plotted the robberies on a map and realized they all took place at isolated country stores surviving on the life support of beer and cigarettes. He directed his night deputies to heavier patrols of the other stores, but in the evenings he pulled a late shift beside Larry's place.

Larry didn't seem to notice the cruiser and continued complaining that his store got no protection. He had a right to be scared since his brother had witnessed at least one of the crooks flashing a gun.

The night was cold, but Tom pulled off his gloves and slipped joggers' wristbands across his palms. He had stuck pins through the cloth so whenever he nodded off and his hands slid onto his lap, the pricks woke him up. Although he sometimes took naps during the day, the double shift and the frigid air were wearing him down. The other robberies had all been pulled a half hour before closing and Tom wanted the stakeout to end.

He sat quiet in his car as he watched Jimmy Knowlton leave the store with two six packs of Rolling Rock and hand one through the window of his younger brother's car. Then Jimmy climbed into his pickup and popped the tab for a long pull before he drove off with the open can balanced on the steering wheel. His seventeen-year-old brother handed cans to his three friends before he drove off in the other direction.

Tom knew he should flash his lights and give them a jolt of siren, should scare the piss out of them, and he ached to smack the kids down. He even touched the siren switch before the pins stuck into the back of his hand. He spoke out loud. "Hold on. The bad guys are coming." Nobody entered the store after Jimmy and the time crept to a quarter to midnight.

Cassie would have told him to lure the thieves with his aura. She liked to wander through the Healing Palace with its crystal pendants, arthritis bracelets, and astrology pamphlets.

In high school he'd told her he wanted to be a state trooper and she'd said, "You going to waste your mojo catching scum? You could be anything, Tom."

"So could you, Cassie."

Then she laughed so hard and long that it hurt him. "Stop it, Cassie." He shook her—gently, and only to make her stop laughing, but he shook her. She quit and shrugged, but her eyes went dead. The same expression shrouded her face when she handed in the note excusing her latest absence without explaining her bruises.

Then, quick as a struck match, she was back again, hiding behind a big smile. "I should teach you to use auras. You can protect yourself with the right aura."

Tom squeezed his hands around the steering wheel until the pricking pins stopped thoughts of Cassie. His eyes watered and he blinked to clear them. Right then a black Chevy pickup slid to a halt before Larry Stevens's store. Tom's heart began slamming around in his chest. His timing must be perfect yet was made more difficult because the store was built over a storage area and, from the ground, he couldn't see inside.

Customers cleared the four front steps or scuttled along the side up the handicap ramp.

Tom slipped off the wristbands and grabbed his hat. He considered a call for backup, but already heard the store's door slam open.

No time. He ran forward, his gun in his hand.

Two men, their heads covered by ski masks, stepped onto the porch. The second man out the door said, "Hurry up."

Tom rushed to the edge of the porch. "Police. Hands over your heads." Instantly he knew he had been too quick.

The second man out the door was taller and wider than the first. He appeared as a black silhouette with the lights behind him and a single porch light above his head. He shoved the first man toward the steps. Tom stepped aside as the shorter man tripped and fell near his feet. Then the big man on the porch stretched up and smacked the overhead bulb, breaking it with his bare hand. Tom clearly saw the man's flapping leather jacket and baggy jeans. As he reached toward the light, his jacket opened over a bright red shirt. Under a shower of glass the big man bolted for the handicap ramp.

Larry Stevens rushed to the doorway and scurried onto the porch. "Get them. Get them." Larry waved his arms and charged three strides down the ramp before he stopped. He looked back at Tom standing there aiming in his direction and said, "Oh, hell." With his hands on top of his head, he ran back into the store.

Too late, thanks to Larry, but Tom fired into the dark anyway. The man at his feet rose and Tom jerked off his ski mask. Since the little crook had dropped his gun and didn't fight, Tom wanted to lock him in the cruiser and chase after the big man. Instead, he called for backup and ordered a search of the entire area.

The next morning the assistant district attorney, Mary Wright, said, "You know the state cops caught Jake crossing his own lawn. I wish he'd been a mile away, but we're stuck. Same clothes you described and he was sweating like crazy."

Tom said, "How'd he explain that?"

Mary smiled. "He was jogging. In the middle of the night."

"Don't we all?"

"I've got three kids. I like to sleep through the middle of the night." She tossed her pen onto her desk. "Your ID will put him away, Tom."

"I know." At the jail Tom had instantly recognized Jake Fletcher,

Cassie's worthless, piece-of-garbage husband. Jake had sat in the interview room with his drying clothes and body stinking up the air.

"I've seen him before."

"But did you see him last night? At the store?"

Tom heard the plea in her voice. He knew she was asking him to step away from his own shadow, leave behind a part of himself. His reputation had remained untarnished, unscathed, inviolate for his ten years in law enforcement. He held to the code even as he wrote the state representative a speeding ticket. Tom Mitchell, the boy scout sheriff who was nothing like his dad. No, sir. Six years ago, Tom had been a lowly deputy until two county commissioners begged him to run. Then he beat his shady predecessor and became the youngest sheriff in Maine.

He said, "The second man stood directly under the porch light until he smashed it and the other lights were behind him."

"Did he still have his mask on? He had to take it off to run, didn't he?"

"People ski in those things." Tom stalled because he knew what she was asking. Always before he'd faced clear, simple choices. Now he felt as slimy as the grease that always creased his father's hands. "What about Larry?"

"They kept their masks on in the store. Besides he was too scared to say fat or thin. He didn't even see the red shirt."

Mary sat on the edge of her desk and tapped a thick file. "This is Jake Fletcher's history. Burglary, battery, OUI. He's never lived a single clean day." She dropped her voice. "Suspicion of wife beating, but she's too scared to charge him."

Tom shifted in his seat, an involuntary movement that turned his shoulder toward the DA. He could never sit still when anyone referred to Cassie.

Mary said, "Four stores and they used a gun. We can finish them now. All you have to do is place him at Larry's store. You recognized him, right?"

The yes lay in his mouth waiting to be flicked out by his tongue.

A word could cut Cassie's bonds. A simple sigh could waft the word out into the air. Yesssss. Only, once released, the seed of yes would dig in and grow, entangling him in its roots, feeding on his mind. Larry Stevens knew Jake Fletcher wore a mask. Tom would need to expand on the yes with a story of Jake snatching off his mask. And why didn't Jake drop it on the porch or the ramp? He was afraid of DNA? A thief running for his freedom thinks about DNA? He felt the yes press on his tongue until it choked him.

Tom said, "He never took the mask off."

Mary sighed. "It'll be tougher for me and he'll get out on bail, but I want to put this guy away."

"What about his partner? Why doesn't he take a deal?"

She picked up Jake Fletcher's file and tossed it into an out box. "He said Jake holds grudges and ratting him out wasn't worth any time off. He said nobody could ever hide that well from Jake."

Tom knew that too. Cassie said the same thing.

Two months later Tom drove his cruiser down the familiar snow-covered dirt road and parked behind his deputy's car. He looked over Cassie's small white cape and its attached woodshed. The wide shed door was open and sunlight glinted across the snow and lit the shed's interior. He wrote "11:45 A.M." in his logbook, then got out and said, "You sure he's dead?"

His deputy, Lyle Baxter, grinned. "I'd like to feel bad, respect for the dead and all that, but I've only got this happy feeling."

Tom and Lyle walked up the driveway and down the path toward the front door. They crossed in front of the open shed and Lyle turned toward the step. Tom said, "Wait. I want to enter through the house. Don't disturb anything."

"It's an accident, Tom. God decided we'd suffered enough and dropped that axe on Jake's head."

"We'll see."

"Tom, the only other person here is Cassie."

Tom spun around on the path. "I'm the sheriff and you're a deputy. We don't know anything until we've looked at the scene. How do you know somebody else didn't leave already?"

Lyle tugged his hat down. "The angel of mercy, maybe."

Tom passed Cassie, who sat in a kitchen chair with her hands gripping a steaming mug of coffee. He squeezed her shoulder, but didn't trust himself to speak more than a greeting. Hope already glowed in his chest. He continued along a passageway and through the door to the shed.

Jake Fletcher had been chopping wood and his body lay spread-eagle behind the broad splitting stump. Almost funny to imagine a person splitting logs into stove chunks, but, instead of the axe in his hand, it stuck, perfectly embedded, in the back of his head. Tom took in the stack of splits and estimated how long Jake Fletcher must have been working. The pile lengthened across the floor as he apparently backed up the splitting stump until he retreated under the tight clothesline. Then when Jake lifted the axe, he caught the blade or handle on the springy rope. An act of God for sure.

Behind him, Lyle spoke. "See? An accident."

"Take pictures before we do anything. And be careful of your footing. This place is a mess." Uncovered barrels of trash and over-flowing cardboard boxes of empty cans rose above a sea of rags, buckets, engine parts, windows with broken panes, and just stuff.

Tom made sure Lyle photographed the entire shed. Then he insisted on photographs of the step and the nearby ground to prove that nobody had jumped down and run away. From his cruiser he brought a tape measure and positioned it for photos floor to clothes-line, stump to clothesline, the length of the axe and anything else he could think of. They worked quickly, since fresh snowflakes blotted the sunlight.

While Lyle snapped pictures, Tom studied the shed and the ground outside. After he approved Lyle's work, he picked up a wooden stick about the same length as the axe and said, "All right. I'm splitting here. You watch and see what happens." Tom placed a fresh log on the stump and positioned himself between the dead man's legs. He raised the stick over his head and instantly felt the rope snag the wood in his hands pulling it free.

Lyle laughed. "See? I told you."

At last Tom said, "Okay. Take down Cassie's—the widow's—story."

Tom had already called the district office of the state police, but he phoned them again. He asked for Dave, the detective who had taught Tom in several classes. Static broke into the connection probably because the weather was changing fast. "Hey, Dave. Tom Mitchell in Barkerville. Nobody's here yet."

The state police detective chuckled. "Isn't it snowing up your way?"

"We had a break, but it's starting again."

"This new storm's a B-52 aboard a rocket-propelled freight train. Over three feet in Portland since eight this morning."

"Those southerners are always whining."

Dave laughed. "You've checked out the scene by now. What do you see?"

"A fatal accident."

"Photographed?"

"Everything but his molars." Tom noticed something about the clothesline's knot, but he didn't know what.

"We've got everybody flat out on this storm. We need to take your word and get a team there when we can."

"What about the body? Rats got to eat too."

"Get your local undertaker to remove him. Can they leave the axe in his head?"

"Yeah. It lies along his body instead of to the side."

"Makes sense if he was chopping wood."

"Okay, I'll take care of things. You're absolutely sure?"

Dave said, "Believe me, I'd walk through this snow to check some guys' work. Understand, we trust you, Tom." He lightened his voice again. "You're our boy scout sheriff—thorough, clean, reverent, honest."

"Cut the crap." Tom stopped the joke but already felt the rush of pride. He had so changed the Mitchell reputation that the state cops took his word as an equal.

Tom called the nearest funeral home then put his phone away. He stepped along the clothesline. The rope was dry all the way to the knot that hung from a metal ring just inside the open door. The knot was damp on the outside, but the inside twists were dry. He had already calculated that the morning flurries had landed six feet into the building with the door left open for natural light. The clothesline was high up and the snow probably couldn't reach it. He had no right to even consider that the line was tied after the axe split Jake's head.

What was the matter with him? The state cops had accepted his word that this death was an accident. Fate had finally blessed Cassie.

The morning snow had stopped at least two hours before they arrived to check the body. The splits farther across the floor bore snow but nearly all those on the house side of the floor were dry. Instead of circling the stump, it seemed Jake shoved the stump along the floor until it rested below the clothesline. It had to be that way. Except the splits didn't look right. A line of pieces among the dry chunks and leading from the snow-covered splits to the stump were dark with damp and bore traces of snow. Why didn't he notice this before? Tom felt the dragging weight of dread.

He wanted to leave the shed behind, to race to his cruiser. He didn't want to be honest Tom, thorough and exacting. He fought with himself, lost, and began shifting pieces of wood across the floor. Moving the stump had created a trail in the dirt, but on either side, smears like small footprints with a distinct circle tread also marked the dust. His heartbeat increased and he felt a stirring in his mind like wheels spinning in snow and struggling to catch.

He flung the wood aside and pieces crashed and bounced off each other and landed in piles of trash. The smeared line through the dust ended in a neat circle of dark floor surrounded by the morning's snow. He stared down at more partial footprints and even places where the feet had slid in the snow and smeared the circle tread because pushing the splitting stump was difficult. Even as he looked, the new storm's snow obliterated the footprints and chilled his face. Snow melted in greasy patches on his cheek and neck.

Tom stood in the space in the snow where the huge splitting stump had surely rested. He pictured Jake Fletcher breaking logs to the left in the early morning then circling the stump to fell pieces to the other side. That way the sun would be behind him. Jake would never have dragged the splitting stump toward the house side of the shed. If he had been that stupid, then during the hours of bright sunshine between the storms, every time Jake lifted the axe, the light would have blinded him.

Tom stepped to the clothesline and gripped it. He squeezed his eyes shut and gritted his teeth. New snow clung to the six feet of rope near the door, but the line had been dry when he arrived. He realized now that the rope should have been damp from the early morning flurries. He placed his hand over his cell phone and then stopped. He should yank the door shut and call the state police. Yet fresh snow already blurred the scene and buried Jake Fletcher's head as though the axe was only stuck in a piece of wood.

White and faint as angel dust, the snow sifted across the proof that Cassie killed her husband. But Tom knew. He felt the firm line of his life snap as Bill Mitchell's laugh seemed to ring around him.

Tom looked behind him and out the doorway into the storm as though seeking his father. As he spun, his feet slid on the new snow and he skidded, feeling that he was falling backward through his entire life.

Tom dropped to his knees and covered his face with trembling hands. He wanted to crouch there until the storm covered him, but he heard a car engine and watched a black hearse fishtail into Cassie's driveway. The undertaker stepped out of the car and said, "Hey, Sheriff." Tom stood and straightened his hat.

Cougar Attack

Ruth McCarty

Chief of Police Erin Donnelly took a sip of her seltzer. What she really wanted was a cold Bud Light and a way to escape Wilfred Dunbar's pressure on how to make Still Water Lake "the boomers' place to be." She didn't mind the fundraisers that she was required as Chief of Police to attend; she just hated when she was on call and couldn't have a decent drink. And she especially disliked the "black tie affairs" and the high heels she had to wear.

"I'm telling you, the town ought to sell the beach rights and the hundred acres we aren't using," Wilfred Dunbar shouted at her over the jazz band.

Erin sipped her drink. It didn't do her any good to get the lake owners pissed with elections around the corner. Most of them had all drooled over the big price tags offered by South County Developers to purchase their abutting land. "It's preserved, Wilfred. You know it's the only place the townies have access to launch their boats."

"Let the townies go to Backwater Pond," Dunbar shouted.

Backwater Pond was her pond. Much smaller in size than Still Water, it had a dozen summer camps, five year-round places, and a half-acre of land owned by the town for swimming purposes.

Dunbar continued, nearly spitting on her in his enthusiasm. "You've seen the plans! Phase Two of Serenity Springs is going to have a private boat launch for the homeowners. Hell, they're providing rack storage and delivery to the dock whenever you want your goddamn boat."

"There are a lot of people who don't want the town to change, Wilfred."

"Yeah and most of them are piss-pot poor. I say we should cater to those self-centered, filthy rich boomers. Think of all the real estate taxes we'll bring in."

And all the money you'll get, Erin thought. Her phone vibrated on her hip. Thank God. She opened it, and glanced at the message. A code 49 followed by an address on the lake. She couldn't be reading it right. There hadn't been a murder in Prosperity in over twenty-two years and of all places, at the town beach she and Wilfred were talking about. "Excuse me, Mr. Dunbar," she said as she hurried out the door.

Erin welcomed the adrenaline rush as her all-wheel drive SUV turned onto the narrow Fire Road 10. She came to a sudden stop when she spotted headlights shining on the lake. She jumped from the SUV, forgetting the three-inch heels she was wearing. "Damn it," she cried as she twisted her ankle.

As she limped to the water's edge, the pounding rock beat from Kick Backs Bar up the road echoed off the water. Erin saw what looked like a woman's body highlighted in the beams of the police car and an officer bending over her. He turned at her approach, and she recognized him right away.

"McDermott, what the hell have we got here?"

"Looks like a cougar attack, chief," Ian McDermott said in his Irish brogue.

"A cougar attack! What the hell are you talking about? You called this in as a possible homicide."

McDermott took in the chief's black dress and three-inch heels, and then looked back at the body. "She's the cougar, ma'am," he said, then mumbled under his breath, "and you sure fit the description tonight."

"McDermott, you'd better explain yourself right now!"

"A cougar. A sexy older woman."

"Have a little respect." Erin kneeled in the sand and felt for a pulse. Nothing. Definitely a head wound. And the body felt cool. She felt a little woozy but she sure couldn't let McDermott see her swoon, so she yelled at him instead. "Where's her ID?"

"I don't know for sure," McDermott said. "I just felt for a pulse. Couldn't find one. I didn't move her."

"Good thinking," she said more to herself than to him. She grabbed his flashlight and shone it around the beach. "Did you call anyone else?"

He looked a little uneasy. "No, ma'am. Just you. I wasn't sure who to call. I've never had a homicide before."

Erin Donnelly turned toward the sound of the music. "Me neither," she whispered, then said aloud, "Let's get this scene taped off. You call backup. I've got to call Portland. Get the Crime Investigator up here. CID handles homicides."

"Chief, I think that's the murder weapon." He pointed to a rock in the weeds.

"Whatever you do, don't touch it. And call for backup now!"

Before McDermott could make the call, two squad cars came rushing up and four officers jumped out. She ignored the look they gave her when they saw her dress and heels.

"I thought you didn't tell anyone, McDermott," Erin said.

He stuttered out, "I only told me partner, chief. He's out sick tonight. He must've called Holstein and . . ."

"Next thing you know the goddamn television stations will be sending their crews up here. We'd better work fast at getting this area secured. She turned to two of the officers. "Back up that car and block off the road, and don't let anyone come anywhere near here. Except for CID!" She turned to Holstein and his partner and yelled at them, "You two head up to Kick Backs and make sure no one takes off before we've had time to question them. And McDermott, I'll talk to you later about the theory of he told one person, and he told one person . . ."

Erin pulled out her phone and punched in her sister's number. Megan picked up on the second ring. "Megan, do me a real big favor and head over to my house and get me a change of clothes . . . I know it's late, but it's real important . . . sorry I scared you . . . Megan! Just get my damned clothes over to Fire Road 10."

She headed to her SUV. At least she had her notebook with her. She jotted down the time she got the call and what the message said. Then she wrote a brief description of the victim and noted that Officer McDermott had called it in. Wait a minute. She rolled down her window and yelled, "McDermott, how did you know about the body?"

"I got a call from that crazy lady who calls in every Saturday night. You know, Mrs. Creighton. She said a vehicle went peeling out of here and she was sure the driver was drunk. And wanted to know why didn't we have a squad car hidden right here to catch the drunks as they leave. So I made a point of hanging around. I started to back in, saw something reflected in my taillights. Thought maybe it was a drunk sleeping it off. So I turned the car around so I could get a better look."

"Jesus, McDermott, not only did you back over possible evidence you turned around and drove over it! Why the hell didn't you use your spotlight?" This was turning into a real nightmare.

She made a note to talk to Mrs. Creighton to find out if she knew what make and model the vehicle was and then made a note to find out the exact time she placed the call to 911. With any luck, Mrs. Creighton would have the plate number of the vehicle too.

The CID team arrived and Erin brought them up to speed. They would process the crime scene and she would start the interviews.

"McDermott here is at your disposal," she said. "McDermott, I'm going to Creighton's. If you see my sister, send her there."

All the lights were out at the Creighton house. Erin pulled into the driveway and was about to head to the front door when she spotted her sister's car approaching. She ran into the road to flag her down.

Megan slammed on the brakes, flung open the door, and yelled, "What are you doing, jumping out like that! I could have hit you!"

Erin walked around the car and opened the passenger door, reached for the paper bag on the seat and said, "There's been a possible murder up the road. I was at the library auction when I got the call and I can hardly interview witnesses dressed like this."

"A murder? In Prosperity?"

"I said possible. And don't go calling anyone yet. I want you to lock your car doors and go back home to Charlie and the girls. And don't stop for anyone, even if you know them."

Erin worried about her older sister. Even though Megan was one year and two months older, she was way too naïve for forty-one. Her sun rose and set on her husband and two girls and she just couldn't see the bad in anyone. "And call me when you get back there," Erin added.

She'd be relieved when Megan called. This wasn't the first time Megan had brought her a change of clothes, but this was the first time she'd brought them to a murder scene.

Erin went back to her car, opened the door and sat sideways on the seat. She took off her heels and threw them to the passenger seat. Then she reached under her dress and pulled off her pantyhose. God, she hated them worse than heels. She pulled a sweatshirt over her head, unzipped the back of her dress and had it nearly off, when a massive outside light from the Creighton house lit up the yard like a state penitentiary.

A voice from behind the light yelled, "I've called the police and they're on their way! Get a room!"

Crap. She yelled, "Mrs. Creighton? It's Chief Donnelly." She pulled on her jeans, then her socks and boots, then grabbed her shoulder bag and cautiously started up the walkway.

"Mrs. Creighton, I was at the library auction tonight. Didn't expect I'd need to change."

By the time she reached the door she was fully dressed, had pulled her gun and holster out of her bag, and was fastening it under her arm.

When her eyes finally adjusted, Mrs. Creighton came into view. She wore a pair of navy blue sweats, a white oversized T-shirt and had her auburn hair pulled back in a ponytail. Her feet were bare and her hair looked wet, like she'd just taken a shower. She appeared to be in her middle forties, and had dark circles under her eyes.

"May I come in?" Erin asked. "I'd like to ask a few questions about your call to 911 tonight."

"I guess," she said.

Erin followed her into living room. "Mrs. Creighton, can you describe the vehicle you saw earlier tonight?"

"It was a dark-colored truck."

"Did you happen to get the plate number?"

"Well, no. It went by so fast I didn't get to see it, but it could've had out of state plates. It went by at exactly 11:14. I know because I looked at my clock as I dialed 911."

"Mrs. Creighton, did you hear anything unusual tonight?"

"No. I keep my television on at night. Don't like being alone."

"Yes, ma'am. I understand." Erin knew her son had committed suicide early last fall.

"Did you hear any screams?"

"Screams? No."

Erin's radio squeaked, and she heard McDermott say, "Chief, we found the victim's pocketbook in the water and we have her driver's license. Her name's Julie Morrissey. She lives on the lake."

"Got that," she replied. "I'll be right there." She turned to the woman and said, "Mrs. Creighton, here's my card. If you think of anything, even if you think it's silly, give me a call."

"Wait, what's going on? I'm a taxpayer and I have a right to know!"

You'll know soon enough, Erin thought as she ran toward her vehicle.

□   □   □

The Channel 7 news team arrived on the scene less than five minutes after Erin left Mrs. Creighton's. They weren't able to get close enough to the crime scene to do any damage, but she was sure the morning news would show the dramatic nighttime scene, which now had the coroner's van parked in plain view.

Erin checked in with CID. "Got anything I can go on?"

"Time of death wasn't too long ago. My guess is less than an hour."

Erin shivered as she realized the killer could be still in the area. Her gut feeling told her to head to the bar. She dragged McDermott along with her.

Holstein and his partner met them at the door. "We've got everyone's identification and phone numbers written down and we've asked each one of them if they saw or heard anything tonight. Most everyone says they've been here since 9:30 or 10:00. Quite a few of them have gone outside for a smoke, but they claim they couldn't have heard anything over the sounds of the band. Can we let them go?"

"Not yet. I want to show this driver's license around. See if anyone knows this Julie Morrissey."

Holstein grabbed the photo ID from Erin's hand. "Christ. It's Julie. She's the victim?"

"Yeah. You know her?"

"I sort of dated her for a while."

Erin turned to McDermott and handed him the card. "Show this around. See if anyone else knows her or has seen her tonight. Holstein, come with me."

Erin walked outside and leaned against the split-rail fence. "Tell me about her."

"There's not much to tell. She owns Hillcrest. Got it in a divorce settlement. Only comes here for the summer."

Erin knew the Hillcrest place. A huge house with a wraparound porch and gazebo corners. A good-sized guesthouse and several garages sat on at least twenty-five acres of land. And it was smack dab in the middle of the land the flatlanders wanted to develop.

"How did you meet her?"

"At a bar. Not here, down in the Old Port. We hooked up one night." Holstein looked down at his feet and kept talking. "We hit it off great, but she ended it just like that," he said as he snapped his fingers.

"You know anybody who'd want to hurt her?"

He shook his head. "No, but she's not very careful who she brings home with her."

"Brought home, Holstein. She won't be bringing anyone home now."

Once back inside, Erin found the owner and bartenders sitting at a table beside the bar. Ed Tillman, the owner, stood up when he saw her.

"Chief Donnelly. Can you tell me what's going on? Why can't anyone leave?"

Erin sat at the table and nodded to Tommy O'Connor and Lisa Fournier, the two bartenders. "We have a possible homicide. McDermott found a body on the town beach."

"A body?" Tillman's jaw dropped open.

"Yeah. A woman. Any of you know Julie Morrissey?"

"Ain't she one of the summer crowd?" Tillman asked.

"She owns the old Hillcrest place," Erin said.

"Where's the Hillcrest place?" O'Conner asked. He'd been in town for only a few months.

"It's that high and mighty place across the lake," Lisa Fournier said. She crossed her arms, leaned back in her chair and yawned. "I'm awful tired, Chief. Is it all right if I head on home? I ain't got much to tell except she came in here sometimes."

"She come in alone?"

"Oh, she comes in alone all right, but usually leaves with one young stud or another."

O'Connor grinned. "How come I never met her?"

Lisa hit him with the wet towel she'd used to wipe the tables. "You idiot. You have met her. She's one of the summer intruders. She turned you down like day-old fish. You're too old and fat for that broad."

O'Connor turned red, grabbed the towel and threw it over the bar. "She was probably too skinny to be any good, anyhow."

"Was she in here tonight?" Erin asked in her most professional voice.

All three of them nodded. Lisa said, "She was here earlier. She sat at the bar. She had three apple martinis."

"You see her with anyone?"

"Yeah," Lisa said. "Those guys with that development company are the ones who bought her the drinks."

"What guys?"

"I don't know their names. I seen them on cable TV the other night, you know, talking about the plans they have for Still Water Lake."

Ed Tillman half stood. "They put that prissy development here and I'm out of business. This ain't no upscale watering hole."

"There are a lot of owners who want to sell their land, Ed," Erin said.

"Well, not this one." Tillman banged his chest with each word.

"I heard her tell those boys she didn't want to sell her land," Lisa said. "Didn't need the money."

"Her land is a key part of the deal from what I see," Tillman said. "She'd be right in the middle of Serenity Springs."

"She leave with them?"

"Can't say," Lisa said. "We were real busy tonight."

Erin made a note to check on the two guys, as well as who would inherit Hillcrest. Then she called McDermott and Holstein over to the table. "You got anything?"

"Some of the guys noticed her, but most of them were with their girlfriends or wives. And they saw her talking to two out-of-towners and it looked like she had a quarrel with Lisa Fournier."

Well, that's a surprise, Erin thought. "That true, Lisa?" Erin asked.

"Oh, yeah, I forgot about that. She wanted another martini. She was already slurring her words so I told her she was cut off. She didn't take it too well."

"What happened then?'

"She yelled something at me, grabbed her pocketbook off the bar and walked into the crowd. I don't know what happened after that."

"There something else you want to tell me?" Erin used the ploy that made most guilty people squirm.

Lisa drew in a deep breath. "Well, I guess it ain't no secret we didn't like each other."

"Why's that?"

"She's a disgusting pig. That's why. She made my Seth . . ."

Erin kept quiet. She watched the anger flash across Lisa's face as she tried to find the right words.

"She picks up younger men and takes them to that, that big house of hers and liquors them up and . . ."

"Seth underage?"

"No. He's twenty-two now, but last summer . . ."

"He would have been twenty-one last summer. No crime there."

"Well he ain't the only one. She's always on the prey for young meat and more than one boy around here has reason to hate her!"

"You saying Seth hated her?"

Lisa paled. "That ain't what I'm saying. You can't think Seth had anything to do with this."

"I'm just getting the facts." Erin put her hand on Lisa's shoulder. "Where is Seth tonight?"

Lisa pulled her arm free. "He's in Bangor and all because of her. Got a job at a pizza place there."

"Give McDermott the name of the place."

"He didn't do it."

"We just need to clear him." She turned, and said, "McDermott, let me know what you find out and you can let everyone go for now. Tell them we'll be round to talk to them in the morning."

Erin walked out of Kick Backs, got into her car, and took out her notebook to update her notes. She hoped Seth Fournier was in Bangor and had witnesses to prove it. She hated to think that it was one of the locals who did this. She flipped back the pages and read her notes from the beginning, making new notes on what she needed to do.

First she'd better put a call in to the station and have someone pick up the two guys from South County Developers. And she'd better find out what they were driving. She wrote down: Black truck? License Plate number.

She'd been at the informational meeting for Serenity Springs and knew that the two guys were in their early thirties. Could they have been "prey" for Julie Morrissey? Or was she "prey" for them? Did they just buy her drinks to loosen her up to sell her land? And did they know that loose meant a whole 'nother thing to her?

Erin knew she'd better contact Morrissey's next of kin before they heard it on the news. She'd also need to contact Morrissey's lawyer to find out who would inherit the land and if that would make a difference in the plans for Still Water Lake. Ed Tillman didn't want the development here, but how many others were counting on the money that her land was blocking?

Then there was Tommy O'Connor. Something bugged Erin about the young bartender. He acted as if he didn't know the victim, yet he said she was probably "too skinny." And skinny she was. So he probably remembered Morrissey and possibly her rejection of him. Look into Tommy O'Connor's background, she wrote.

And Holstein knew the victim. But he'd been on duty all night and his partner was his alibi. He couldn't be thirty if he was a day, and Julie Morrissey had slept with him even though he was young enough to be her son.

Her son, she wrote. That left Lisa Fournier. Had Julie Morrissey screwed up Lisa's son enough for Lisa to pick up a rock from the beach and smash Morrissey on the head? Her son. A chill went up Erin's spine. Her son. "Oh, shit."

 Erin left her car at the bar and walked along the shore of the lake to avoid the newscasters waiting on the fire road. Her route took her past the crime scene. She walked in the water so as not to disturb any of the footprints left by the killer and she stopped to tell the CID where she was headed. She didn't tell them why. She had a mother to confront and she knew it would be painful.

She focused her flashlight on the small prints in the sand leading to the now dark house. She walked quietly toward the back porch. She heard the squeak of the rocker before she saw the figure sitting there. Erin shone the light on her. She had a blanket wrapped around her now. Her hair was loose and dry and she ran a comb through it as Erin approached.

"He didn't have to die," she said. "He thought she loved him. I could have told him about whores like her."

"Mrs. Creighton," Erin said.

Luck of the Draw

S. A. Daynard

The steak was overdone, the broccoli barely cooked, and she'd gone more than a bit heavy-handed with the oregano on the garlic bread. Still, Mae Del Vecchio couldn't keep a smile from her face. They were three weeks into the lottery without a winner being drawn and tonight Mae felt lucky. She sat at the kitchen table fiddling with an arrangement of fresh-cut blue hydrangeas, pink oleander, and white fairy roses, daydreaming about how the lottery could change her life. She'd rebuild the greenhouse in the backyard, open the little café she'd been dreaming of, and once and for all be rid of Joe.

A slam of the bathroom door brought her back to reality. Every Monday through Friday for the last twenty-four years Joe stomped through the front door at exactly 6:10, grabbed the paper from the credenza, a beer from the fridge, and headed to the john for a twenty-minute read. No kiss on the cheek, no "How's my girl," no acknowledgment that she even existed. When he emerged, he expected another cold one waiting for him, dinner on the table, and Mae to keep her useless thoughts to herself. When dinner was finished, he skulked into the living room with a bottle of whiskey and turned on the TV. He ate his dessert watching "Wheel of Fortune" and picked his teeth through most of "Jeopardy."

With a grunt, he took his seat across from her and grabbed the salad. Mae watched as he poured the poppy seed dressing, waiting for him to notice the mandarin orange segments. According to Martha Stewart, dinner companions would be tickled with the splash of color and whimsy they provided. Joe didn't look tickled. Joe looked pissed.

"They were Martha's idea." Mae defended her culinary walk on the wild side. "She calls it Goldfish Salad."

One by one, Joe harpooned the tiny orange segments with his fork, stalked to the john, flushed them, stomped back to the kitchen and stood behind her. Her stomach tightened waiting for his fist to connect with the side of her face, the back of her head, or the middle of her shoulder blades. She'd almost gotten used to it over the years. The sooner the first punch was thrown, the sooner he'd drink himself into oblivion. It seemed like he stood there forever, his rancid breath on the back of her neck, reveling in her fear. He grabbed a fistful of hair, snapped her head back, shoved his ugly face to hers, and smirked. He jerked her head back hard, twisted it as far as flesh and bone would give, watching tears stream down her checks, waiting for her to raise her hands to push him away.

"Come on, Mae, I dare you," he taunted. "Give me a reason to snap it." With a sickening laugh, he released his grip and took his seat.

It didn't take long before he found fault with more than just the goldfish salad. "What does Martha call this?" Joe asked, dragging his knife through the tough cut of meat. "Elephant Ass Au Jous?"

"Red wine and rosemary grilled flank steak." Mae found it hard to talk above a whisper.

"Flank steak," he groused, his mouth full of broccoli. "I find out you're pocketing the grocery money for that lottery you're gonna be one sorry bitch."

A tear traced the contour of her face as she shook her head and handed him the plate of garlic bread. Joe threw a hand-monogrammed napkin at her and told her to wipe her snot. "Someday, Mae, someday you're gonna push your luck and it ain't gonna be pretty what happens."

Mae wiped the tears from her face, knowing for the first time in his miserable life Joe Del Vecchio was right.

□   □   □

"Mae!" Joe hollered from La-Z-Boy in the living room. "I'm dying here."

"Coming," she called back, watching the seconds tick down on the microwave's timer. When it dinged, she dumped the hot popcorn into an oversized ceramic bowl she made for Joe for his birthday. She ran her fingers along its blue and green glazed surface and smiled. It'd taken her hours to painstakingly glue the pieces back together, but it was perfect.

Her hands fumbled along the spice rack, settling on dried thyme and rosemary. She shook what she estimated to be a teaspoon of each on the popcorn and gave it a shake.

"Popcorn?" Joe looked at Mae as if she'd finally lost her mind. "I friggin' work my ass off all day and you give me popcorn for dessert? What's the matter? We all out of peanut butter on a spoon?"

"It's savory popcorn." Mae's voice cracked. "Alton Brown—"

"It's popcorn." Joe cut her off, snatching up the bowl. "I swear you're just itching for a split lip. That it, Mae? The last go-round not lively enough for you?"

"I could make Jell-O." Her eyes darted around the room, avoiding his.

"Jell-O! Now there's the food of kings. Maybe Mr. Bill Cosby himself could come over, plunk some whipped cream on top for me, and spew gibberish 'til I up and blow my brains out. Oh, Mae, it'd be a friggin'dream come true. Sit down."

Mae took her seat on the sofa and watched the clock tick the minutes away while Joe ate fistfuls of popcorn and downed a shot every time someone bought a vowel, lost a turn, or went bankrupt. Ten more minutes and he'd enter the tooth-picking portion of the evening, and with a little luck, pass out before "Final Jeopardy."

"Got somewhere to go?" Joe asked, flicking a piece of popcorn at her. "Can't take your eyes off that clock."

"I was thinking about the lottery. It gets drawn around seven-thirty."

"Like you're gonna win." Joe flicked another piece.

"It's been three weeks. The odds are in my favor."

"In your favor!" Joe gave a hoot. "You don't even know how a lottery works. It don't matter how much time goes by without a winner, the only thing that increases your odds is increasing your number of chances."

Mae shrugged her shoulders. "I know."

"Really?" Joe snorted. "How many chances you got for tonight?"

"One a day for the last twenty-one days makes twenty-one chances mine will be drawn tonight."

"It gives you one, you moron," Joe snapped.

"One's all it takes," Mae mused.

"Yeah, and what are you going to do when you win?"

"Lots of things." Mae smiled thinking about it.

Joe made the annoying sound of a game show buzzer. "Wrong! You're handing it over to me. You know what I'm gonna do? Take an early retirement, buy a kick-ass car, a boat, high roll my way through Vegas, and get rid of you. I'll be living the good life and you'll be shit out of luck. It's what they call a win-win situation."

Mae brushed away a tear, Joe snatched a wooden pick from a porcelain toothpick holder, and Alex Trebek introduced the contestants. "Tonight's drinking word," he informed Mae, "is *sorry*, as in my sorry-ass excuse for a wife plays a magic lottery."

Mae watched Joe down shot after shot, pick at his teeth, and spit bits and pieces of dinner and popcorn onto the coffee table. Still, she couldn't keep a smile from her face. She had twenty-one chances in tonight's lottery.

☐   ☐   ☐

Mae sat at the kitchen table planning Joe's dinner: BBQ ribs, grilled corn on the cob, and Dijon-dill potato salad, and for dessert, toasted coconut-coated, caramel apples when the oven timer sounded. Two hours at 225° had nicely dried out the toothpick she'd fashioned from a deadly oleander twig. She picked it up with a pair of tweezers and deposited it in Joe's porcelain toothpick holder. That made twenty-two.

They were twenty-two days into the lottery without Joe drawing a poisonous toothpick and tonight Mae Del Vecchio felt lucky.

The Flagger

Louy Castonguay

The gentle June breeze fluttered the hem of her pansy-print, voile dress, gluing it to her still-slim legs, as Doris walked out of her home. The rain-washed leaves shimmered under the rising sun as she started her Camry. Windows down, she inhaled the succulent morning air. For once, she would let her short, blond hair blow with the wind and fix it at work. Checking her lipstick one last time in the visor mirror, she backed out of her driveway for her hour commute.

She found herself braking when she spied the girlish woman with fluffy carrot hair wearing an orange-and-green flagger's vest. The past three mornings, she'd thought the slight figure under the yellow rain gear with a thumb out was a young man. The woman was obviously also headed for work. Wanting to share the bounty of her recently acquired Toyota, Doris came to a stop. The woman could only be headed to one place, since there was only one major construction site in the area. Doris was going right through it. "Hi, I'm Doris."

"I'm Molly. It's Crawford, now." She took a moment in the busyness of getting in the car to smile at Doris. "It'll be Saunders soon. As soon as my fiancée gets out of prison! We're flaggers for True Construction." She'd finished getting buckled in, her three water jugs arrayed at her feet. The equipment took more space than the bird-like woman with the hard hat over the bottle-orange frizz of hair.

57

Not noticing Doris's frown at the mention of prison, she continued. "They sent him to Windham. He can get work release there."

The visibly sun-baked skin, which reminded Doris of a pair of Doe buck shoes she'd once had, made her appreciate her education and a good, clean desk job.

Molly didn't occupy much space physically, but she wasn't recessive. "He asked how much time to get out without parole. So he's in for nine months. I sure miss him. We used to work together. We'd mess with people's heads, 'cause some people pick up the two-ways on their scanners, you know."

No, I didn't know, thought Doris, as she wondered what had possessed her to pick up this harmless-looking, working woman, who was older than the seventeen she'd looked roadside, employed at a young person's job, and with a jailbird boyfriend.

Oblivious, the other chatted on. "He lost his license OUI, though he'd only had a drink or two. Our boss knew and kept having him drive, first from one end of the worksite to the other and then running other errands. He got stopped for driving without a license. Go figure. So one weekend I visit with him and the other, I visit with my daughter. She was acting out and DHS put her in a group home. She should be coming home soon 'cause they said it would only be for four months and it's been like six."

More like the boyfriend grabbed a handful of the daughter, thought Doris. How many kinds of ways is your life out of control, she wondered. As the other woman kept up the spew of information, Doris clandestinely stroked the leather on her armrest.

"When we was flagging together, Tom and me came up with codes for some of the regulars: Goldie for this woman in a gold Audi and Blondie, and Mustache. And the True's trucks we called Blues. 'Got a Blue coming through.' Flagging, you keep traffic going good and keep the lanes open for the construction equipment so they can get the work done. Trucks are hauling all day. If you hold them up, they can't do what they need to."

Doris could see flagging traffic was a little more complicated than she had considered while chafing at traffic delays in construction zones.

"They put me in charge of the crews the last few days. I'm running my crew and trying to work the other crew and watching the trucks, too. Somebody mouths off about waiting, we remember and hold them extra long on the rewind."

It was with some relief that Doris stopped to drop off the Chatty Cathy she'd picked up.

"See you up and down," said Molly with a final wave as she sauntered away.

Doris dealt with people like the bushy-haired Molly all the time in credit counseling. The house Molly claimed to own was probably in hawk to the bank or was one of the broken-down wrecks that blight small towns, filled with equally broken-down furniture or rent-a-life things. No money was available for bills, but the overflowing trash would be filled with pizza boxes and dog-gnawed steak bones and stenchy paper diapers.

The next morning, Doris couldn't think of a reason to drive by Molly. Some people, she thought, even as she braked, really ought to get their life together. Wishing to recall the words even as they poured out of her mouth, she said, "I come by every morning. I'll gladly give you a ride, as long as your clothes are clean." She could see that not only were Molly's jeans clean, but pressed. Even she didn't press her jeans.

"Oh, neat. Yeah, wouldn't want to mess up this gray upholstery," she said, as she squashed her yellow hard hat onto her frizzed hair.

Doris corrected her. "It's silver."

"Oh, yeah. I'll be getting my license soon, I think. As soon as I'm finished the DEEP program. Then I gotta get the car inspected and registered. Sam, the local cop, saw I'd moved it the other day and stopped by to harass me and ask where'd I been with it."

Doris had a burning question for Molly. Finally she pushed it into the flow of chatter. "How do you get where you're going?"

"I live right in town. Like, what do you mean?"

"Like work. I mean, usually." Her voice sounded snappy. "And to see your daughter and boyfriend?" How could someone be so dense?

Molly answered as if this were normal chatter. "Well, DHS pays Community Concepts to take me to see my daughter, except when they forget. Then, my mother-in-law, I call her that even though we're not married. She takes me along when she goes south to see her son."

The answer spawned another question. "What have you been living on, with him in jail and flagging just starting up again?"

"Oh, this and that. I've been getting unemployment, but that was about to run out. And I've been doing some painting for this other guy I know. And last week I picked fiddleheads. I picked seventy pounds one day. That pays sixty cents a pound. This other guy picked like two hundred, but I think he was taking from others when no one was looking."

Doris had thought Molly would claim welfare or child support. Food stamps were mentioned, as if everyone had them. With food stamps came MaineCare, some form of child welfare, and usually a host of unpaid bills. Most likely, Molly's finances would be a challenge to straighten out, for sure.

The third morning, Doris stopped again and, for her effort, received a blow-by-blow account of the ongoing struggle with the DHS worker who handled the daughter's case.

"So, I told Susie, the worker, she was breaking a court order by not letting her call me. I finally got through to her, I guess. She's sending me a phone card. I wish she'd just pay my phone bill, but I guess a card is better than nothing." The monologue was delivered matter-of-fact. "Anyway, you gotta stay on these people. Wish I could get someone to pay for the calls to Tom. Now I gotta get after them to let her come home for weekends. We have a court date next month and I should be able to convince the judge she'd do better at home."

By the fourth morning, Monday of the following week, Doris was looking forward to the outlandish stories Molly told. The topic was visits to the boyfriend and the struggles to convince the warden to allow this and that privilege. "There was no one to fight for this old fella', so I talked to the warden. He was carving beautiful little wooden things, but not at the prison shop, but I told the warden he should be allowed to sell his stuff there anyway. They use the money for junk food, cigarettes or whatever. I think he's gonna let him do it, too. He oughta be allowed. He needs the money."

The fifth morning, Molly was running out to the road when Doris arrived. As she tried to push a comb through her drying hair, the talk was about a stalker, someone who was around the house. "Almost overslept. Was up half the night. I've got a coupla dogs and they barked on and on. They don't usually bark much. I know someone was out there. They better not come in, though. What the dogs don't get, I'll kill." Her voice carried convincing passion, but the threat seemed comical, coming from such a small person, like a braggart teenager. "They're messing with the wrong woman."

Doris worked hard not to laugh as Molly quit the combing, jammed on her hard-hat and continued her story. "I know I can't go out in the yard and shoot them, but they put a foot in the door, they're done for. My dad taught me to shoot. Clay pigeons, at first. I can hit anything." Sounded like a bad B-rated movie.

Nuts. Certifiable, Doris had thought. And yet, under the rough exterior, every now and then, some little icon poked through, like clay pigeons, that suggested a way of living that wasn't receiving welfare, painting houses, and working construction.

Doris breathed a sigh of relief when Molly wasn't out at the road Wednesday morning. These types didn't hold jobs long. Yet, Molly talked like she'd been flagging for a few years. Thursday, Molly again wasn't there for her ride to work. Maybe she's starting work earlier, Doris thought to herself.

When she arrived at work, she bought a paper, as usual. The headline was in big, black bold letters.

ATTORNEY SHOT—WIFE FOUND MURDERED
Flagger Held For Assault

Leslie Rowe, a prominent attorney in the town of Avalon, was report-ed in stable condition at Franklin Memorial Hospital, where he was transported by AMPS after receiving a gunshot in the leg while in the home of Molly Crawford. Sheriff's Deputy John Small went to notify Mrs. Rowe of the shooting and found her body. Sources close to the case state that the state crime lab is investigating the death as possible murder.

Attorney Rowe claimed he knew nothing about the death of his wife until informed at the hospital. He further stated that he went to visit Molly Crawford, a flagger with True Construction, on his way home from a trip, after receiving a voice mail that she had an urgent need to see him about on ongoing DHS case.

Ms. Crawford, currently held at the Franklin County Jail, claims she never called him and that he'd been stalking her for a day or two, and she shot him in self-defense, after he entered her house uninvited and approached her in a threatening manner. She told the press she couldn't be involved with the death of his wife because she has no clue where they lived.

The article startled Doris, and as she read, before starting work at Consumer Credit Assistance, she remembered the first time she met

Molly Beale Crawford, just a week ago.

"Not so nuts," thought Doris, as she glanced back over the headlines of the Thursday morning newspaper. She'd grown to like the crusty redhead who ironed her clothes to go to work as a flagger.

On impulse, Doris pulled up a credit check for Molly Crawford-soon-to-be-Saunders. No credit cards, no charge cards showing anywhere, and no evidence of a checking account. No outstanding bills except the telephone. That would be the calls to the daughter and collect calls from the boyfriend. Maine prisons only allow prisoners to make collect calls to someone who has already phoned in. They can't receive incoming calls.

Doris was bothered by a seeming conflict in the article. Attorney Rowe claimed he'd been out of town for a week. Molly claimed someone had been stalking her for a few days. Doris reached for the computer keyboard, then withdrew her hands. This was more than just a friendly credit check, such as she'd just done on Molly. If Mr. Big Shot Attorney Rowe had been out of town, he would have left a paper trail, credit card charges, checks, hotel receipts, maybe airline tickets, or toll slips, something to show he'd really gone somewhere.

It really was illegal to go into someone's personal life electronically, without their permission or a warrant. She'd go see Molly or the investigating officers and ask if she could help. Do it legally, so the information would be legal, binding and put the son of a gun away.

She knew, somehow, at a gut level, Molly was telling the truth. Rowe had been stalking her. He had the bullet wound to prove it.

Doris didn't have any trouble getting into the jail to see Molly. "Hey, Ride Lady. Sorry I haven't been out the past few mornings." She was smiling. The orange jumpsuit looked oversize but neat on Molly, whose hair looked a little frizzier than normal without a hardhat to shape it. "Hope you didn't wait or nothin'."

"No, I didn't wait or nothin'." Doris felt a smile of friendliness creep across her face. "So, they treating you right?"

"Yeah. I'm getting out this afternoon. They just have to, you know, process stuff. The shooting was legal, 'cause he was in my house and I asked him to leave and he didn't."

"What happened? Why would he come after you?"

"I talked to him the day he killed her, but I don't remember, you know. Flagging. So many people come through. He thought I could finger him and ruin his alibi. Go figure. Heck, if he'd left it be, I wouldn't have remembered."

"And he told you that?"

"People say funny things when they're on the floor, looking up the barrel of a gun. Now I got to get him to say something in court. Right now, he refuses."

"You don't seem afraid of the murder charge, and him a lawyer."

Molly smiled. "Naw. There's no connection. He did it. I'm sure. I got to prove he didn't go anywhere on a trip, like he says."

"I might be able to help. It's what I do."

"Prove where people were?"

"Not exactly. I work with paper trails. He'll have to account for his whereabouts. There should be paper trails, like credit card charges, stuff like that."

"Oh, man. I hadn't thought. I just always pay cash. I get in so much trouble with even a checking account. I just pay cash. Great. And maybe someone else saw him, or something. Or he used the card."

Doris laughed along with this slight woman who was really so very in charge of herself and of her world. So much for first impressions.

"So, maybe I'll see you tomorrow morning?"

"Don't wait, but I'll probably be there. My boss was in and said he needed me as soon as possible. He ain't got any other flagger can run more than one crew and the Blues, too."

Runaway

Judith Green

When Agnes pulled into the dooryard in her metallic blue P T Cruiser, Margery Easton laid down the clippers she'd been using to deadhead the lilacs at the corner of the house. Agnes, her head with its tightly permed hair hardly high enough for her to see over the dashboard, sat hunched over the wheel, unmoving.

This was an event. Agnes Littlefield could often be found in the back of Nesbitt's Store in the village, selecting canned soup and canned cat food with equal care. She attended church every week, and drove daily to the post office at a stately 35 per. But she never went visiting.

The window came down halfway. Agnes's rheumy eyes, like a pair of fried eggs, stared out at Margery from behind her thick, round lenses. "It's my cat," she croaked. "Fluffy's been taken!"

"Taken? Who would take your cat?" Margery often saw him, all thirty-odd pounds of him—he was big even for a Maine coon cat— draped magnificently along the front railing of Agnes's porch, his long glossy fur shining in the sun, eyes closed, tufted ears pivoting in the ever-vigilant radar of cats.

"Taken," Agnes repeated.

"Well—" Margery adopted a look of concern. "When's the last time you saw him?"

"Last night. I let him out about seven o'clock to do his business,

65

and when I went to let him back in, he was gone."

"Well," Margery said again, "it's June. Nice night. Maybe he thought he'd take a stroll, do a little hunting—" Fluffy probably ate better than Agnes did, judging by what Margery had seen stacked on the counter at Nesbitt's Store, but a little fresh mouse on the menu from time to time might be appealing.

"He'll come back on his own," Margery assured her. "He's probably on your doorstep right now, wondering why you don't open the door."

"No." Agnes shook her head solemnly. "I'm going around and telling everyone: he's been taken. You need to keep your ears open."

And with that she slammed the P T Cruiser into reverse and roared down the length of the driveway, across a corner of the lawn, and out onto the road.

"Okay." Margery watched the metallic blue end of the car disappear around the curve. "I'll keep my ears open."

□   □   □

It was too darned nice out to cook dinner. Nachos, Margery decided. Nachos as a meal was a concept brought back from college by their youngest daughter. Superbly easy. Margery loved it.

However, as she peered into the murky depths of the refrigerator, with her own orange cat enthusiastically buffing her shins, she hit a snag. Hiding behind a six-pack of Shipyard, the half-jar of salsa had taken on a dark, malevolent look. She sure as heck wasn't going to feed that to anyone.

A trip to Nesbitt's Store, then. Still easier than cooking, and she could pick up some sour cream—oh, yum—for the nachos.

When she was a kid, the little store in the village had sold everything: groceries in bulk, grain, machinery parts, and where the pizza counter was now, broad shelves held overalls, shirts, bolts of cloth. Now here she was, dashing in just for a jar of salsa.

A semi tractor without its trailer sat smack in front of the store, and beyond it an advance car with WIDE LOAD signs fore and aft. Both vehicles bore the logo and name of Just-Rite Homes.

Margery maneuvered between the two vehicles, bristling at the company's name: what a tacky thing to do to the English language. She tried not to think of modular homes themselves as tacky, since a number of her friends worked at the place, or called their product home, but still—

As Margery let the store's ancient screen door slap shut behind her, she spotted the drivers perched on stools at the counter, wolfing down Erlon Nesbitt's famous pounder hamburgers. "Yeah, they're looking for a couple more guys to make trips out of Maine," one of the carnivores said around a large mouthful. He was big, broad-shouldered, already building a paunch beneath his Fryeburg Fair t-shirt, but the face under the shock of blond hair was soft and unformed, somehow, like a baby's.

Still chewing, the baby-faced man swung around on the stool to face someone curled over a cup of coffee at one of the tables. "And it don't take much training to drive the advance car, does it, Calvin?" He planted a jovial elbow in the ribcage of the man on the stool next to him.

Calvin wiped his fingers fastidiously on a paper napkin before turning around to face their audience of one. "The training's not the point. You gotta be able to drive with one eye on the road and one eye on the rearview, see if that damned truck is gaining on you. Going down a steep hill, I keep both eyes on the rearview. I just watch Troy's face." Calvin jerked a thumb at his companion. "His eyes start bugging out, I know I got a couple of tons of house trail-er about to ride right up over the top of me."

Margery had been absent-mindedly following the conversation as she rooted about in the cooler for a pint of sour cream. Now, approaching the counter, she realized that the man the truckers were talking to was her cousin Norris. Last she'd heard, Norris had found a job as a long-haul trucker. If he was back home again, then that job hadn't worked out either.

"Remember last week going over to Vermont?" Troy asked. "What's that mountain—Searsburg? I think I hit that runaway ramp doing about eighty."

Vermont, Margery thought. In fact, she'd been over Searsburg Mountain. Phyllis, her best-friend-in-all-the-world from grade school, had married a Vermonter and settled in Brattleboro. How long since she'd seen Phyllis, anyway?

"Yeah," Calvin was saying, "You scared the shit right out of that damned animal you had in there, and then you left me to clean up after him. But seriously," he added, turning to Norris, "you oughta go over to the factory and put your name in."

Norris nodded. He kept his face turned away from Margery. "I think I might do that."

□   □   □

As she came out of the store, Richard Davis pulled his tan pickup into the driveway next door. "Evening, Margery," he called. He jerked his chin toward the Just-Rite vehicles. "Is that Troy and Calvin in there?"

"Troy's a big guy, kind of young-looking? Calvin's a little older, dark hair?" Margery asked. "Yes, they're having supper."

"Figures. The foreman's waiting for them. Those guys—" Richard shook his head. "Get a meal while they're on the clock, twenty miles from the plant. Anybody else'd bring the truck in and go home for supper."

He climbed down from the pickup, tucked in his shirttail all the way around, then kissed his wife, who had come out on the porch, flushed from the heat of the kitchen. "You smell like pot roast." He grinned. "Sexiest kind of perfume a woman can wear."

"Just like you asked for," Sandra said. "I've just got to whip the potatoes."

Richard pulled his lunchbox off the seat and handed it to her, then elbowed the truck door shut. "You go ahead if you want," he said. "It's too hot to eat a heavy meal. I'll just make me a sandwich later."

□   □   □

"Agnes Littlefield stopped by today." Margery reached for a particularly cheesy section of the plate.

"Hey! Pig!" Laughing, Jenny snatched up a plain chip and filched a drooping pennant of cheese before Margery could get it to her mouth.

"What did she want?" Tom smeared a chip through the sour cream.

"She's lost her cat. It didn't come in last night, and she's already convinced it's been catnapped." Margery grinned at her own joke.

"That big gray tabby of hers?" Jenny asked. "That's a Maine coon cat. They can be very valuable."

"It's just a cat," Margery said.

Jenny bristled. "You wait a minute!" She lunged across the kitchen to the table under the window where the family computer sat still flashing "You won!" across a completed game of Spider solitaire. "And stay away from my side of the platter," she said over her shoulder. "I've got dibs on that part by the beans."

Margery sighed. Her husband and daughter often used the Internet to settle disputes. The mid-meal dash to the computer had become commonplace. She was glad the family still ate together— if you defined hanging over the computer, still chewing, as togetherness.

"Come here and look, Mom!"

The computer screen displayed a half-dozen photos of cats in haughty poses, perfect coon cats in the slant of their enormous eyes, the tufts of fur on their pointed ears, the ruffs of fur down their proud chests. Below each photo were the words GRAND CHAMPION and the name of a cat show.

"Well, yes, champions," Margery said vaguely. "But no one would pay—"

"Watch." Jenny clicked back to the original Google screen. "Here's where they sell things," she said in a you-should-know-this tone of voice. She clicked on the first advertisement, for a breeder in southern Maine. "This kitten available for adoption" unscrolled above a photo of a particularly adorable ball of fur with enormous slanted eyes.

Margery pointed at a notice on the bottom of the screen: "Our kitty's are certified." She said, "All that fancy web page stuff, and they can't spell their own product."

"Mom, can't you leave your English teacher head at school? Anyway, this coon cat's in Maine, and look, it's on sale for a thousand dollars."

"You win," Margery said. "Now come eat your dinner. Your father's scarfing all the salsa."

□   □   □

An hour later, Margery found herself back at the computer. Some people, she discovered, believed that the sturdy, long-haired coon cats came from interbreeding between housecats and bobcats. Or raccoons. Other theories involved the Vikings arriving in the Maritimes, long before Columbus—with their sturdy hunting cats at their sides. Or the smuggler Captain Coon, who sailed in and out of the thousands of lonely inlets of Maine's rugged coast with a shipful of long-haired cats.

Maine coon cats had been very popular in cat shows in the 1800s. Suddenly they were in demand again. Breeders not just in Maine but all over the country demanded prices in four digits for tiny kittens.

Big as he was, Fluffy never seemed anything more than a cat that did a good job of keeping a lonely old lady company. But if he were an exceptionally good example of a Maine coon cat—

"Here's something," Tom said suddenly from the kitchen table, where he sat reading the *Portland Press-Herald* over a cooling mug of decaf. He pointed to a box at the bottom of the page. "REWARD," read the heading, and below that: "Lost: Maine coon cat, female, smoky, green collar," with town and phone number.

"Jeezum," Margery said. "Do you suppose Agnes was right? Fluffy was stolen?"

Tom shrugged and refolded the paper. "Here's an interesting column on the school board reorganization."

"Spare me," Margery said.

□ □ □

When she pushed open the screen door at Nesbitt's Store the next afternoon, Margery found Agnes Littlefield's stocky frame planted in the aisle between the ice cream cooler and the newspaper rack, blocking her way to the counter.

"Have you seen this?" Agnes thrust a newspaper clipping into Margery's hands. "Look!"

The clipping had been worn as soft as a bit of fabric. The words at the edges had blurred, but the headline was clear: PET THEFT RING SUSPECTED IN PORTLAND AREA.

"Oh, Agnes," Margery said. "So Fluffy hasn't come back."

"No. Like I said from the start, Fluffy wouldn't just run off. He's been taken."

"Have you reported it to the Sheriff's Department?"

"Hmph. They just say to call them back when I have a definite lead."

Margery looked down at Agnes. Her eyes seemed smeared, somehow, and Margery realized that behind her huge glasses Agnes was weeping.

□ □ □

Margery pulled out of the high school parking lot the next afternoon with the back seat stacked with themes to correct, including five woefully late term papers. Her juniors were finally getting to work: there was something about watching the seniors lined up for marching practice that could squeeze the last few assignments from the laziest juniors.

She paused at the exit, ready to make the right turn for the familiar fourteen miles home. But suddenly she heard that fellow Calvin's voice again, buzzing between her ears: You scared the shit out of that damned animal you had in there.

Someone's pet, scared to death, shoved into some hidey-hole in that rolling, shuddering house on wheels?

Where? Where would they hide a stolen pet?

She swung the steering wheel to the left, away from home. And toward the supermarket, the Pizza Hut, and beyond them to the wide, squat building that was Just-Rite Homes.

She didn't exactly pose as a customer. After all, dozens of her neighbors and former students worked in the place. She just asked the nice fortyish man with the pocket protector and fresh wad of pencils if she could have a peek at the production line.

In the factory, the air hung with sawdust, through which, from all directions, the sounds of nailguns and men's voices moved with muffled urgency. At the end of the line, distant in the gloom, men were assembling a wide, flat trailer frame. One step nearer, a similar frame already had its linoleum stapled down in a ghostly dance floor of kitchen, bathroom, laundry room. Nearer yet, prebuilt partition walls were being lowered in and nailed down. "The linoleum can't ever curl up," her guide informed her, "because the walls are actually sitting on it."

"Very nice," said Margery, picturing the gaping cracks between the pine floorboards in her ancient farmhouse.

The partition walls seemed to huddle together for protection in the center of the open trailer as a forklift roared down the shop floor and shoved a shower/bathtub combination into place in the future bathroom. "Once we've got the appliances and cabinets loaded in," her guide said, pointing to the next station, "the outer walls and roof go on."

Margery nodded. This one looked like a house already, walls and roof in place. Men crawled about on top of the peak, laying in wire off huge hanging reels, while packages of insulation seemed to unroll themselves between the joists. "How long until a house is completed?" she asked, just for something to ask.

"Ten days, including testing the wiring and plumbing. Then out it goes."

Margery stood still in the din of the nailguns and staplers, the roar of the forklift heading back for the kitchen stove. The houses at the far end of the line were complete with window trim, carpets, even drapes. They were houses.

Plenty of room to hide a cat.

□ □ □

For Friday night fare, Margery made sloppy joes to please Tom, and a huge salad to keep Jenny from grumbling about the nutritional hazards of living at home. As soon as both had their mouths safely full, she told them about Agnes posting herself like the Ancient Mariner with her newspaper clipping. "I've known Agnes all my life— although I think she was already old when I was a kid. Anyway, I feel as if I've got to help her."

Jenny laughed. "My mom the cat detective!"

"What are you going to do?" Tom asked. "Stake out Agnes's front porch in case they come back?"

"Listen. The truck driver from Just-Rite Homes had an animal in the trailer. They had to clean up after it in Brattleboro, and I think they wanted Norris along so he could do it next time. Next time! So there's some connection in Brattleboro. Maybe it's a link to New York City. All we need to do is to find out where the transfer is made. And I think I know." Margery hopped up from the table to snatch a sheet of paper from the computer printer. "See?" She waved the paper at Tom and Jenny. "There's a modular home dealership right on the outskirts. All we have to do is go—"

"To Brattleboro?" Tom's eyes registered panic.

"Now, come on. Phyllis was my best friend all the way through grade school, and I haven't seen her in ages."

"Margery, be reasonable for once. We're not going to Brattleboro looking for Agnes's cat."

"Then I'll go by myself."

"Knock yourself out." And Tom wrestled his sloppy joe off the plate and up to his mouth, decorating his shirtfront with tomato sauce in the process.

"But Mom," Jenny asked, "how are you going to know if they're transporting cats to Vermont?"

Margery smiled. "I'm going to take Phyllis with me to the dealership in Brattleboro. She's terribly allergic to cats. When I was a kid, I had to choose between having a kitten of my own and having her as a friend."

And she bent down to give Marmalade, who was entwining himself about her ankles, a good rub behind his ears.

"Mom!" Jenny's tone was awestruck. "You are positively Machiavellian."

Margery smiled. "It'll be lovely to have Phyllis all to myself for a quiet evening."

□ □ □

"Omigawd, it'll be so good to see you!" Phyllis's voice came through the receiver loud and clear. "Are you sure Tom can't come?" Across the kitchen, Tom slid down behind his newspaper.

"No, he's got some projects here," Margery said.

"Too bad. Sheldon," she shouted, evidently to the next room, "Margery's coming! Margery Easton. We've got a couple of the grandchildren over this evening," she explained, "and Sheldon's in the living room giving horsie-back rides. This is perfect. I'll get on the phone to the kids. I'll just bet they'll all be free for dinner tomorrow night. They like to rally round when there's food involved. We'll have our first cookout of the summer. Well, it's supposed to rain, so it'll be more of a cook-in, but you'll get to meet all the spouses and—let's see—nine grandkids, including the baby."

Margery didn't dare look at Tom. She could feel his smirk right through the newspaper.

□   □   □

Margery stood beside her car in the parking lot of the Mountaintop Restaurant, looking out over the vast sweep of lush June treetops undulating over rounded hills and into sheltered valleys to the horizon. According to the sign, the view took in parts of four different states. Searsburg Mountain might not be tall by western standards, but for New England, it was high enough.

Well. Onward.

As she pulled open her car door, she heard the roar of a truck engine climbing the hill she had just come up. She climbed in, started her car, and pulled to the edge of the road, just too late to cut in front of him. Actually, she realized, it was a familiar entourage: advance car emblazoned with the yellow WIDE LOAD sign, truck with modular home, and rear car following patiently behind. As they passed, she found herself staring at the Just-Rite Homes logo on the truck door. And there was Troy behind the wheel, window cranked down to the sill, thick elbow emerging, sticking out from a green t-shirt sleeve into the sunshine.

Margery paused. Should she tail them into Brattleboro, or pass them by and wait for them at the dealership? Suddenly she realized that she'd better hurry up if she was going to do either. The rear car was still in view, but the advance car and the truck had disappeared around a curve.

She pulled out and stepped down on the gas, watching the speedometer needle move up to forty, fifty. She still hadn't caught up with the rear car.

She swung around a wide curve. Below her she could see the two cars, now spread wide apart on the long mountainside, the advance car tiny in the distance. Between them the truck roared downward, the house behind it seeming to swell with momentum. Two cars coming uphill on the other side of the road pulled over to give them room.

Was it safe to get the trailer going this fast? Troy had boasted about hitting the runaway ramp at eighty. What a cowboy!

Another curve was coming at them. The trio disappeared, then reappeared as Margery rounded the curve. Below them a runaway ramp slashed a steep track up into the forest. Margery shuddered. The ramp looked vicious, somehow.

The truck pointed toward the ramp, brake lights flashing on— then rocketed by the end of the ramp and continued downward, the trailer jostling along behind in its own private earthquake.

Margery's heart clenched in her throat. What was Troy thinking? Had he lost his brakes? Or his mind?

Margery realized she, too, was plummeting down the mountain. Heart racing, she pumped the brake, and steered into the next curve. There they were—the rear car with its WIDE LOAD sign, and beyond it the house. Suddenly the back wall slewed sideways, as if the whole house had boarded a merry-go-round. The front windows swung across the lane in a mad dance. Then the whole thing righted itself, aligned itself with the curve, hung for a long moment pointed down the mountain—then flipped over on its side. Margery could hear the frantic blasts of the air brakes as the house skidded, swerved, the trailer wheels sticking out like little legs kicking. Shattered pieces flew off into the woods: shutters, window frames, bits of siding. A home. Someone's home was slaloming down the road, tearing itself to shreds as it went.

And in it somewhere was someone's pet.

At last the truck managed to stop the slide, or perhaps the trailer dragged the truck to a stop. The entire lane was blocked with debris and the long, black undercarriage of the trailer.

As the rear car pulled up at a safe distance, Troy was already jumping out of the cab. He stood looking at the wreck, muscular arms dangling at his sides. He made no move to check inside the trailer to see if anything were still alive.

Margery braked, braked, then pulled up behind the rear car. Her heart was beating so fast that she felt faint and sick. She crawled out of her car door, only to grab her rearview mirror for support as the grassy shoulder swayed and turned beneath her.

She looked past the rear car toward the wreck and spotted a window on the end nearest her. Laid out sideways, the window hung ajar, its drapes flapping in the breeze. In the next instant, Margery was pelting down the hill.

She poked her head into the window. Inside was a bedroom, beige carpet running up what was now a wall. Closet doors hung crazily from the newly assigned ceiling. Oh, she hoped they hadn't put an animal cage in there—

"Hey!" a man's voice barked. Margery was vaguely aware of cars pulling up, doors slamming. A jumble of voices. And shrill in the distance, a siren.

Somewhere in the depths of the wreckage, something whimpered.

"Hey, lady!" the voice shouted again. "Get away from there!"

Margery thrust her arms and torso through the window. "Hello? Hello?" she called. The whimper sounded again. A mewling cry, like a baby's.

"Lady!" Boots scrunched in the gravel. A hand grasped at the back of her jacket.

Galvanized by the touch, Margery lunged forward and fell into the room. She landed heavily on her shoulder in the corner, her head thudding against the carpet rising behind her, her legs spraddled against the wall.

Above her, Troy's cherubic face poked through the opening, flushed in astonishment. He reached for her, the huge paw coming at her, fishing for her, grasping for her ankle.

She rolled over and crawled away, then scuttled toward a door in the opposite wall. Beneath her feet, glass crunched, and she stepped down through a shattered window frame onto the pavement of the roadway. Behind her she could hear Troy struggling through the opening she had come through.

In two more steps, she reached the door—laid out sideways, its doorknob like a decoration at the upper edge. She yanked the door open, letting it fall downward to form a wooden ramp, and crawled through the horizontal opening.

She found herself hunched in a corridor barely three feet from side to side—now bottom to top. A dented appliance—a dryer, she thought—lay tipped on edge, blocking her way. Directly above her, a washing machine hung precariously from its plumbing. Next to it, a door formed a pale green rectangle of low ceiling.

Above the door, the mewling cry sounded again.

She rose as best she could and grasped the doorknob, using her back to heave the door upward. A scrabbling of claws, an excited yip, and a golden retriever puppy slid through the opening and landed between her feet—along with a bit of old blanket, a water dish, and other bits and pieces that must have originally been set out on the bathroom floor for the puppy's comfort.

Margery grabbed for the dog's collar. She'd been right! Troy and Calvin were smuggling pets out of Maine. She had the proof, the warm, furry proof, right here.

"Queenie!" Troy's voice boomed from beyond the doorway.

"Queenie, you're all right! Here, girl!"

And the puppy pulled out of Margery's grasp, dove through the sidelong doorway, and leapt messily into her master's arms.

Margery dropped where she was and sat leaning against the dryer, her face in her hands. She was suddenly exhausted. What an idiot she was.

She heard footsteps coming through the end room, then a scuffling at the open door, as if someone were crawling through. She looked up, expecting to see Troy.

It was Calvin. And gone was the placid philosopher she'd seen at Nesbitt's. Calvin's face was rigid with fury.

She scrabbled backwards against the cool, hard surface of the dryer, her heart pounding. What? her mind shouted. What?

And then she saw it. Just beyond her foot, lying in a fold of the puppy's blanket, was a fat packet of white powder.

Calvin's eyes followed her gaze. In the dim light filtering in around the dryer, Margery watched the eyes turn hard. He looked back up at her.

Then he lunged.

His shoulder drove into her stomach, jamming her back against the dryer. She could not move, could not breathe. "I don't know what you're doing in here, lady," Calvin snarled, "but I think it's time you had a little accident of your own."

He shifted his weight, and she realized that he was reaching upward, toward the washing machine that hung from its pipes just inches above her head. It creaked as he grabbed at it by its open door.

Suddenly his weight was wrenched away. Gasping for air, she scrabbled away from him. He lunged after her, but with a cry he fell face downward. His feet disappeared, then his legs, and she realized that he was being dragged backwards through the horizontal doorway.

"Help! We need some help in here!" a man's voice shouted. "Someone's hurt!"

The voice sounded familiar, Margery thought hazily. In fact, it sounded like her cousin Norris.

And then the tiny space under the washing machine got very busy indeed. Voices sounded in the other room, footsteps, the crunch of wood as the window opening at the far end was broken out. Strong arms drew her out through the doorway and held her close for a moment, someone wearing a John Deere cap, and she was fairly sure it was her cousin Norris. But now there were so many men moving around her, talking to each other in deep voices. Men in police uniforms. One of them crawled through into the corridor beside the fallen dryer, and Margery heard him scrambling upward into the space the dog had fallen from.

"Well, well, well," she heard him say. "Better put the cuffs on that guy. Looks like there's a real haul of the stuff in here wrapped up in the shower curtain."

□   □   □

"The boss fired all three of us." Norris sat hunched at the back table at Nesbitt's, his big knuckles ridged around both sides of a coffee mug.

Margery pulled out a chair and sat opposite him. "I'm sorry."

"Yeah, even though the accident was all on Troy. Troy said all's he was trying to do was break his own record for getting over the mountain. Guess he forgot for a moment he'd put his own dog back there."

"Jeezum." Margery sighed. "All that mess. And, Norris, I never really got a chance to thank you for—"

"Calvin?" Norris shrugged. "I saw him dive through that window, and I figured I'd better check on you. Just in case."

"Oh, Norris."

"Well, you know. Blood is thicker'n water." Norris looked away, suddenly shy.

She patted his elbow. "Thanks," she said. "You won't—well, you won't tell Tom about me going into that wreck, will you?"

Norris glanced at her, a twinkle in his eye. "Nah." He took a sip of coffee. "I can't figure those two," he added. "Calvin and Troy, I guess they both just like excitement. Anyway, it don't matter about the job. I wouldn't of gone back today anyway."

"Really?"

"You know how much one of those houses weighs? Prob'ly close to twenty tons. I had to follow that trailer all the way up that damned mountain, wondering the whole way if Troy'd ever bothered to check the trailer hitch." Norris took a swallow of his coffee. "If that trailer'd come loose, there's no way in hell I could've got the rear car backed out of the way before all twenty tons of it just flattened me right into the pavement."

He grinned up at Margery from under the bill of his John Deere cap. "They said the rear car job was dead easy. All I could think about was the dead part."

Of course as Margery drove by Agnes Littlefield's house on the way home from Nesbitt's, she saw that the front railing was entirely covered by the familiar gray-tabby fur, surmounted by the magnificent tufted ears of Agnes's cat.

She almost passed by. No, she had to ask.

"Oh, yes, he came home on Friday," Agnes said. "I knew he was here when I found a dead mouse on the doormat. A little gift, you know. Oh, yes, Fluffy knows how to look after himself."

Margery looked over at the cat. He regarded her for a long moment, then closed his eyes.

Thirty Days

Woody Hanstein

Peggy didn't say anything after I hung up the phone and asked how she'd feel about driving me over to the coast on Friday to serve a thirty-day jail sentence for some guy Lloyd Carter knew.

She was feeding applesauce to the baby, and she put the spoon down and shook her head. I was sitting across the kitchen table from them with a cup of instant coffee and the help wanted ads from Sunday's paper. It was Wednesday and the fact that my broken right hand was in a cast wasn't doing wonders for my job prospects.

In the glow cast by the streetlight outside the trailer, snowflakes were falling as big as nickels. Peggy's eyes got narrow as she watched me, and she set her mouth like a question was coming. It was the same look she gave me back in the fall after she found out about me and her younger sister.

Peggy kept shaking her head, but she still didn't say anything. The baby started fussing and she fed her some more applesauce. Peggy still had on her waitress uniform. It was robin's egg blue and cut snug so it showed off her nice breasts and her strong, freckled arms. Peggy turned thirty-five back in December, but she was still easy to look at.

"It'd be two thousand bucks," I said, trying to sound indifferent, like it was just a number. "That's good money for a couple weeks' work."

"You said thirty days a minute ago."

"Lloyd's cousin says Rock Harbor's so full everybody's getting two-for-one. I keep my nose clean and push a mop around, he says I could be home in fifteen. Maybe even less they get crowded and run out of room."

"So, why doesn't Lloyd go push a mop around if it's such easy money?"

"His divorce. He's got mediation next week and he no-showed last time. His lawyer says if he's not there Tuesday, Julie will get the woodlot for sure."

Peggy shook her head. "She oughta get the woodlot." Then she mumbled something to the baby I couldn't make out but which didn't sound complimentary. Peggy didn't think a whole lot of Lloyd.

"We could fix the furnace," I said. "And put some new tires on your Bronco. Even pay your mom back the $600 we still owe her."

Peggy didn't say anything to that, but I could see her doing the math in her head as she looked through the cracked kitchen window at the snow coming down. She was an honorable woman, but she also had her practical side.

"It'll never work," she finally said, but I could see from the way she held herself that the idea was starting to lose some of its distastefulness. "You can't just show up at jail and pretend you're somebody else."

"Who's going to know the difference?"

"I thought they had mug shots?"

"Not of this guy—he never got arrested. He rolled his Jeep like six times and the EMTs just bagged him and dragged him. Straight to the ER. He's never even been booked."

"So what happens when they ask you for ID? Won't they fingerprint you and want to see your license?"

"That's the beauty of it. Since it's an OUI, I just tell 'em the DMV down in Mass already took it. Hell, it's foolproof."

"It sounds messed-up to me," Peggy said. "What's this guy doing with a whack-job like Lloyd?"

"Maybe none of his doctor friends could get the month off."

"But, Lloyd?" Peggy made a face like she just tasted something bad.

"His cousin Mike knows the guy."

"Mike, whose tattoo parlor burned down last summer?"

"Hey, that was an accident. They proved it."

Peggy shook her head. "It still sounds foolish to me."

By this time Sara had lost interest in eating, so Peggy put her down on the living room floor and went in to take a shower. I finished up with the classifieds, but if anybody else was paying two grand to lie around reading magazines for a couple weeks, they didn't put an ad in last Sunday's paper. Later on Peggy made macaroni with real cheese sauce, and after dinner she bathed Sara and put her down for the night.

Neither of us said any more about Lloyd's offer, and after things got quiet in the baby's room we watched some TV until the news came on at eleven and then we called it a night. We went to bed, but I lay in the dark for a long time listening to the snow blow against the skin of the trailer and thinking how badly we could use that two thousand dollars. Things hadn't been great between me and Peggy for a while, and I was sure that money could help get us back on track.

I must have fallen asleep at some point, because I was awakened at three in the morning by a clanking noise that turned out to be the sound of the furnace cutting out again. When I went in to check on things Peggy was out of bed already, sitting on the couch breast-feeding the baby.

I took the cover off the blower motor and tightened up everything that had a screw. When I hit the switch the blower kicked on again. Out in the living room Peggy said our hero, and I could hear her clapping the baby's little hands together. I went in to join them, but my glory didn't last long because five minutes later the heater shut down again, this time for good.

Peggy opened her robe and shifted Sara over to her left breast, but she didn't say anything.

"I'll call that heater guy in the morning," I said. "Maybe I can get some of that money Al owes me." I went to the window and looked out. In the dark it looked like the snow was starting to let up.

"Oh, the hell with it," Peggy said after we'd been quiet a while. "If Bev will switch shifts with me, I'll drive you over to Rock Harbor on Friday if you're still set on the idea."

We didn't talk any more about it, and after the baby fell asleep in Peggy's arms she put her down and we went back to bed. The trailer was already starting to cool off.

□ □ □

I didn't hear Peggy get up and head off to work and when I woke up the baby was fussing in her crib. Outside the sun was shining, but the trailer was cold as an icebox. I could hear a snow blower somewhere in the trailer park, and in the kitchen Peggy had left the oven cranked on high and its door wide open. I changed the baby and warmed a bottle in the microwave. Then I called and left a message with the heater man that we needed that new blower as quick as he could get to us.

I didn't feel like eating, so I poured some boiling water over a couple teaspoons of instant and then called Lloyd's cell phone. When he picked up I told him he could count me in for Rock Harbor but that I needed to meet the guy in person.

Lloyd started telling me how that would be impossible, and before long I knew there was more to the story so I told him I'd be over in a little while. Lloyd was the kind of guy who could lie to you better over the phone than he could to your face.

I shut off the oven and went out and brushed off the truck. When it had warmed up, I went back inside for the baby and we headed over to see Lloyd.

Since Lloyd's wife, Julie, had kicked him out, he'd been staying at his Uncle Kent's farmhouse out on the Tozier Road while Kent was down in Florida for the winter. The baby and I headed over that way, but everybody in town with a plow was out clearing driveways and parking lots, so the traveling was slow.

The dooryard to the old farmhouse had been freshly plowed, and a big black lab lay on top of a mountain of snow where he was going to work on an old baseball bat. I parked by the porch and carried Sara inside. Lloyd Carter was sitting at the kitchen table in a gray t-shirt and blue coveralls so faded they almost looked white. On the table in front of him was an old double-barreled shotgun disassembled in a dozen greasy pieces.

Lloyd was sucking smoke from the top of a bong made out of three feet of PVC drain pipe. The woodstove at the far end of the kitchen was so hot it crackled, and the air was smoky and sweet with the smell of the marijuana. Sara looked over at an orange cat sitting on the counter by the sink and giggled.

"We could have done this on the phone," Lloyd said after he exhaled half a roomful of smoke. He was a bit taller than me and had a muscular build and a ponytail that ended halfway down his back.

"I came because I think you're bullshitting me," I said.

"Alls I said was this guy wants to go through me. For me to make all the arrangements."

"This guy have a name?"

Lloyd shook his head and took a second big hit from the bong. He closed his eyes and shook his head but didn't answer until he'd exhaled again. "Not 'til I know you're in, he doesn't." On his right forearm was a tattoo of a coiled snake and below it the words Live Free or Die.

"I told you I'm in," I said. "What's his name?"

"Charles Burnham."

"What's he do?"

Lloyd scratched his jaw. "Something with real estate, I think. But you're not meeting him. Like I already said, he wants me to make the arrangements."

"What arrangements? I show up at jail tomorrow night and say I'm him. What arrangements are there besides that?"

Lloyd didn't answer. I watched him fiddle with the shotgun parts and pretend to look bored and suddenly things were clear.

"What's he really paying?" I asked.

"Two grand. I told you already."

"No, Lloyd. What's he paying you?"

Lloyd didn't say anything. The cat batted a bottlecap halfway down the kitchen counter and Sara squealed like life couldn't get any better.

"Look, I gotta get something out of this," Lloyd finally said.

"Right. Because you're making all the arrangements."

"You don't want the money, just say so. I'll find somebody else. I just figured, especially with your hand and all, I'd steer this your way first."

"You're a real saint," I said. I pulled the hood of Sara's parka back onto her head and zipped her up tight. Then I headed for the door. We needed that two grand, but you've got to draw the line somewhere. I had my hand on the doorknob when Lloyd spoke up.

"Three grand," he said, his voice whiny. He set the bong down on the floor by his chair and stood up. "He's paying three grand. I figured two thousand for you was fair."

"You know, if something goes wrong with this deal I got to stick things out. Or else I'm looking at an aggravated forgery charge. That's a felony, and with my record that would be time down in Harlow. Some pissed-off judge gives me three or four years to serve there, you going to come do a third of it?"

"Look, nothing's going wrong."

"Easy for you to say. Once I walk into that jail, there's no turning back for me."

Lloyd frowned and looked down at the floor. The cat drifted over to the bottlecap and batted it off the counter. It skittered across the kitchen floor and under the woodstove.

"I want $2,500," I said. "Five hundred bucks is plenty for what you're doing."

Lloyd shook his head and hitched one of his coverall straps back up higher onto his shoulder. "$750 is as low as I'd go. That's rock bottom."

Outside, a sand truck rumbled past the farmhouse heading south toward town. I turned the doorknob and opened the door.

"Okay, okay" Lloyd said. "If you're gonna be like that, take the $2,500. But that still don't mean Burnham will see you."

"Well, he needs to."

"Why's that?"

"First off, to give us our money. This deal is strictly cash up front."

Lloyd nodded. "You got a point there," he said.

"Second, I want to see this guy. Know something about him. And I need to see his signature."

"His signature?"

"When they do the intake, there's all kinds of crap they make you sign."

Lloyd nodded some more and his eyes narrowed. "Smart," he said, still nodding. "I'll call Mike to try to set it up. You free in the morning if Burnham can come up?"

"One way or another, he's coming up," I said. "Either to hand me my $2,500 or else to go do his own goddamn jailtime."

□   □   □

I knew it would be cold at home, so Sara and I drove over to the Wal-

Mart and I pushed her down the aisles until she started squawking. I bought a jar of strained carrots and fed her at the snack bar while I ate a tuna fish sandwich a skinny red-haired girl had made with too much mayonnaise. Around noontime I bundled Sara back up and we bit the bullet and headed home.

Parked by the trailer's front steps was a navy blue van marked GIL'S HEATING. Inside it was still cold, but things looked promising. A paint-speckled radio on the kitchen table was playing country music, and an open metal toolbox sat next to our old blower motor on a drop cloth by the heater closet. The furnace man was down on one knee, his back to me.

"Almost done," he said without turning around. A minute later, the heater came on with a rush. The man stood still and listened for another minute or two. Then he made a couple adjustments and he loaded up his toolbox and carried it out to his van with our old blower motor. He came back inside and handed me a bill for $440. Then he unplugged his radio right in the middle of a Johnny Cash prison song, and he headed out the door.

Peggy wasn't due home for a while, so I sat down on the couch with a little bourbon to celebrate the extra $500 I squeezed out of Lloyd. I thought for a minute about keeping that last bit of good news from Peg, but I needed all the brownie points I could get, especially with her ex-husband, Danny, sniffing around again.

Danny and Peggy had been divorced for five years, but a blind man could see he still had the hots for her. Back a couple months ago he'd sent a Christmas card from Lexington, Kentucky, where he'd moved to go work for some computer sales outfit. He was the only person we knew from down that way, so the afternoon the card came, I steamed it open over a tea kettle before Peg got home.

Danny was about the biggest liar I ever met, so I took it with a grain of salt when he wrote about the seventy grand a year he was pulling in and how his new condo had central AC and a kidney-shaped swimming pool. Danny was offering Peggy a plane ticket so she could come down in May for the Kentucky Derby and they could drink mint juleps and catch up on old times.

Trying to get that Christmas card steamed back closed again was harder than I thought. It looked so bad when I got done I had to pour a cup of coffee over the whole stack of mail and when Peggy got home make a joke about being so clumsy. Peggy never did mention Danny's invitation after she'd opened the card and read it, and when I saw it in the trash later that night I figured the best thing was to just let sleeping dogs lie.

As I sat there drinking bourbon and waiting for Peggy to come home, I thought about how it was probably a good thing the Kentucky Derby was a still a few months away, and how by then we'd be all caught up on our bills and this thirty-day jail deal would just be something for me and Peggy to have a good laugh about. The baby woke up and I gave her a bottle while I watched the rest of a "Gunsmoke" rerun. When the baby was happy I put her down on the rug and got the chicken in the oven and helped myself to a little more bourbon. When Peggy finally did get home the trailer was warm as toast and filled with the good smell of the roasting chicken.

"It's nice in here," Peggy said.

I turned the sound off on the TV just as Matt Dillon and a one-armed cowboy with a three-day beard were getting ready to square off in front of a burned-out railroad station.

"Nice day?" I asked her.

She held out a hand and rocked it back and forth. "Not as nice as the one you got going," she said. She was eyeballing my drink on the coffee table. She picked up the glass and swallowed half of it. Then she picked up the baby and started dancing with her around the living room. Outside it had gotten dark and I could hear someone slamming a car door by the trailer next door.

I went over to the sink and made Peggy a drink of her own and freshened up mine while I was at it. We sipped our bourbon and made small talk for a while. When Peggy began nursing the baby I cut up some lettuce and made instant mashed potatoes that for once turned out halfway decent. While I was finishing up in the kitchen Peggy helped herself to more bourbon, and by the time we sat down to eat she was glowing like a neon sign. Seeing her smiling and looking so beautiful suddenly gave me second thoughts about being apart from her for so long, and once that thought took hold I was homesick for her already even though she was sitting there right in front of me.

After a while Peggy could tell I was feeling low, because all through dinner she did what she could to cheer things up. She was laughing and eating chicken with her hands and rubbing her foot against the inside of my leg in a way that made me feel horny and sad at the same time when I thought how long thirty days apart from her would feel.

"I don't have to do this," I suddenly heard myself say. "I could call Lloyd and tell him something's come up."

Peggy put her drink down. "It's up to you," she said. "I never liked the idea from the beginning." She drained her glass and then tapped it lightly against my cast. "We'll get by either way."

I looked at her for a long time. "Screw it," I finally said. "The change of scene will do me good."

Peggy got up to refill her drink. She poured some more bourbon, and then I watched her unbutton the top couple buttons of her blouse and walk over to my side of the table. She set her glass down next to mine and started rubbing my neck. "Why don't we go to bed early. Maybe I can give you a little something to remember me by when you're over there in Rock Harbor."

Peggy was already asleep when Lloyd called to tell me Charles Burnham would meet me in the morning at the Burger King out by the fairgrounds. I figured it'd be a couple weeks between drinks, so I sat up watching an old war movie and polishing off the last of the bourbon. Then I went to bed.

□   □   □

When I woke up Friday morning Peggy was gone and the baby was crying and my head felt like it was two sizes too small. It was already past nine, so I got Sara dressed and we split a bowl of Cheerios and then I drove her over to Peggy's sister's place out past the Ford dealership. When I pulled into the Burger King parking lot my head was still pounding and I was wishing I knew of a better way to earn $2,500.

I walked inside and saw Lloyd sitting in a booth by the back wall with a guy about my size wearing a black leather jacket and a Harley Davidson ball cap. When I got up to them they both stood and Lloyd made the introductions. Burnham said to call him Chuck. He had a handsome, narrow face and short brown hair and gray eyes that stayed on you long enough to make you uncomfortable. Underneath the leather coat he had on a white western-style shirt with pearly buttons and blue jeans creased liked he'd ironed them that morning.

The restaurant was nearly empty, and the two of them were drinking coffee out of white styrofoam cups. When I sat down Lloyd slid me an envelope that felt like it was an inch thick. Inside it was a stack of twenties bound together by a green rubber band.

"It's your first $1,500," Lloyd said. "We get the last grand after Chuck knows you've reported."

I looked at Lloyd. "So you've taken your $500 already?"

He nodded.

"It's nothing personal," Burnham said to me. I could smell whiskey on his breath when he spoke. "I'd just feel silly paying you the whole three grand and you have car trouble or maybe forget to show up." He handed me a blank envelope, already stamped. "Put your address on this and I'll mail you out a money order in the morning."

The guy had a point, but I wanted to mull it over anyway.

"I won't shaft you," he said after I'd been thinking for a while. "I can't afford to. If this falls apart it will be bad for both of us."

"With my record, it'd be worse for me," I said. "A whole lot worse."

"Maybe so," Burnham said. He put a hand on my shoulder. "You start my sentence tonight, that last thousand bucks will be in the mail by morning."

There didn't seem much point in arguing, so I counted the money and stuffed it in my pocket and then put Peggy's name on the stamped envelope with our address. I spent ten more minutes asking Burnham about his accident and who his lawyer was and about a couple other things I should know in case anybody asked. I wrote most of it down on a place mat so I could memorize it later, and I got him to sign his name a couple of times so my signature would be at least halfway close when I got processed that night. When I had all the info I thought I needed he thanked me again and we said goodbye.

I drove by the truck stop and walked inside and sat in Peggy's section. I watched her smiling and joking with her customers, a coffee pot in each hand. She finally came by and slid into the booth across from me. She looked tired in the restaurant's hard light, but she looked beautiful too. I slid the envelope with the money across the table toward her.

Peggy pulled out the slab of twenties and her eyes got big. Then she balanced it in her right hand like she was trying to guess its weight.

"There are seventy-five of them," I said. "And you'll get a $1,000 check in the mail on Monday."

She thought for a minute. "But that's $2,500."

I nodded and watched her slip the envelope into her apron pocket. Then she leaned across the counter and kissed me on the cheek. "I'll be home by four," she said.

I drove over to bowling alley and drank a couple of beers and fed a few quarters into the pinball machine and then went home and stared at the walls. After a while I got out the Burger King placemat and memorized Charles Burnham's birthday and address and his social security number. Then I grabbed a pen and dug around the trailer for a while until I finally found a piece of lined notebook paper folded in a romance novel on Peggy's night stand. I spent a few minutes working on Burnham's signature until I had it down pretty good and then put the paper in my pocket in case I felt like working on it a little more on the drive to the coast.

Peggy showed up at four on the dot in a brand new pink sweater that looked so good on her it put a lump in my throat. She asked me if I was ready to go, and although my heart wasn't in it, I said let's hit the road like we were headed to Mardi Gras.

Peggy wanted to drive, so I sat beside her in the Bronco listening to her chatter on about finally fixing up the kitchen while I watched the snow-covered hills slide by in the fading light. While she drove I thought about how things had been between us and all of the ways I'd let her down in the three years we'd been together. Midway to the coast it dawned on me that my thirty days would pass a lot easier if I somehow made them mine—if I accepted them in advance as something I had earned for the things I'd done wrong. As Peggy drove I thought of the little blonde bartender I'd hooked up with deer hunting in November and about hurting Peggy's wrist Fourth of July weekend and about the time I'd lost my head and given tiny Sara a shake after she'd cried all night long. As Peggy drove through the dusk a feeling of peacefulness came over me, and the notion of me serving those thirty days suddenly seemed as fair as anything could be.

It got dark and the land flattened out and lost its snow cover as we neared the coast. Neither of us spoke those last few miles. We passed a sign that said Welcome to Rock Harbor—A TOWN ON THE MOVE! The jail sits on the west side of town, out across from a salt marsh. Peggy pulled into the parking lot as far from the front door as she could get. She shut off the engine and looked over at me.

"I guess this is your stop," she said.

I opened the door a crack and the dome light came on. "I guess it is," I answered back.

"You want me to visit?"

I looked at Peggy in that pretty pink sweater and felt a powerful urge to start over, to do better by her. I leaned over and kissed her hard on the mouth. "No," I said. "I'll be home before you know it."

I got out and walked over to the jail's front door and hit the buzzer and watched Peggy wave as she drove off. I had a few months to regret ever going inside, a few months to wish that before I'd walked through that jail door I'd first remembered the piece of paper in my back pocket that I'd used to practice my new signature.

I wished every day until summer that I had pulled that paper out and unfolded it and checked both sides of it before I'd hit the jail's buzzer and walked inside to pretend I was someone I'm not. Maybe then I would have seen where Peggy had written lightly in pencil in her cramped, grade-school hand next Tuesday's date and a time and the words UNITED Flight #236 and where, below that, she'd printed CALL LLOYD CARTER with his phone number and, finally, in letters bigger than the rest—180 DAYS!!

Just Try Again

Glenda Baker

I've dreamed of being a writer ever since I learned to read, but I've also known that to achieve my dream, I needed a plan. So when I got the job at *New England Mystery Magazine*, I was delighted. Assistant to Editor-in-chief Claudia Prescott-Newman! Claudia published the magazine out the basement of her home in Laconia, New Hampshire. I figured I'd get some experience at *NEMM*, then move on to a larger publisher in Boston. After a couple of years there, Random House would be begging for me.

I was also working on my own breakout novel, "Liz's Story," that would set Stephen King and the entire horror world spinning on its eerie little ear. I'd made my plan and was ready to work it. In eight to ten I'd be a literary success.

But things didn't go exactly as I'd planned.

Claudia didn't pay a hell of a lot, so I had to get a job evenings and weekends at Lakes Region Feed and Grain to make ends meet. Well, at least to get the ends within stretching distance of each other. It didn't take long to become bored as hell at *NEMM* as secretary, mail-opener, and personal gofer to Claudia. But hey, I was working in the industry. I may not have had Claudia's MFA in fifteenth-century Irish madrigals, but I did have a brain and I knew how to use it. I could handle a couple-year sentence at *NEMM*.

What I couldn't handle, I soon realized, was Claudia. Talk about your bitch on steroids! It was one demand after another:

"Get this in the mail yesterday!" she yelled.

"Why do writers submit stories without SASEs?" Scruuunch. She stuffed another writer's disposable copy into the shredder along with his dreams.

"My Dr. Pepper's warm!" Claudia drank Dr. Pepper like it was the elixir of youth. Tasted like poison to me. "Get me a cold one—now!"

Never a "please" or a "thank you."

Never, "What do you think?" or "I'd like your opinion."

But I didn't complain. Just did as I was told.

Claudia was good at what she did, no doubt about that. Under her editor-in-chief-ship *NEMM* became the magazine for mystery writers in New England to be published in. Circulation soared as fast as Claudia's delusions of grandeur. But Claudia didn't have a kind bone in her body. She didn't even make a pretense at being nice.

Well, in public she did. She took me to the Crime Bake last year. There she was, sitting up there on a panel. "Oh yes," she purred, "we love to help new writers."

I saw all those writer wannabes taking down the *NEMM* website as fast as their tired little, note-taking fingers could scribble.

"Everybody thinks they can write!" Claudia growled as she peeled us out of the conference hotel parking lot in her 2006 BMW, almost wiping out two excited conference attendees trying to find their car.

Back in the office on Monday morning, it was the same old bitching.

"Doesn't he know how to use a semicolon?" Claudia stuffed a manuscript into the SASE and tossed it in my general direction so I could seal it up.

"The guidelines say double-spaced, not one-and-a-half!" she bellowed.

I ducked just in time to be missed by another incoming.

"Using peel and seal SASEs should be required!" She slammed her Dr. Pepper bottle down, sending brown foam all over her desk.

I guess she had a thing about licking an envelope and getting a paper cut on her tongue. Or maybe she was paranoid that somebody would put arsenic or strychnine on the flap. I'd heard that poison lady at the conference; I knew it was possible.

Claudia never read the cover letters that the writers took so much time and care to write. "I don't give a damn who they are or what their frigging backgrounds are," she'd informed me on my first day. "If the story doesn't work, it doesn't work!"

"But their contact information . . ." I tried to tell her.

"If their contact info isn't on the first page, they aren't following the rules. Send it back. Just give me the story and the SASE. I've got enough damn paper to deal with."

"Yes, ma'am,"

"Her character's are flat, flat, FLAT!" Another manuscript came flying across the room.

"It's all a dream?" Claudia detested this ending the most. "IT'S ALL A BLOODY NIGHTMARE!"

I just kept my mouth shut.

I was honored, however, when she tossed me the keys to her BMW one day. "Take my car to Frank's Foreign Motors. Frank's waiting for it. He'll give you a ride back."

The Beemer went to Frank's every Friday to be washed, waxed, and probably massaged.

"Tell Frank I want it back here by five on the dot and to leave the keys under the mat. And for the love of God," she added, "BE CAREFUL! I don't want any dings."

"I'll treat it as if it were my own."

"And empty the damned shredder and take the trash on your way out."

"Yes, ma'am." I shed a metaphoric tear as I threw the bag of rejected manuscripts into the Dumpster.

After several months of this treatment I started doing a slow burn mainly because I didn't have time to work on "Liz's Story." I know, I know, all writers complain they don't have time to write. But between the hours I put in for Claudia at *NEMM* and Jake at the Feed and Grain, I was left with only Sunday nights to complete my break-out book. By then writing was the last thing I wanted to do.

But I'm not a whiner. I'm disciplined, made myself write as much as I could, but I wasn't making anywhere near the progress I wanted. I know things usually take longer than we plan. At this rate, however, I'd never get the book done.

Most of all, I felt really bad for all those unpublished writers working so hard, hoping for even a little break. Hoping to get one story published so they could prove to their friends that they really were writers. So I started reading the incoming submissions. A lot of them just needed a little more work. The writers needed a little help, a little support. Maybe the dialogue didn't ring true. Or the story really started on page three. Or the ending fizzled. The kind of things that could easily be fixed if someone just told the writers. So I added a little hand-written note to Claudia's form rejection slips:

Story needs a better ending. Just try again.

Cut the chitchat out of your dialogue. Just try again.

Start story at top of page four. Just try again.

Well, the writers started following my advice. They made the changes and resubmitted their stories. What I didn't know was that Claudia had a memory like a whole herd of frigging elephants.

"I've read this story!" she bellowed. "Why are these idiots sending the same damn stuff back? Get me another Dr. Pepper!"

She obviously didn't take the time to realize that the stories were better, that the writer had made changes—my changes.

Then I made my big mistake. One Friday I forgot to remove the cover letter from a manuscript, and for some reason Claudia read it.

"What do you mean 'thanks for the constructive comments!' " she yelled. "I don't make constructive comments! I never have and I never will!" She glared at what I knew was my hand-written note. Then she glared at me.

I didn't have to say a word. I knew guilt was written all over my face in 24 point Times New Roman.

"You're fired!" she said with a finality that Donald Trump would have envied. "Be out of here by five. And get me a COLD Dr. Pepper."

I didn't. I just walked out, right past another trash bag of shredded manuscripts waiting to be dumped and out the door.

I could have fought it, I suppose, but I was just plain fed up by then.

Now, I know you think you can see what's going to happen. The clues are there: The Dr. Pepper that tastes like poison. The fact that I learned about poison at the Crime Bake. The fact that I work at the Feed and Grain where they sell rat poison. Or even the fact that she didn't like to lick envelopes. You put it all together, didn't you? I poisoned her Dr. Pepper. Or I put rat poison on the flaps and she licked herself to death.

Wrong.

I'm too impulsive to do something that sneaky and precise. And I knew I'd get caught whatever I did, so I made a plan as I drove home.

I called Frank and told him Claudia needed the Beemer immediately. Then I drove back to the office and waited across the street until he'd parked it precisely where Claudia insisted, at the top of the drive parallel to the office door and heading down the driveway. Claudia didn't like to have to back up. Frank put the keys under the mat and hopped into the truck that had accompanied him. They peeled out fast. I got the feeling Frank was just as happy not to see

Claudia.

As soon as Frank left, I walked across the street and up the drive and got into the Beemer. I got the keys from under the mat, then slouched down and waited. It wasn't long before Claudia came storming out of the office, unbuttoned coat flapping, swearing at the top of her lungs and carrying the bag of shredded manuscripts. She walked past the Beemer's passenger side and crossed in front of the car to the Dumpster on the other side of the driveway.

That's when I revved 'er up and gunned it, slamming Claudia against the Dumpster.

I didn't kill her the first time. Try again! Just try again! I backed up several times (I don't mind backing up) and rammed her again and again until she finally lay quiet—under a covering of manuscript shreds.

I turned off the Beemer, put the keys under the mat, walked down the driveway to my car, and calmly drove myself home.

Took the cops the whole weekend to figure out I did it, but by then I had everything packed and ready to go. No, I didn't escape to Canada.

I confessed. Yup, as soon as I opened the door for the cops, I said, "I did it." Surprised the you-know-what right out of them.

I'm a practical person, you see. I didn't want to waste the tax-payers' money on some long, drawn-out trial where I'd be found guilty anyhow. And I didn't want to waste any more time.

So here I am in the clink for twenty-five-to-life.

Now I have all the time I need to write.

I re-titled "Liz's Story" to Claudia's Story. It hit the *New York Times* Best Seller and got me a three-book contract with Random House. I'm working on number two—"Murder in the Feed and Grain."

I'm also teaching fiction writing to some of the other gals in here. I tell them how to make their writing better. "Try again," I say, "just try again."

I'm even doing some editing. I'm putting together an anthology of crimes all the other inmates insist they didn't do, which gives me an endless supply of stories. I'm calling it "If We Had Done It."

The Copycat Didn't Have Nine Lives

Ang Pompano

When I got the text message saying that Rupert Allan was dead, I hit the brakes on my '69 Camaro so hard that my grandfather fell off the back seat.

Sorry 'bout that, Gramps, I thought as I reached behind the passenger seat and tapped around on the floor until I found his urn. I placed him back on the seat where he'd been for the past year and a half. One of these days, I'd have to paddle out to the islands and spread those ashes. Today, obviously, wouldn't be the day.

I looked at the message on my cell again. Rupert is dead. Emergency Meeting, 7:00. Lazarro be on time. That's me, Quincy Lazarro. I give kayak lessons in the Nutmeg Islands, off Sachem Creek, Connecticut, but my dream is to be published. That's why I belong to the Sachem Creek Writers Group.

We usually meet every Wednesday, so I figured the message wasn't a joke if they called a meeting two days early. What the hell could have happened to Rupert? He seemed healthy enough for a guy of fifty-something.

A shame too, since he was about to become the first of the group to be published. Who would have thought? When Rupert joined the group about a year ago, he came to the first meeting straight from a cottage he was rebuilding out on the islands and he still had sawdust in his hair. He told us he'd always wanted to be a writer and passed out a story he had been working on.

The next week we returned with what we thought were helpful comments. I tried to say something positive, but it wasn't easy. "That's one of the best first lines I ever read. But you've got to punch it up a little bit in the middle. Follow though on that great opening."

Even Kate Goodman, the pudgy former-actress with a fondness for Cuban cigars who brought Rupert to the group, seemed at a loss for words. "Interesting," was all she could come up with.

Betty Frome, a perpetually mellow teacher who dressed like she expected the 1970s to come back, took a metaphysical approach. "I don't get the sense that you're imaging success. You must have a positive mind frame when you write."

I know where her mind frame was. Someplace under a mushroom stool.

Senior member and founder of the group, Walter Burns, slapped his hand on the table. Walter has poppy eyes like a goldfish and they bulged, as they usually did when he got out of control. "Interesting, my ass! It read like a thirteen-year-old kid wrote it." He practically threw the story back to Rupert.

Rupert shrugged his shoulders and thanked us for the advice. Later, as we walked out to our cars, I took Rupert aside.

"Look, Rup, you can't go by what Walter says. He's a little . . . well, you know, old and all."

"I'll think about the suggestions," Rupert said. Then he got in his car and took off.

I walked over to the others, who were chatting by their cars at the other end of the parking lot. Betty was pressing her fingers to her temples as if she was channeling someone. "I'm afraid he didn't take that well. I detected bad vibes."

Kate lit up a cigar. "Well, goodness knows we didn't intend to hurt his feelings. That's not what we're about." That was her way of saying he should've been grateful that we gave any encouragement at all.

Walter's reaction was typical. "If he can't take the criticism, he shouldn't be in the group."

I suggested that we give Rupert a chance. Personally, I thought he would never return.

But he did come back, faithfully every week, although I couldn't figure out why he bothered. On the few occasions that he did join the discussions, he just reiterated other members' comments. And he never submitted another piece. His excuses ranged from "dry spell" to "too many remodeling jobs" taking up his time. Each week we'd encourage him to write, telling him that he had to get something, anything, down on paper.

Then at last week's meeting, he came with a large manila envelope which he placed on the floor next to his chair. Throughout the evening, he seemed like he wanted to say something, but he wasn't the type to just jump into the conversation.

Kate was chairing the meeting that night. She had written a murder mystery that took place on a nineteenth-century New England farm. After we gave her feedback she proceeded to adjourn without even asking if there was any other business. "Okay then, we'll meet next Wednesday at 7:30. Quincy, it's your turn to bring refreshments. And dear boy, a half-empty bag of Doritos isn't considered refreshments, if you don't mind."

Before I had a chance to ask why not, Rupert picked up his envelope from the floor. "I have something I'd like to share. I won a short-story contest."

Betty was ecstatic. "You imaged! I knew you could do it."

Kate looked doubtful. "What story?"

"You write like a kid. What did you win? A bicycle?" Walter said under his breath.

Rupert may not have heard him, because he beamed, although he made an effort to be modest. "Just a small contest, $500. But someone liked my work. That's worth a million bucks to me. And, the story will be published in the *Connecticut Literary Review*."

That last bit of information blew us away. *CLR* is one of the most respected magazines in the country. It would be safe to say that any one of us would kill to be in his shoes. Still, we all congratulated him as he passed around the confirmation letter.

We don't usually read our works out loud, but I thought this was a special occasion. "Read the story to us, Rupert."

At first he hesitated, but then he read the story about a man who went back to Tahiti, a special place that he shared with his wife in their youth. But by this time his wife had passed away, and he found that the place wasn't as special as he had remembered it.

I was sitting across from Walter, and I thought his eyes would grow to the size of bowling balls. I knew exactly what he was thinking. I'm sure Kate and Betty did too.

Finally, Walter stood up and got right in Rupert's face. "That's a rip-off of my story, 'Return to Amalfi.' "

Rupert looked like he really didn't understand the accusation. " 'Return to Amalfi'? I never read that. It has to be a completely different story."

"You're going to have a completely different face if you don't admit you copied my stuff."

I stood in front of Walter to save him from doing something rash. The shouting went on for several minutes before Rupert stormed out, vowing never to return. If the text message was true, he had been right about that.

□   □   □

When I got to the meeting in the parlor of the old granite church in Sachem Creek, the others were already there.

As usual, Betty sat barefoot and cross-legged on the antique horsehair couch, under a foreboding painting of a snowbound Puritan village. The other end of the sofa was anchored by Kate. She rummaged through her purse and took out a Montecristo. Walter sat hunched in a high-backed wing chair, looking at the floor and mindlessly tapping the leg of the coffee table with his shoe. The next matching wing-back was empty, Rupert's place. Out of respect for Rupert, I walked to the window and dragged over a straight-backed chair, the most uncomfortable in the room. It was the one that I usually sat in because I was almost always late.

"What happened?"

Kate puffed her cigar and watched a smoke ring twist and spin as it drifted toward the ceiling. "He's dead, dear boy. Someone murdered him."

I wasn't expecting that. "Murdered? How? Where?"

Betty waved at the air. "I wish you'd get rid of that filthy thing. There's no smoking in here." Betty grabbed the cigar from Kate's mouth and crushed it out in a saucer on the coffee table.

"Ladies! Tell me what happened to Rupert."

A tear crawled down Betty's cheek and she wiped it with her sleeve. "They found him in his skiff at the Sachem Creek dock. Shot."

Kate examined the end of her crushed cigar. "You ruined it, bitch." Then almost as an afterthought, she said, "Maybe you can 'image' him back to life."

I couldn't believe it. "Shot? Who would shoot Rupert?"

Betty glanced at Walter. "I guess that's up to Marcus to find out."

Marcus Page is the Sachem Creek sheriff. Last summer I had been on his suspect list when I found a young woman's body while kayaking in the islands.

Walter stood up, bristling. "Stop looking at me. I had nothing to do with it."

Kate was fooling with the end of the cigar, seeing if she could save it. "Just because Walter looks guilty, it doesn't mean he did it. Necessarily. Isn't that right, Quincy?"

I wasn't about to answer Kate's question. I knew the drama queen would twist my response into something that I never said. I'd take a neutral route.

"Well, Rupert is . . . was . . . a nice guy, and a fellow writer. We have to do something to remember him."

Everyone looked at me like I had three heads.

Walter plopped back into the chair. "Remember him?"

"I assumed that's why you called this emergency meeting."

"Get real, Quincy. We have to cover our asses and come up with a strategy for when Marcus questions us. That's what we have to do!" I thought Walter was going to have a stroke.

"You have to come up with a strategy, you old coot." Kate's face was getting red.

Now it was my turn to look at them with disbelief. "So you think we have to come up with a strategy. Why?"

"You know how news travels in the village. Everyone will know Rupert won the contest. Walter thinks that Marcus might try to build a case that we were jealous that Rupert got published. We'll all be suspects," Betty said.

Kate must have decided saving her cigar was hopeless. She tossed it into the trashcan. "He almost missed the contest deadline. Too bad for him that he didn't."

Walter's foot jerked, moving the table. "It's too bad for me, too. Who do you think is going to be the prime suspect?"

Betty locked eyes with Walter. "Well, you did practically call him a plagiarist. That created a negative atmosphere, very negative."

I held up a finger to interrupt. "Would you guys excuse me? I'm going to hit the head. I shouldn't have had that second coffee."

The two women snickered. Walter just continued to tap the table leg with his shoe.

When I returned, the three of them were bickering again. Time for me to take charge. "I think you're right. We have to come up with a strategy for handling Marcus."

Betty fidgeted on the couch. "It's Walter's fault. He's the one that sent out all the bad vibes when Rupert read the story."

"He stole my idea and then goes and wins a contest with it. Why shouldn't I be ticked off?"

I was beginning to feel sorry for the old guy. "Walter, Rupert didn't steal your story."

"Are you saying that his story isn't like mine?"

"No, the two stories are very similar."

"Wait a darn minute, here. You're not saying that I stole the story from him, are you? Because if you are—"

"Cool your jets, Walter. I'm not saying that at all. I'm just telling you that Rupert didn't steal your story, because Rupert never read your story. He never read any of our stories. He wasn't really interested in our work."

Walter looked surprised. "How do you know?"

"Because the only feedback that we ever got from him was, 'I liked your story. Nice job.' Or, 'Keep up the good work,' scrawled on the last page. At least that's all I ever got, and I'll bet that's what everyone else got too."

"Well, yeah. But if he didn't read my story, how did he steal it?"

"He didn't. Did he, Betty?"

Betty was still sitting cross-legged, but now with her head hung forward, her hair falling toward her lap. She was emitting a low "ohmmmmmmmmmm" sound.

"Betty?" I said.

Finally she straightened up. "Well, I may have helped him to image a winning story. He got writer's block after we criticized him so much at that first meeting."

"Aw, the poor baby," Kate said. "We gave him post-traumatic stress syndrome. So we criticized him! That's what this group is about."

"Well now I've heard everything," Walter said. "Betty, what's the idea of stealing my story and giving him credit for it? If he couldn't write on his own, he didn't belong in the group."

"I told you I only helped him image," Betty said. "I didn't know his piece was anything like your story until the night he read it to us. I just wanted to encourage him."

"You didn't have to encourage him with my story. What? Were you sleeping with him or something?"

Betty stood up, reached across the coffee table, and slapped Walter's face. "If I was, you'd be the last to find out."

So much for peace and love. I tried to move on before the two came to further blows. "Maybe she did only coach him, Walter, just like Betty coached you. She did. Didn't she? That's why you had the same theme. I figured the teacher in her gave the same assignment to both of her students."

Kate looked at Betty in disgust. "Walter, too? You certainly do get around. I guess you must have been a hit at Woodstock."

Walter and Betty together was a sight I didn't want an "image" of. "Kate, I only meant that she was helping Walter with his writing."

If Walter did have something going on with Betty, he wasn't sentimental about it. He was more concerned with fixing the blame on someone other than himself. "I don't believe her. She gave him my story and when it won she got jealous and killed him."

"Stop flattering yourself," Betty said. "He promised to stay in the group if I helped him write. I didn't know he entered a contest. After he won he broke his promise. He was going to leave just the same."

I tried to help her explain. "He wasn't only leaving the group.

He was leaving Sachem Creek, right, Betty?"

Betty looked small and fragile. The laidback façade was stripped away leaving a broken, desperate woman. "More than that, he wanted money so he could move. He said he'd tell my husband about us if I didn't give him $5,000."

Walter jumped to his feet again and jabbed his finger in Betty's direction. "So then, you did kill him, Betty!"

"No! I confessed to my husband and I told Rupert to go to hell."

"Believe her, Walter. She didn't kill Rupert," I said.

"Well if she didn't, and I didn't. Then we're back to square one."

"I thought so, too," I said. "But then I realized that there was another possibility. This group should be called the Peyton Place Writers Group. Betty, you were 'encouraging' Rupert, but you weren't alone. Kate was helping him out as well."

Kate got up and confronted the three of us. "I don't have to stay here and listen to this fairy tale." She headed for the door.

I grabbed her by the arm. "But that's what we're all about, Kate, listening to each other's stories. Let's see if this one plays out to be fact or fiction. Rupert didn't care about writing. You convinced him to join the group so he could be near you. When you found he was also fooling around with Betty you decided to kill him. But first you had to set it up to look like someone else had a motive. You cleverly fed Walter's story to Rupert bit by bit. Poor Rupert probably thought the story was all his. That's why he was so proud of it and wanted to read it to us. Of course, when Walter heard it he blew his top and that left the door open for you to get rid of Rupert."

Walter was indignant. "You wanted to kill him for playing with Betty. So why set me up?"

There was hate in Kate's eyes. "Because you're a pompous ass, and no one would have trouble believing you did it." Kate seemed very satisfied with herself. "He believed he wrote the story himself. I built up his confidence enough that I knew he'd bring it to the group eventually. And I knew that Walter's reaction would be violent. When Rupert won the contest that was just an added bonus."

I let go of Kate's arm.

Marcus stood in the doorway. "That sounds pre-meditated to me."

"Where in hell did you come from?" Walter wanted to know.

"I called him when I went to the bathroom. Kate tipped me off when she mentioned that Rupert almost didn't make the deadline. Supposedly, none of us knew that he had entered the contest. Since Kate knew, she must have been the one to give him the story."

After statements to the police, and some rehashing of the evening's events, we headed for our cars. Betty, Walter, and I would meet again in two days, as originally scheduled. Whether we met again after that was anybody's guess, but we needed that next meeting for closure.

When I got in the Camaro, I thought of Rupert's broken promise to Betty. Before my grandfather died a few years back, I promised him that I would spread his ashes out in the Nutmegs. Somehow, I never got around to it. So I understand broken promises. I took Gramps off the backseat and put him on the front passenger seat. "Lookin' good, Gramps. Lookin' good." I reached over and fastened the seatbelt around the urn. The next day I'd take him out to the islands in my kayak and keep my promise.

Visual Field

Leslie Wheeler

Late again. It's disgraceful, absolutely disgraceful." A silver-haired, perfectly coiffed woman tapped her foot impatiently outside Dr. Peter Strattner's office as Margaret approached.

"You would think he'd have the courtesy to show up on time," the woman said to an older man, also waiting outside the small, one-story building. He did not reply, but stared into space with a bored expression.

Margaret wondered if they were husband and wife. She had never married, but the long-married couples in her acquaintance tended to ignore each other.

"Wouldn't you?" The woman trained inquisitive eyes on Margaret.

Margaret was not sure how to reply. Tardiness was no sin in her book. She had learned patience long ago during the nightly vigils of her childhood. While she hesitated, the woman whipped a cell phone from an embossed leather case, and punched in a number. "Yes, by all means, page him," she snapped at the person on the other end. Moments later, she flipped her phone shut. "Dr. Strattner isn't answering his pager. This is totally unacceptable. He's always late. And when he does arrive?" The woman paused and glanced at the man, who continued to stare into space. Nevertheless, she lowered her voice in a conspiratorial manner. "When he does arrive, he looks like he's slept in his clothes. And his breath—" She wrinkled her nose. "He's a doctor, for heaven's sake. Don't you think he should pay more attention to his personal hygiene?"

"This is only my first visit," Margaret replied mildly. "I've never met Dr. Strattner before."

"You'll see," the woman said. "If it weren't for the convenience, I'd go to someone else."

Margaret nodded. Convenience she understood. Dr. Strattner's Belmont office was only a five-minute drive from her apartment. She had not had to battle traffic to get here, nor had she had any trouble finding a parking space on the street in front. Her previous eye doctor had been a dapper, efficient Chinese man with the unlikely name of Valentino Wong. When she first started seeing him, his office had been in Brookline, twenty minutes away, but then he'd moved to Needham, forty minutes away, and finally, the Cape, too far a drive for someone who was getting on in years.

"Do you live nearby, too?" the woman asked.

"Cambridge," Margaret replied.

"So do I." The woman smiled approvingly. "I'm Cornelia Schuyler, by the way."

"Margaret Pickering."

"The only other reason I keep coming is Suzy," Cornelia said. "She's his nurse. Such a sweetheart. And so organized. She's the one who keeps the office going . . . But look, here she is now!" Cornelia gestured toward the sidewalk, where a pretty, petite young blonde ran toward them, a ring of keys jingling in her hand.

Margaret was sitting in an examination room with a magazine she'd picked up in the waiting area when the door opened. A tall, darkly handsome, disheveled man started to enter before Suzy stopped him. They stood silhouetted in the doorway, Suzy balancing on tiptoes as she straightened his tie. Inclining his head toward her, he mouthed thanks. She made a face, he nodded, and they separated. He removed a small, foil-wrapped package from his pocket, and popped something into his mouth. Then, apparently realizing that Margaret was watching, he strode over and held out the package. "Would you like a mint?" He smiled disarmingly.

Margaret beamed. "Why, thank you."

While Dr. Strattner reviewed the file from Dr. Wong, Margaret sucked on the mint and studied him. There was something familiar about his tousled hair, rumpled suit with the tie still slightly askew, even his sour breath, barely masked by the mint. "Diagnosis of borderline glaucoma," he said. "Well, you've come to the right place. I specialize in glaucoma and cataracts."

The sense of familiarity grew as he began the eye examination. Then, Margaret was aware of the strong, masculine odor that lay behind his cologne.

Her father had smelled that way as he bent to kiss her when he returned late from work and came into her room to say good night.

"The pressure in both eyes is on the high end of normal but holding steady," Dr. Strattner said. "That's a good sign. But on your next visit, I want to do a visual field test."

Lulled by his scent in the darkened room, Margaret suddenly snapped to attention. "What's that?" She had reached the age when the very idea of anything new made her nervous.

"It's just looking at some lights on a screen," Dr. Strattner said.

"That's all?"

"Yes. You'll do fine."

Margaret was reassured. She could handle this. She had often gazed at the stars on those long nights of her childhood.

That summer, Margaret stood in front of the meat counter at her local market, selecting a single lamb chop for her dinner, when a woman's voice asked, "Don't I know you from somewhere?"

Cornelia Schuyler squinted at her. "Dr. Strattner," Margaret replied. "We waited outside the office together."

"That's right. Have you heard the awful news?" Cornelia looked at Margaret with the bright, keen eyes of a born-gossip.

"No. Did something happen to him? He didn't die, did he?" Margaret felt a clutch of fear.

"It's worse than that," Cornelia said in a hushed voice.

"What?" Margaret wondered how anything could be worse than death, except perhaps extreme and prolonged suffering.

"Suzy's left him."

"Too bad." Margaret was relieved that was all it was.

"For him, yes, but not for her." Cornelia's chin tilted upward and came down again with the finality of a courtroom gavel. "I always thought she was too good for him, and now she's finally cut loose and moved on to greener pastures. Without her, his practice will go to wrack and ruin. He'll lose the few patients he has left—the ones like us who only come because of the convenience."

"Have you switched to another eye doctor?" Margaret asked.

"Not yet, but I'm working on it."

"Good luck," Margaret said. She had no intention of changing doctors herself, nor did she believe Cornelia's dire prediction of what would happen to Dr. Strattner's practice without Suzy. The young woman had seemed pleasant enough, but she was no paragon. She, too, had arrived late on the day of Margaret's first visit. As for Dr. Strattner, despite his shortcomings in punctuality and personal appearance, he did not lack charm.

On a chilly November morning, Margaret again waited in front of Dr. Strattner's office. She had come for the visual field test. She wished someone would arrive soon because she was anxious to get it over with. Dr. Strattner had told her she would do fine, but what if she didn't? It had been years since she had counted the stars.

They had lived in a large house in the countryside around Concord, Massachusetts, then, and on clear nights the stars shone as brightly as they did in a planetarium. Margaret felt a pang at the memory of those nights. After her father's death, she and her mother moved to an apartment in North Cambridge, where Margaret still lived. There, the street lights and surrounding buildings made it almost impossible to view the night sky.

She was not only out of practice, but worried that her vision had grown worse. Margaret dreaded the thought of becoming like Rufus, the family dog when she was a child. Rufus whose big, Spaniel eyes were too cloudy for him to see the strangers who might be a danger to Margaret and her mother. In old age, Rufus had also grown hard of hearing, a problem Margaret now shared. He had stopped barking when anyone, including her father, had come to the door.

No, she did not want to become like Rufus. Margaret peered in the direction that Suzy had come running the last time. But today there would be no Suzy, Margaret reminded herself. Instead, there would be Dr. Strattner's new nurse, whose voice, nasal and unfriendly, had reminded Margaret about the appointment over the phone yesterday.

Then, to Margaret's surprise, she glimpsed Suzy hurrying toward her, the ring of keys jangling. The keys to the castle, Margaret thought. She was so glad to see Suzy that she could have hugged the young woman. "Suzy, what are you doing here? I heard you'd left," Margaret said.

"Well, I'm back." Suzy gave Margaret a half smile, but she didn't sound or look pleased. Her face was red and her eyes were watery, almost as if she'd been crying. Perhaps the job Suzy had taken upon leaving Dr. Strattner hadn't worked out as she'd hoped. But then again, the redness and even the wateriness could be from the cold. It was late November, and after a delightful stretch of Indian summer, the temperatures had plummeted. Whatever the reason, Margaret chose not to pry.

Suzy unlocked the door and they went into the waiting room. While Margaret hung up her coat, Suzy consulted the appointment book on the desk. "You're here for a visual field?"

"Yes." Already Margaret felt the pre-test jitters she remembered from her schoolgirl days.

"I just need to use the bathroom, then I'll get you set up," Suzy said. The door closed behind her, and Margaret heard her blow her nose loudly, then the sound of running water. When Suzy reappeared, her face looked redder than ever.

"Is something the matter?" Margaret asked, abandoning her customary reticence.

"No, it's just . . ."

Margaret couldn't hear the rest of the sentence because Suzy had turned away from her and gone into the examination room. "What did you say?"

"My allergies," Suzy said in a louder voice.

"I'm sorry. Will Dr. Strattner be here soon?"

Suzy shrugged. "Probably, but you don't need him for the test. I can do it."

"Oh." Margaret was disappointed. She had assumed Dr. Strattner would give her the examination, and had been looking forward to being in the room with him.

"Sit down here, please." Suzy guided Margaret to a black leather swivel chair that was positioned before a screen like that of a TV monitor, only recessed. Margaret noticed that Suzy looked a bit disheveled herself. Perhaps Dr. Strattner's untidy habits had worn off on her.

After Margaret sat, Suzy pushed the chair close to the screen and told her to rest her chin on a plastic cup-like device in front of it. "Is that high enough for you?" she asked. "Would you like a tissue to put under your chin? Some people find that more comfortable."

Reassured by Suzy's solicitous manner, Margaret accepted the offer of a folded tissue.

"This is how the test works," Suzy said. "Small lights will appear on different parts of the screen at varying intervals. Whenever you see a light, however faint, press this." She handed Margaret a button attached to a cord. "We test one eye at a time, and each test lasts for fifteen minutes. But if you get tired, you can stop whenever you want. We'll start with the right eye." She placed a patch over Margaret's left eye and told Margaret to stare straight ahead at the screen.

At first, all Margaret could see was a black inverted "V" with a vertical line extending from its apex. Then a largish lighted dot appeared on the screen. Margaret pressed the button excitedly. This was going to be easier than she had thought.

"That was only a trial," Suzy said from behind her. "The actual lights will be smaller and less bright."

"Oh." Margaret flushed with embarrassment.

"Ready?" Suzy asked.

"Yes."

Another light appeared. Although smaller than the "trial" light, it was bright enough to be readily discernible. Margaret pressed the button. One down, and how many more to go? The next light was not only fainter but located at the outer edge of the screen. That one is meant to keep me on my toes, Margaret thought. It's trying to slip past me, unnoticed, but I've got it. She pressed the button with a feeling of triumph. It was good to know that after all these years, she had not lost the ability to detect specks of light. But her prey was elusive and unpredictable, sometimes coming one after another in a brilliant cluster; other times, appearing wan and distant after what seemed like a long wait.

Focused on the lights, Margaret was only dimly aware of what was happening around her. She heard Suzy doing something in another part of the room, then the door closed. From the waiting room came voices, Dr. Strattner's deeper tones mingling with Suzy's higher ones. So he had arrived. Margaret hoped he would come into the examination room. She wanted him there, silently cheering her on while she pressed the button again and again, his prize pupil.

The voices rose in volume. Suzy sounded agitated, Dr. Strattner angry. Margaret was surprised. She had been under the impression that doctor and nurse got along well. But perhaps Suzy's allergies had made her cross, and she was taking it out on poor Dr. Strattner.

Their raised voices were distracting, but also, Margaret realized, oddly familiar. Her father and mother had often quarreled on the nights he came home late. Her mother had called him a drunk and a philanderer—names that Margaret had not understood at the time, though she knew from her mother's angry tone that they must be bad.

The voices became even louder, but Margaret could not make out what Dr. Strattner and Suzy were arguing about. The audiologist she'd gone to a few weeks earlier had explained that her hearing was deficient in both volume and clarity: even if the volume was turned up, she would not be able to hear what was being said unless the speaker took care to enunciate each word. Now, the voices were loud but fuzzy, as if Suzy and Dr. Strattner were shouting with chewing gum in their mouths.

This, too, was familiar to Margaret. When she complained to her father that she hated hearing her mother yell at him, he told her to plug her ears. "Don't listen to her; it's all lies anyway. You know that, don't you, sweetheart?"

But even with her hands clamped over her ears, her mother's words sometimes penetrated the barrier. Ugly-sounding words like "bastard," "slut," and "whore."

It was better with the earplugs—small pieces of wax that she molded to fit inside her ears—her father brought her after she told him she still occasionally heard her mother.

Now, Margaret was glad she had not yet gotten a hearing aid, because if she could have understood what Dr. Strattner and Suzy were shouting about, it might have been upsetting. She needed to concentrate on the task at hand—on the lights playing hide and seek on the screen. Now you see me, now you don't. Now you see me, now you don't. Winking at her like the stars she had watched while she waited out her parents' quarrels all those years ago.

Margaret's fingers were sore from gripping the button, her right eye was dry and scratchy with strain. Her left eyelid and lashes beat against the black cloth patch like a bird caught in a trap. How much longer would this take? Margaret was afraid that if she looked at her watch she'd miss one or more of the winking lights. Now you see me, now you don't.

At least it was quiet now. Whatever Suzy and Dr. Strattner had been arguing about, they must have settled their differences. Any moment now, one of them—Dr. Strattner, she hoped—would come into the room and end the test. Or maybe it would simply stop by itself.

At last the lights stopped flickering on and off. The test was over. But just to be on the safe side, Margaret kept her eyes trained on the blank screen a while longer, lest a stray light should sneak onto it when she wasn't watching. She wanted to do well, not only for herself but for the doctor whose approval she craved. Her father had often brought her candy or a trinket. Margaret did not expect a reward from Dr. Strattner, but she wouldn't mind a mint.

Finally she ended her vigil. She removed the patch from her left eye, rubbed her right eye, stood, and stretched. They seemed to have forgotten about her. Perhaps Dr. Strattner was with a patient in the other examination room. Margaret went to the door and listened. Nothing. The whole building was strangely quiet, and the silence made her uneasy.

Her parents' quarrels usually ended with an interval of silence, followed by the thud of her father's footsteps as he strode upstairs to her room. But one night, the silence had stretched on and on—until Margaret could bear it no longer and went downstairs to see what the matter was. The front door was closed, and her mother stood in front of it like a grim sentinel with her arms folded across her chest. When Margaret asked her where her father was, her mother said he'd gone away.

"But he can't have gone. I heard his voice just a little while ago," Margaret protested.

"He was here," her mother said, "but when he realized he couldn't get in, he left."

"Why couldn't he get in?" Margaret asked.

"I had the locks changed," her mother said.

"How could you do that? Where will he go?"

"Back to his whore, I imagine," her mother said coldly.

"No!" Margaret tried to push past her mother to the door. Her mother caught her and they struggled. They were still struggling when a knock sounded. Thinking it was her father, Margaret broke free of her mother and opened the door. The man standing there was not her father, but a police officer come with the news that her father had been killed when his car swerved off the road and crashed into a tree.

"Suzy? Dr. Strattner?" Margaret called. No answer. With a mounting sense of dread, she opened the door to the other examination room and peered inside. Empty. She went into the waiting room. It also appeared to be empty. But with the blinds drawn and the room in shadow, she couldn't be sure. When her eyes had adjusted to the dimness, she saw that a calendar, pens, and other desk accessories were strewn every which way, as though a whirlwind had swept through. Dr. Strattner slumped against a wall in a far corner, his collar open, and his shirt stained red with—was it possible?—blood.

Margaret gasped. How had this happened? Where was Suzy? Dr. Strattner's mouth flapped like that of a grounded fish struggling for air. He was saying something, but she couldn't make out the words. She knelt beside him, turning her head so her good ear faced toward him.

"Stabbed . . . Suzy . . . Help."

□   □   □

"I don't understand why she would want to kill him," Margaret said to the policeman who'd stayed behind after the ambulance had taken Dr. Strattner away.

"No?" The officer had rough features but a kindly expression. "I got a pretty good idea from what you told us. Doctor having an affair with his nurse, won't leave his wife, so the girlfriend leaves. But then she comes back, hoping he'll change his mind. He won't, and she flips out."

"If only I had known," Margaret said slowly, "I might have . . ." She left the sentence unfinished.

The policeman shook his head. "This kind of thing, it's best not to get involved. 'Specially a lady like you." He did not say elderly but Margaret heard it.

"Un-uh," he went on. "Bad enough you had to find him like that. Want to sit here a while longer? Or shall I drive you home?"

"I'm ready to leave, but you needn't drive me. My car is parked just outside."

"Walk you there then." He got up and held out his hand.

Margaret rose unsteadily and let him help her to the door. Outside, she blinked. She felt as if she had stepped from a darkened theater into the bright sunlight. She wished it were night so the transition would not have been so abrupt, and once outdoors, she could have taken refuge in the cool, impersonality of the stars. But here, there was no escape from the glaring light that threw everything into sharp relief, illuminating shadowy corners of her mind, where old feelings of guilt lurked.

Had she been wrong to cover her ears and gaze at the stars while her parents fought? Should she have tried to make them stop? If she had, perhaps her father would not have been killed.

And now, could she have done something to avert this new tragedy? What if she had stopped the test and gone into the waiting room at the first signs of trouble? Margaret wondered if it was even possible to be an innocent bystander. Or did the very act of standing by make one to a certain extent responsible?

"Sure you don't want a lift home?" the officer asked. "You seem kinda dizzy."

"Thank you, but I'll be all right," Margaret said. He opened the car door for her and she got in, gripping the steering wheel tightly, as she pondered questions that until now had remained outside her visual field.

The Big Picture

James T. Shannon

W hy is the ranch called The Flying A?" I said. Since his name was Tex Henderson, the question seemed a reasonable one, although the old guy squinted a narrow blue-eyed frown at me as if I'd just asked him if he knew how to do a moon dance. He was average height and pushing seventy, probably pushing it a few years behind him. But he had that corded-wire outdoor-living toughness that never goes away. He rubbed at his white chin stubble, raised his sweat-stained Stetson up off his forehead and said, as if the reporter who'd come to interview him happened to be six years old, "Why, because of Gene, of course."

"Gene?"

"Autry, Gene Autry. I named this place after his spread."

"The guy who used to own the Angels?" I'm a big baseball fan and figured that must be what the *A* meant.

Tex shook his head and kicked gently at a weathered fence post. "Gene was a cowboy first," he said. "A movie cowboy, way back when. His horse was Champion and his ranch was The Flying A."

Oh, right. I vaguely remembered something from one of those old TV shows I'd stumbled over on an obscure channel late at night.

"His horse was a big palomino?"

"Nope," he said, frowning with disgust. "That was Roy Rogers."

Bobby O'Neil, a twenty-something staff photographer with hair dyed the color of a ripe plum, had been off taking pictures of the buildings and came up to us just in time to hear the mention of Roy Rogers.

"My grandfather used to talk about him. The king of the cowboys," he said with a confident grin.

Then he snapped a shot of Tex's grimace as the old guy said, "Nobody asked for my vote."

"Right," I said, deciding it was time to stop pretending I knew or cared what he was talking about. But I still needed a hook to hang my article from, so I plodded on, saying, "How long have you been here?"

"The land's been in my family a hundred years, give or take, the ranch a little over fifty."

Bobby wandered off to take more shots of the ranch, which was actually not much more than a dozen acres of mostly woods about halfway between Boston and Providence. We were standing on the dirt drive lined on either side by worn four-rail ranch fencing. Up ahead were a half-dozen buildings. They were all in various stages of near-collapse and formed a rough horseshoe shape in front of the woods. At the right tip of the horseshoe was a small ranch house, maybe four rooms with a wide porch that seemed to be held up by nothing more than sheer indifference. Toward the middle was the long, low Flying A Bunkhouse, its old sign dangling precariously. Once upon a time Boy Scouts had come down from Boston or up from Providence to stay there on weekends. It must have been an adventure for the city kids in their Hollywood hats and chaps. Ride the horses, learn roping, build a fire at night and sing songs written for radio and movie cowboys. And less than an hour from Back Bay.

There were a few other outbuildings and the stable, which looked to be the sturdiest and best maintained, at this end of the semicircle of ageing structures. Behind it were a couple of corrals for riding, and off to the left was the beginning of a trail, hardly more than a wide path into the woods. A faded sign out near the highway had promised trail rides, but I could see grass growing down the middle of the path. Tex might have done better business advertising his place as a ghost town.

"When are you leaving?" I said.

"Scheduled for a week next Wednesday," he said and then, after a significant pause, added, "'Least that's their plan."

" 'Their plan?' Aren't you planning to leave?"

Hey, maybe this could turn out to be more than one of those nostalgia pieces I thought I'd been stuck with.

He turned his head, spat in the dust, the classic western gesture spoiled somewhat by the fact that the only holster on his wide, silver-studded belt held a cell phone.

"Nope."

"But I thought this land was taken by eminent domain."

"Eminent domain? Sonny, this here is my domain. Been in my family over a hundred years, and there ain't no fancy commission can take it away from me just to give it to some fat cat biotech company."

The speech, like the man, was an odd mixture of idioms. But his meaning was clear, and so was my interest when I asked him, "Have you told the commission or Veri-Chem that you aren't moving?"

The commission was the state's Economic Development Commission. Veri-Chem was the big biotech firm the EDC had lured here with promises of cheap land near a major highway connecting two state capitols.

Henderson, shaking his head, apparently was planning to be the fly in the ointment.

"Didn't they pay you?"

"They sent a check. I tore it up."

"But you didn't tell them."

"They know."

Of course they'd know. But I sure as hell hadn't heard anything about this.

"Y'know, back when I was a kid," Henderson said, "There used to be a lot of western movies, mostly in black and white, just like the morality in 'em. Republic was the studio made most of 'em, had a whole string of cowboy heroes to star in 'em. But half the movies seemed to have the same plot—the railroad was comin' through and some town guy, usually the banker, knew about it and was trying to get some poor rancher's land cheap. Looks to me like that's what we got here. 'Course, there was usually a pretty daughter in the mix, and I got no kids. No kin at all, really."

"And the EDC's the rich town guy?"

"In a way, I suppose so. Especially the chairman, Wilson. Y'know him?"

"I've seen him on TV."

Byron Wilson was an oily fat guy with one of those comb-overs that began near an earlobe. There were rumors that the Chairmanship of the EDC had been a payoff for political services rendered, an appointed position that Wilson was reputed to be using to prepare for a very comfortable retirement.

" 'Course, in this scenario, the town guy's gonna get the land," Tex said, "so he can give it to the railroad, not sell it."

"Veri-Chem's the railroad."

"Right," he said, with an impatient look at his slow student. "I never said the analogy was an exact one. But if you know who Wilson is, then you know he's gonna make a lot more off my land than Veri-Chem's offered me."

"So what are you going to do? Shoot it out on Main Street?"

His quick, angry look was a warning that he didn't much cotton to smartass young reporters. And maybe being old wasn't the same as being helpless.

"Nope," he said after he saw I'd gotten his warning. "Veri-Chem wouldn't fight fair anyway. They'd send someone else out to the showdown, some three-piece shyster with a lawbook more deadly than a buckboard full of dynamite."

"But you're not planning to leave."

"I dunno," he said. "Wilson's come by here a couple of times with his flunkies on the commission, telling me my problem is I don't see the big picture. Guess they're right. I musta spent too much of my youth watching the little pictures, the ones in black and white where the good guys won in the end."

"Is there anything you can do legally? You have a lawyer?"

But he was shaking his head with disdain.

"You think I can afford one?" he said, looking around his spread. "Y'know, I've been doing some checking on the Internet down to the library. This eminent domain thing has gotten out of hand in a lot of places. Used to be it was only used for highways coming through, airports, maybe, or military bases. Now, the rich firms like Veri-Chem get to use it to grab up land for practically nothing. And the EDC says it's okay because they'll generate more economic growth than I do. Hell, Wilson told me my buildings aren't worth the time it would take to knock 'em down."

Bobby, who had come wandering back, said, "Isn't Veri-Chem going to have about fifteen hundred people working here?"

"Hey, if somebody wants to put up a strip mall where your house is or slap up a McDonald's, won't that generate more economic growth than your taxes?"

"Right," I said. "So what are you gonna do?"

"You fellas want to see the horses?"

"Yeah!" Bobby said, not concerned that Tex hadn't answered my question. I reluctantly followed them to the stable. It was dark in there, lit by a few low-watt bulbs, and it smelled of hay and leather, dirt and horses. There were a dozen of them, their stalls on either side, a couple of them snuffling in the shadows. I've only been near horses a few times and have never felt comfortable. They're always bigger than I think they'll be, intimidatingly big. And while I know they're not carnivores, those enormous teeth, not to mention those long legs and big hoofs, have made me nervous ever since I was a kid. There's a good reason that metropolitan police departments, even today, will assign mounted officers to riot duty.

Tex went to one of the stalls, patted the neck of a big reddish horse that responded with that nodding thing horses do.

"I board a few of them for the owners," he said. "Most are mine and, like Bangles here, older than me in horse years." He held something on his palm for the horse to lick off, its big tongue sliding out between those bucked teeth. "They can't do much anymore, but I still have to feed 'em, muck out the stalls, pay a vet. Should've got rid of most of 'em years ago."

"You going to sell them?"

"They're too old," he said, patting the horse again. "Nobody'd want 'em."

"Do they really use them in glue factories?" Bobby said, snapping off some more pictures.

Tex looked as if he was measuring the distance between his fist and Bobby's chin.

"Well, what are you going to do?" I asked quickly.

He let out a slow breath, looked away from Bobby and said, "I don't know, Sonny. Guess we'll have to wait and see."

We ran the piece in the Sunday edition, the lead on the Neighbors page, including a color picture of Tex, a booted foot up on one of his rail fences. Bobby had used a profile shot, which hid the old guy's cell phone holster. I had tried to get responses from both the EDC and Veri-Chem, but was shot down. I checked out the Internet, however, and Tex had been right about some misuse of eminent domain, so I included a few examples that I'd found. I thought it was a pretty good piece, building up a nice sense of tension and leaving the resolution uncertain, ending with Tex's "Guess we'll have to wait and see."

My follow-up piece would have to wait until I went to the ranch on the day Tex was going to be told to get the hell out of Dodge.

I called him on Tuesday, and he told me he'd been contacted by three different lawyers, all willing to take his case pro bono—one of them was well known for taking on David versus Goliath cases, the other two probably wanted the free publicity.

"Turned 'em all down," Tex said.

"Why?" I said, not masking my disappointment very well.

Sure, bringing in the lawyers would stretch out the stand-off, give me a juicy series of stories, but I also thought Tex should fight this and was surprised that he had given up so quickly.

"Once you bring in the lawyers, Sonny, it's all about them and about what they have to say to the television cameras, and it's about language and courts and that kind of nonsense. It won't really be about my ranch anymore or about what's right or wrong. It'll be the Veri-Chem lawyers fighting my lawyers with words. And that fat weasel, Wilson, won't have to face up to what he's doing."

"So you aren't going to do anything?"

"Well, one of Veri-Chem's lawyers wants to talk to me before I'm supposed to vacate the spread. I guess they'd rather not have some kind of showdown with the cops and the TV people here and all. I'm pretty sure they want to give me another damned EDC check, make it all formal. So I told him I'd see him Friday. Told him just him and Wilson, nobody else. But if you want to stop by, they're gonna be here at ten. Might be something you can use in a story. Don't want that purple-haired picture taker with you though. Just you."

Friday was overcast, but mild, and I was at the ranch a little before ten. Tex was hitching his horses to the rail fence near the stable as I drove slowly past him and parked beside the ancient Flying A pickup near the ranch house. There were no other cars around. Tex was bringing the last two of the horses out of the stable when I walked down the dirt driveway.

"What's up?" I said.

He shook his head, patted the rump of the nervous black until it had calmed down, and he looped the reins once over the fence.

"They're not coming?" I said.

"Oh, no," he said quietly. "They'll be here all right. They're just letting me know I'm not important enough for them to be on time. A business strategy, I guess."

But he sounded more sad than angry, and that bothered me. And not just for the sake of my story. I could write it any way it happened, but I suppose I was still holding out for a showdown.

"Why are the horses out here?" I said.

Instead of answering, he nodded toward the front gate, where a black Mercedes was turning in slowly, as if reluctant to get the dirt from the driveway on its hubcaps.

We walked down the narrow, fence-lined driveway and the car stopped to meet us. Two men in dark pinstripe suits got out. The lanky driver had to be the lawyer because there was no mistaking Wilson. His rotundity on television had always made me think he was taller, but he was a short, fat guy with a three-thousand-dollar suit and the few dark strands of his remaining hair combed carefully flat to his scalp.

"Parking's up there," Tex said, pointing toward my car and his truck.

The lawyer shrugged, got back in, and drove slowly up toward the ranch house.

Wilson waited, his small, dark eyes frowning at me.

"Who's this, Tex?"

"Just a friend."

"Are all your friends reporters?" he said.

I wasn't surprised. Wilson was the kind of guy who'd want to know about the reporter who'd written a story sympathetic to his opponent. But he didn't seem too concerned about me, not when he had his own lanky legal gunslinger walking back down past the horses toward us.

"Jess Baxter," the lawyer said, reaching out his hand. "Pleased to meet you, Mr. Henderson."

Tex nodded, but his hands stayed in his pockets.

"Jess Baxter," the lawyer repeated, turning to me, the hand still out there.

"Pleased to meet you," I said, shaking the damned thing so he could finally put it away.

"Can we get down to it . . . Tex?" Wilson said, his sarcasm thick as he pronounced the name. "Have you decided to see reason?"

"And what might reason be in a case like this, Mr. Wilson?" Tex said.

But Baxter, his voice as smooth as the engine of his Mercedes said, "I think reason is the very reasonable offer the state has made for your property, Mr. Henderson."

"And what are you getting out of all this?" Tex said, eyeing Wilson.

"A first-rate firm locating in our state and fifteen hundred jobs for our citizens," Wilson said.

"That's the big picture you're always talkin' about?"

"Yes, it is ... Tex. And I think it's time you saw it that way."

"So you hand this slick firm all this land, the state pays me a fraction of what the land's worth, and you get nothing out of it but the satisfaction of a job well done?"

Baxter started to interrupt, but Wilson stopped him with a hand on his sleeve.

"I don't know what kind of story you're trying to concoct for your friend here," he said, nodding toward me. "But I didn't come here to be accused of anything or badgered by you. You're getting a more than fair market price for your land. Look at this property! Is it really worth anything to anyone?"

"Y'know, Wilson," Tex said, "you've said that a few times on a couple of TV news shows since this young fella's newspaper story came out. And I began to think, maybe you're right. Maybe I've lived here too long to really be able to see the ranch. Maybe I just keep seeing it the way I want it to be."

Wilson and Baxter relaxed, clearly pleased with the way this seemed to be going. There'd be no good quotes for me, no showdown on the day Tex lost his land.

"I've been thinking about that big picture you keep talking about, and I've finally decided you must be right. So I also decided it was time I did something about it."

"Very wise, Mr. Henderson," Baxter said, his smile the one the man in first place gives to the runner-up.

"If you'd just wait here a second, gentlemen. Sonny, you come with me."

I walked with him up the wide dirt path toward the horses, where, with a series of quick snaps, he loosened each horse's reins from the railing.

"What's up?" I said.

"Setting 'em free," he said. "Lookin' at the big picture."

The horses stood still.

Tex motioned me on. A few yards beyond the horses was a battery with a switch on top and wires running off into the stable.

He took a deep breath, knelt at the battery, muttered, "Thought I'd save them some effort," and flipped the switch.

The charges must have been circuited because the stable was the first to go, the explosion shattering the roof and spraying wall boards out as the building collapsed in on itself. A second later a large shed exploded. Then the bunkhouse, two other outbuildings, and next the ranch house roof blew off and that porch finally gave in to gravity. They were all gone within a few seconds. It wasn't like the movies, no gasoline fueled fireballs wafting up in slow motion. But the explosions going off one after the other were deafening. The boards rattled and banged to the ground, a few of them thunking on my car, the pickup, and the Mercedes, setting off its alarm. But through all the noise I could hear the horses behind us whinnying wild with fear. I turned and saw them rearing from the sound and then running away from it in the only direction open to them, down the narrow, fence-lined lane straight toward the two men frozen in the middle.

Baxter's quick thinking and long legs saved him. He raced for the rail fence and vaulted, clumsily banging himself sideways over the top. Wilson stood transfixed. He looked more annoyed than fearful, frowning and offended that these large clattering beasts were coming toward him. He must have realized at the last second that, my god, these large clattering beasts were, in fact, coming toward him because, just before the horses blocked my view of him, Wilson turned and ran a few awkward steps. Then there were just the horses in the narrow lane. Then there was just the dusty, trampled heap of Wilson's body in its three-thousand-dollar suit.

"Jesus," I whispered, watching the horses shouldering each other through the gate and racing down the narrow country road away from the highway that connected the two capitol cities.

"Knew they'd turn right," Tex said. "We never ride 'em toward that damned highway."

I ran down to Wilson, but he wasn't moving, and his comb-over had shifted so you could see where the hoofs had cracked his skull. I knelt down to feel for a pulse, although I knew it was a wasted effort.

"My God!" Baxter said, his black wingtips dusty at my side.

"I'll call 911!"

"No need," I said.

Still kneeling, I saw Tex's battered boots arrive before I heard him say, "He dead?" the way you might ask if those clouds looked like rain.

"What the hell were you thinking?" Baxter yelled, his cell phone out and open.

"I was obliging him," Tex said calmly. "The man kept saying my buildings weren't worth the price of knockin' 'em down."

Baxter wasn't listening. He was telling 911 about the emergency, though there really wasn't an emergency anymore.

I hate to admit it, but I was already mentally writing my story. I'd have to call the paper to get a photographer out here quickly. We'd have to find out where the horses had stopped running. And I'd have to get some quick answers from Tex before the police showed up, maybe ask him if he'd planned it this way. I wasn't sure about that question, though, because I wasn't sure about his answer, and the wrong one could land him hip deep in trouble. After all, he had told me to go with him, out of the path he knew the horses would take.

"Y'know, if Wilson had thought faster," Tex said quietly, staring down at the body as if it were lying at high noon on some dusty western street, "he coulda got out of the way real easy. Guess he was just too busy thinking about the big picture."

Running on Empty

Stephen Liskow

Kristen let Tom accelerate into the westbound traffic before she spoke.

"I want a divorce."

Tom pulled out to pass a Buick with a white-haired driver and Massachusetts plates, accelerating long after he'd cleared it. He only drove fast when he was upset. Wilco moaned on the CD player and Drew slept, his blond curls bobbing in his car seat.

"We're falling apart," Kristen said.

"Certainly sounds like it."

Tom never took his eyes off the road, but he turned down the CD. His voice held just a hint of tension, like the hint of garlic in Kristen's special marinade in the Tupperware in the back seat. His parents expected them at four-thirty, they'd eat at seven, and the fireworks would start at nine-thirty. Tom worshipped schedules.

"You're never around anymore," Kristen said.

"You traveled a lot, too," he replied. "Until you wanted to be a mom."

"I thought you wanted to be a dad."

"I did. I do. I am." In the back seat, thirteen-month-old Drew dangled a silver ribbon of drool on the chin he'd inherited from Kristen. She reached back and gently dabbed at it. He murmured but didn't wake up. He had Tom's nose.

"Let's face it, Krissy, we got used to living pretty well when we were a two-income family. I love you and Drew, but one of us has to pay the bills."

He turned up the CD again. Family or career, Kristen thought. Who the hell said you can have it all?

"I never feel like you're here anymore, even when you're on the couch or holding Drew. It's like I'm looking at a video or something; there's no connection."

"I need a little down time when I get home. You ought to be able to understand that. You most of all."

Wilco went into a loose jam that reminded Kristen of Neil Young. She hated Neil Young. The sign by the roadside commanded, "Remove sunglasses at tunnel."

"We never talk anymore."

"Sure we do. Drew did this, Drew did that, Drew hates solid food. Drew's fussy because he's teething. And you know damn well what my day was like."

I miss it, Kristen thought. I didn't think I'd miss it this much, but I do.

They slid into the tunnel, echoes surrounding them until Tom guided them to the white dot at the other end and slid his sunglasses down on his nose again.

"I bust my butt so you can stay with Drew, then I come home and you carry him around like a shield. You won't even put him down so I can hug you."

"That's because you never just want to hug anymore. You hug me, and the next thing I know, I'm on my back on the kitchen tiles or bent over the dining room table. What ever happened to cuddling?"

"I cuddle. You snuggle up next to me on the couch—or you used to, anyway—and we'd cuddle like teenagers at a movie. Two hours, my arm feels like a pipe full of cement. The blood dies there. Hurts like hell."

"Don't curse in front of Drew," she said.

Drew shifted again, surrounded by his supplies: formula, jars of strained vegetables and fruit, clean t-shirts, another pair of shorts, his stuffed dinosaur, three books, and God knew what else. The paper bag against the armrest held the Tupperware and a bottle of zinfandel. Mom and Dad Harrison liked red wine, but it always made Kristen's head feel like an echo chamber. The fireworks tonight wouldn't help that, either. They'd sit in lawn chairs and watch from the hilltop, perfect seats overlooking the village a mile away.

The Showcase Cinema sign approached, and Kristen examined the juxtaposed titles. *De-Lovely White Chicks Before Sunset, I Robot Anchorman,* and *Dodgeball Sleepover* all sounded worth seeing. Maybe *Spiderman 2: A Cinderella Story,* or *King Arthur Prisoner of Azkaban.* Her favorite was still *Four Weddings The Cowboy Way.* They even tried that in bed—when they still did anything in bed.

She remembered meeting Tom on a job in—Seattle? Tacoma?— somewhere in the northwest, a guy who'd been a real problem, but they'd discovered they could work together, her flashing a little leg, distracting him so Tom could close things. He'd sent her an e-mail after that and they'd corresponded for a month before meeting again in Kansas City and deciding to form a partnership. It was perfect until Kristen's biological clock turned off the snooze alarm.

Another hour to the Harrisons, tickled to see the next generation carry on the family business. Dad Harrison still liked to tell Kristen how he and his wife conceived Tom while celebrating the handling of a particularly difficult client.

"Tom," she said. "I'm going crazy."

"Ah ha," he said. "I should have known, shouldn't I? Saying you want a divorce is a dead giveaway."

"Don't be sarcastic." It made her feel eight years old. She was a grown-up now, with a thirteen-month-old son and three-hundred-sixty-month-old husband.

"Sorry," he said sarcastically. "Why don't you tell me why you want a divorce, Kristen? I won't say another word until you finish, okay?"

She heard the change from his usual "Krissy." "I'm Drew's mother, and I'm your wife, and I'm your family's good little daughter-in-law, but I'm not Kristen anything. I feel used up, empty."

I used to be someone, she remembered. They used to call me for a tough client as often as they called you.

"You're still Kristen," Tom said. "And I still love you."

"No, I'm not the same person. I know, I've—we've—got Drew now, and that changed things, but it feels like I gave up a lot of stuff I didn't know I was going to give up and didn't know I'd miss until it wasn't there anymore."

The CD changed to Metallica while Tom grappled with her syntax.

"You don't have to spend every second with Drew, you know. It's better for both of you if you don't. Teach him you won't always pick him up the second he cries. Start taking back your own life."

She shook her head. "You make it sound like you just find the car in the long-term lot, stick the key in again, and it starts up. What if the battery's dead?"

"You get cables and jump it. It may take a while, but that's okay. It took you a while to lose the weight after you were pregnant, but you did it. You're more beautiful than ever."

Actually, she was ten pounds heavier than two years ago. Tom didn't mind because now she had cleavage. Not that they took advantage of it. The fields on her right glared bright gumdrop green. Corn didn't really grow that color, did it, knee-high or not?

"What if I've lost the edge?" she asked.

The car felt stuffy and she stuck her head out the window, the seventy-mile-an-hour wind blowing her short hair and whumping in her ears. You're afraid, you're afraid, you're afraid.

"Are you getting your period?" he asked. "You're always a little crazy before you get your period."

"You don't even know?"

"You started wearing those stupid pajamas. You used to sleep naked, remember?"

You'd think having a baby would make her feel warmer, but it hadn't. She looked back again, Drew's hands clenched into little pink knobs. The best thing she'd ever done. Tom's voice came like he'd been inside her head.

"Look at him, Krissy. He trusts you and loves you holding him, he makes noises at you. Hell, he's almost walking, almost talking. I don't get to see that. Some night, I'll come home, he'll open the door, say, 'How you doing, Dad?' and I'll look at this kid I never got to know."

Taillights grew large ahead of them and Tom eased his foot off the accelerator. The exit to his parents lay seven miles ahead, then twelve miles on a road too insignificant to have a route number. Kristen knew the feeling.

"Leave him at day care once in a while," Tom continued. "We'll get a sitter. A nanny, something. And you should find a hobby."

"Hobby," Kristen said. "You mean like knitting or painting?"

"Whatever. Collect something."

"Matchbooks? Moving violations?"

"Maybe sports, get some exercise. Tennis, golf, whatever. Meet people, make some friends."

"Oh, fine. 'And what does your husband do?' "

Her voice's edge could peel apples, long red curls twirling into the sink. She fought down the explosion trying to happen under her shirt, the one she didn't know how to get rid of anymore. Tension never built up when she worked, always on the go, always dealing with different people, she usually didn't even know their names and they never were around long enough to drive her crazy.

She squinted at the license plate she couldn't quite read through the windshield. A pair of senior cits in their Mercury Marquis slowed down for the exit three miles ahead. Tom pulled out and passed them.

"I need to work," she said. "Not full-time, maybe, but at least carry a little bit of the load. Feel like I'm helping us. Right now, I feel like I got into the back row and it's the wrong ticket."

And suddenly she was crying.

"Krissy . . ." Tom's hand squeezed hers.

Drew woke up and grunted; the smell filled the car in seconds. It had to be those strained beets.

Tom pulled off the exit and turned right, twelve miles of boulders big as pool tables. He opened all the windows, but Drew's effluvium still battered them. They'd never survive twelve miles. A Jiffi Mart loomed near a copse of trees, paint peeling, the only car in the lot a decrepit Pinto, mostly rust with occasional faded green. The faded bumper sticker supported Dukakis.

"Think it's open?" he asked.

"I'm not even sure it's still in business," she said. "Do you think that car even runs?"

"It's a current plate."

Tom pulled up next to the gas pump and Kristen unbuckled Drew from his seat.

"I don't believe this," she said.

"What?"

"We forgot his pampers. We've got his formula, food, books, toys, blanket, pacifier, but no pampers."

"Here." Tom handed her his wallet.

"You might as well fill up while I change him," she said. "If the pumps work."

He read the pump. "The prices are up to date."

Kristen pushed her way through the raspy screen door and into the stale Styrofoam smell of cheap air conditioning. Cartons of cigarettes peered at her from behind the girl at the cash register, pudgy with stringy brown hair and impossibly pale skin. She wore jeans and a man's blue work shirt with a patch that said "Darla" over the breast pocket.

"Do you have pampers?" Kristen asked. The girl nodded at the aisle to her left, next to aspirin, throat lozenges, and decongestant. The shelf had more colors than a carnival.

"Jesus." The girl's nose twitched. "Something die in his pants?"

"We had an accident," Kristen said. "At least he had his seat belt fastened."

"Damn, lady. My kids never stunk like that. What you feeding him?"

Count to ten, Kristen told herself. Darla didn't ask to be fat and stupid, she just is.

The restroom sign was left of the counter, under the security camera.

"And fill on the SUV out there, please."

"Which pump?"

There wasn't another vehicle in sight. Kristen pointed, Drew's smell filling her head.

"Out there, the second one on the outside."

Darla stared and Kristen waited for her to stick a finger in her nose.

"That would be pump four."

Kristen handed her two twenties.

"Put the rest on the Pampers, please?"

"You got it." The woman's voice could kill plants. "Clean up the place good before you come out."

Kristen watched Darla start the pump and wondered if she fed her kids rats and let them coil up in the sun. Then she pushed through the restroom door.

Tom watched the letters on the pump change to "Please Begin Fueling" and let the fumes fill the humid air around him. Half an hour to Mom and Dad's place, ten minutes on a real road, but they loved their privacy. Go over fifteen on this path and you'd break an axle.

He squeezed the nozzle, wishing he could choke away Kristen's misery. He knew she missed the old life, and she'd been good at it. She was a terrific mother, too, but it wasn't enough. She was putting all of her life into the little guy, and the rest of her was beginning to atrophy. Some careers you can balance with a baby, but some you can't.

He had nineteen gallons in the tank when Kristen returned, biting her lip and blinking her eyes. Drew gurgled something that sounded like "Elmo" in her arms. She sat him firmly in his seat and jerked his buckles tight.

"Krissy?" Tom asked. "You okay?"

"That, that . . . bitch." Kristen's face grew strawberry blotches.

"What happened?"

"Nothing. I'll take care of it myself." She snatched the keys out of the ignition, then rummaged in the trunk.

"Don't you keep an emergency gun here anymore?"

"Under the spare tire."

Kristen's face gleamed when she found it, a Smith & Wesson .32 revolver.

"I'll be back in a minute."

She handed Tom a screwdriver from the tool kit.

"God, I didn't realize how much I've missed this."

Tom took the screwdriver over to the rusted out Pinto, already putting the plates on their SUV when Kristen emerged. She wore a blue work shirt with "Darla" stitched over the pocket, bills peeking out, a twenty on top. One hand held the gun and the other had the videotape from the security camera.

"They sell shirts now?" he asked. "But only with certain names?"

"I liked the look," she told him.

The Moneylender

Susan Oleksiw

Anita Ray brushed her hand over a stack of brightly printed brochures till they fanned out across the reception desk. She ticked each one until she could see every cover, then she tapped each one with her forefinger. Without looking up, she said, turning her head slightly toward her left shoulder, "Are you seeing what I'm seeing, Auntie?"

"How can I see what you're seeing, Anita, without losing my mind. I dare not look most of the time." She brushed against her niece and leaned over the tall counter. She scanned the brochures with an expression mingling anxiety and curiosity. "I see no trouble here, nothing, nothing at all. Why do you have them?"

Anita Ray was not surprised at the slightly hysterical note in her aunt's voice. Ever since Anita had moved in to help the newly widowed aunt run her hotel in this South Indian resort, her penchant for crime had unnerved Meena. The woman now jumped at every new idea, and openly blamed Anita's Irish American father for corrupting a good Hindu woman and Meena's older sister.

"These are from some of the other hotels. Can't you see? They have something we are missing!" Anita leaned back and waited.

"Hotel Delite missing something? Not possible, not possible at all!" She glared at Anita, but her expression hinted at a certain wavering doubt. "No, please don't tell me we are in decline. Please, Anita."

146

Anita took pity on her aunt, and rubbed her back affectionately. "No, Auntie Meena, we're not in decline."

"No, we cannot be," Meena said, leaning her head on her hands.

"Auntie?"

"The complaints people come up with! I knew it would happen." She raised her head, her face twisted in torment. "Such complaints! This room is too loud—the ocean keeps me awake. This room is too dark and the mosquitoes come in. This room requires a net and there is none. This room has a rattling fan. Oh, Anita, they never stop."

"Come with me for a massage, Auntie. It'll take your mind off your worries. Other hotels all list massage as one of their amenities. We should too. Our guests will be so mellow they won't even notice if there's no power."

"Massage! We should offer massage!" Meena looked at her niece with widening eyes and a mouth working to find words to express her feelings. "Do we not have the women walking here and everywhere with almost no clothes, and now we are to persuade them to lie among strangers with no clothes, only the oil covering that pink flesh." Meena's face suddenly went pale, then flushed a deep red.

"I knew you'd agree." Anita winked at her aunt, gathered up the brochures and stuffed them into her purse. "Leave it to me. I'll talk to Jayan about it." She picked up her camera, and headed out the door.

Despite her show of confidence, Anita wasn't sure where she was going to find a masseuse who would be willing to work occasionally at Hotel Delite. Right now, demand was high and supply low.

Anita jumped onto the stoop of a small house made to look like a traditional Kerala hut but given a polished stone floor, wood-framed windows with screens, and a door between the two rooms. Anita swept aside the curtain and started to call out when she heard voices of a man and woman coming from within. The door kept out eyes but the tightly woven and framed palm-leaf walls let sound flow.

"Where have you been?" Anita heard a soft female voice, petulant and pleading. She couldn't place the accent—French or Swedish, perhaps—but the voice sounded familiar. "You were not here. You promised me."

"I had to be away." The man's voice was carefully calm, to Anita's ears. An Indian man's voice. "I have obligations."

"But you promised." The door handle turned; Anita stepped back onto the sandy lane just as a woman emerged into the outer room.

"It is not . . ." A young man followed the woman into the room, then stopped abruptly when he saw Anita in the doorway. "And you are wanting follow-up massage? I will tell Jayan."

"No, I don't want another massage." The woman flipped away the curtain on the front door and pushed past Anita. "You are asking too much. I know you are." Anita recognized the young woman as Kristen, a former guest at Hotel Delite who had moved, just a few days ago, to a lodging house, at a daily savings of about twenty dollars. Anita gave her a warm smile. The woman paused as though just noticing Anita. "They are not honest," she said. "They're very tricky." She gave a little jerk of her chin and stepped around Anita, her bright pink skirt swirling out as she pulled the strap of her cloth bag over her shoulder. The morning light glinted on the pattern of gold threads along the hem.

"You are wanting massage?" the young man offered. His thick silky lashes swept down over deep brown eyes. His face still held the beauty of youth, which signaled how handsome he would soon be as a man.

"Good morning, Ranju. I have a seven-thirty massage, but," she turned away, hoping to catch sight of Kristen before she disappeared around a corner, "I also wanted to speak with Jayan. Perhaps later?"

"But he is coming just now." Ranju sounded alarmed at the impending loss of business.

"Ah, well, okay," Anita said, still looking over her shoulder for signs of Kristen.

An hour later, as Anita handed Jayan a wad of rupees and marveled at how wonderful she felt under his ministrations, she tried to figure out what she had meant to ask him about.

"Your next massage, perhaps?" Jayan said.

"No, not that."

"Another customer for me, perhaps?"

"No, don't think so."

Jayan's face fell with every reply until he finally ran out of suggestions.

"I've got it!" Anita said, still feeling dreamy. "Kristen, the tourist who was here when I arrived. She said something rather harsh and I was wondering what's upset her so."

"Who is this?"

"A young tourist, European, who said it was all trickery, but I don't know what she was referring to." Anita lounged in the only comfortable chair in the outer room while Jayan studied her from a bench set along the opposite wall. The only other piece of furniture was a small table serving as a desk.

"European? The blonde hair?" Anita nodded. "Ranju!" Jayan said, but not so loud that his assistant sitting outside would hear. "It is never good for the tourist to become involved with us. It is not meant to be conducive to good relations."

"So, Ranju and Kristen are involved? A lover's spat?"

"They come and want to see the true India, so they make friends, they think, and soon they are having the same problems they have in their own country. Why do they think life will be so different here?"

Jayan shook his head in disapproval.

□   □   □

By the end of the evening, when she was closing up her photography shop, Anita had all but forgotten about the pouting foreigner in the pink skirt. She had sold a number of photographs and was pleased with her take for the day. She pulled the metal shutter down, locked it, and turned to the narrow lane. Just above her Kanjappa was leaning over the parapet outside his tiny bookstore.

"No business tonight," he said when Anita looked up and waved.

"A quiet evening down here also," she said.

"Only few books today. The mystery novels." He gave an exaggerated sigh, then leaned farther over the parapet as a young woman walked by. Anita recognized Kristen in her pink skirt. "Hallo!" he called out. Her eyes flickered upward for barely a second before she jerked her head forward, chin up, and marched on past Anita without acknowledging the greeting.

Anita looked up to Kanjappa for an explanation. "One of your customers?"

"Soon going, I am thinking." he said. "To Goa going. She is just purchasing *Tours of South India.*"

"Ah." Some people can't be happy no matter how much beauty surrounds them, Anita thought. The sour, pouting one was clearly one of those. Anita waved to the bookseller and left.

The following morning Anita settled down at one end of the breakfast table. It was early, barely seven o'clock, and the guests were rarely up at that hour unless they were scheduled for an early departure for a tour or flight out of the country. She spread *The Indian Express* in front of her and settled down to enjoy the quiet.

"Juice, Memsahib," Moonu said, sliding a plate with a glass of juice toward her. "Such excitement this morning." He placed an empty plate in front of her, arranged a pot of tea, and stepped back.

"And toast. Today toast is very good."

"I should hope so. What excitement?" Anita lowered her newspaper and looked up.

"The corporation is meeting today. The business owners are gathering," he said with a broad smile.

"Yes, that will be exciting. I can just imagine the owner of the Shiva Palace Hotel sitting down next to Jayan the masseur to talk about tourist amenities. Toast sounds good. Auntie Meena didn't mention it, did she?"

"She is only just learning about it, Memsahib."

"All right, Moonu, what are you holding back?"

"They are talking about the canal that runs at the back of the tourist village." He held the menu close to his chest and closed his eyes. There had to be more to this, Anita knew, than landscaping.

"They have found someone in the canal?" She felt a sudden despair.

"A foreign lady—once so pretty. Now . . . " He shrugged, as if to say, What more is there to know about life? All is fleeting. "She is the one who was staying here, and moved to that lodging house. Why are they such fools?" He headed back to the kitchen.

"Moonu, wait! Do you mean that young Swedish girl Kristen, with the long blond hair and she wore that pink skirt all the time. Is that the one?"

"Yes, yes, it is her. And now she is gone."

After a hurried breakfast Anita went straight to the lane twisting beside the canal; she soon came to a section roped off, with a constable standing guard, or rather sitting, in a bright red molded plastic chair. He moved to stand when he saw her.

"What happened here?" Anita asked. "I've just heard the news."

"She is falling into the canal." He clucked in dismay at the carelessness of foreigners.

"That's all?" It couldn't be all, Anita thought. The path is wide enough for two people to pass, though just, the area is well lit, and the water is not deep here. Anyone falling in could simply stand up and climb out. "How did she come to fall in?"

"She is hitting her head."

"You saw signs of that?"

He waggled his head slowly, his eyes falling shut. Yes, he had seen the evidence—blood matted in her hair and on her clothing. Which meant, Anita forbore from telling him, that the victim had sustained the blows before she fell in, not after. She had stuck her nose into enough murders to know what to make of the evidence— but also to know the police would not welcome her opinions.

Anita thanked him and moved away, scanning the area. Opposite her was an old compound wall, and behind that an old farmer's house. The owner had managed to hold onto his property despite the burgeoning tourist business around him. But it couldn't last forever. The offers to sell would soon be too tempting.

Anita moved to the wall and peered over. Inside was a typical compound, with a low-slung house fronted by a broad veranda with by a hip-high parapet, a dirty white chicken and dark brown rooster scratching in the dirt in front, trash piled in a corner, ready to be burnt, and a small boy squatting by the side of the house, his wide eyes watching her. She waved. He waved back and came skipping over.

"I know you," he said, and proceeded to prove that he did. Anita also knew him, and they exchanged news of their families.

"Did you see the accident?" she asked. He shook his head; she hadn't expected more, but she was hoping he knew something. "Were you here?" He nodded.

"He was angry," the boy said.

"Who?"

"The man who was with her. He came one way and she came the other. He called out to her. And he was angry."

"Was the woman angry?"

The boy shook his head. "She said no, just no, she didn't have to do anything he wanted."

"Then what happened?"

The boy shrugged. "He yelled and left."

Yes, thought Anita, stepping back and studying stains at knee-level on the wall. He would leave, wouldn't he? She knelt and peered closer, her index finger hovering over a string of reddish brown spots. She rose and scanned the ground, then peered into the canal. Disappointed, she turned away.

□ □ □

Well, thought Anita, as she walked back along the lane to where the dead woman had been living, well, well, well. Kristen's last words must mean something. She turned left down a dirt path, passed an open-air restaurant, and turned onto a narrow lane rising up the hillside and leading to a number of modest hotels, including a small lodging house. At Ganapati's Rest, a constable slouching against the compound wall pushed himself upright as she approached.

"More trouble?" Anita asked when she reached him.

He shrugged. "Someone broke in last night and searched one of the rooms."

"Whose room?" She was pretty sure she knew the answer. "The dead woman's?"

"Yes, the one who was found in the canal. But no one can say if anything is missing."

"She stayed at Hotel Delite for a while," Anita said. The constable raised his eyebrows, apparently surprised. "And she didn't have anything valuable there that we knew about. She was quite concerned with costs also."

"And so she has moved here," he said, nodding to the lodging house.

"About what time was the break-in?"

"Very early. One of the other guests was getting ready to go to puja and it was not yet light, he said, and he saw someone climbing down from upstairs, at the back. He called out but the man ran away." He paused to look up at the second floor. "But he wasn't carrying anything, so perhaps he is not finding what he wanted—nothing valuable there."

Anita also looked up at the lodging house. It was the simplest of buildings for travelers—a row of five rooms on each story, with a long balcony on each level, reached by stairs at the side. There were no amenities—guests shared a row of bathrooms behind the building, and each room had a single overhead light. Even the compound wall actually belonged to an abutting guesthouse. Anita thanked the constable and went back to Jayan's massage hut.

It was still early, not yet ten o'clock, and Anita knew this was the end of Jayan's busiest time—in this weather, massages were best given early in the morning or late in the afternoon. Anita rounded the bend to see two men standing in the doorway of Jayan's hut, one, a large man, leaning against the wall with his foot up bracing himself, peeling a banana, and the other with his palms out and his head tilted, pleading, it seemed to Anita. When she saw their faces, she knew she was right. Anita recognized the large man as Bhaskaran, a well-known moneylender, and the other was Jayan's assistant, Ranju, and the last time she'd seen him he'd been arguing with the dead woman, Kristen. The moneylender walked off, giving Anita a cursory glance, and Ranju disappeared into the hut.

"We are fully booked," he said the minute Anita poked her head in.

"That's all right. It's you I want to see anyway." Anita stepped in, noted that the massage room was empty, and pulled up a chair. "That was your girlfriend who was found dead this morning, wasn't it?"

"No, no, just someone who came for massage. I have already

spoken with the police. I don't know anything about it." Ranju looked morose enough for Anita to believe him—almost.

"What did they ask you?"

"I told them I only knew her slightly, and I spent the entire night in the hospital watching over my sick mummy. First I am making her some rice and then I am giving her sponge bath with my sister-in-law, and then I am lying there all night to give her peace of mind. The nurses are seeing me and giving me a pillow." For a man with an airtight alibi, Anita thought, he didn't seem very relieved.

"The man you were talking to," Anita began, "is Bhaskaran, the moneylender. Your mother's bills are very high?"

"As the Amrikans say, Huge! Like a house." He covered his face with his hands and looked ready to cry.

◻ ◻ ◻

The second-floor, open-air café was filled with tourists chatting over coffee in a dozen different languages and the waiters wandering among the tables, in no hurry to get people served and out of the restaurant. Anita took a table along the side, out of the sun, but where she could catch a breeze and think. Somehow Kristen's death was tied to Ranju, but he seemed more concerned about his mother's care than the death of a tourist he knew. And what about her room being searched? What could Kristen possibly have of any value?

Anita recalled the morning when Kristen had first arrived, tired, jet-lagged, and worried about someone stealing her plane ticket, as though that was all anyone needed to leave India and start a new life overseas. Meena did her best to calm her, but it took the young woman several days before she seemed to settle down. Foreigners had such strange ideas about India, as though we are a different breed of humans, Anita thought. When they are the ones who are so odd.

The moneylender walked by just then. Probably on his collection rounds, Anita thought. She was so used to seeing him dodging in and out of shops that she barely noticed him anymore. But he did a thriving business, and he was a talker. Curious about how much Ranju and his family owed, Anita paid for her coffee and hurried down the stairs. Bhaskaran wandered through the lanes and stopped at a small restaurant boasting a roof but no walls except the back one that shielded the guests from the kitchen. When he saw her he waved to the chair opposite him. Anita nodded as she sat down.

"You have had coffee already this morning, I think," he said.

"You don't miss much, do you?"

"It is my business."

"And your business is thriving, I hear."

He inclined his head in modest acknowledgment. "And you are wishing to make use of my services?" He leaned forward with a hopeful smile.

"Not exactly." Anita paused while the waiter took Bhaskaran's order and moved away. "About Ranju and his family."

"Ahhh." The moneylender leaned back and nodded. "Yes, a large debt, and requiring more."

"But they can't afford it?"

"Yes, they can afford, but without surety I cannot give." The waiter placed a tall glass of coffee teetering on a saucer in front of him and left; Bhaskaran stirred his coffee, then looked up with a twinkle in his eye. "A foolish man pays many times."

The combination of a cryptic remark from a moneylender and a dead woman was all Anita needed to order something to nibble on while she tried to decipher Bhaskaran. He smiled and sang softly to himself while she worked things out with the waiter. He had a beautiful singing voice, which Anita had heard at a wedding some years ago. It was a talent he reserved for his family, but since his family was large, many had an opportunity to hear him.

"I don't know what Ranju's mother's illness is, do you?" Anita asked when silence fell. Bhaskaran nodded. "How much will the whole thing run to?"

Bhaskaran shrugged and lifted his palms up in a graceful arc. "Who knows? Ten thousand, twenty thousand rupees? She is very sick."

Anita winced. This was a fortune for someone in Ranju's position. "How much is the debt so far?"

Bhaskaran shrugged again. "Who knows? Five thousand, six thousand rupees? Perhaps so much."

"I thought moneylenders always knew to the penny how much they loaned out." Anita wrapped a swatch of appam around some vegetables. She frowned at Bhaskaran's mischievous expression.

"And so I do. I am most meticulous about my loans." He raised his coffee glass to his lips. "My ledgers are accurate to the paisa, and not one transaction goes unrecorded in both ledger paper and ledger computer. I track everything most carefully, each week. Each rate of interest is calculated daily. Nothing is left to chance."

"You're not the lender on this loan, are you?"

"Alas, Missi Anita, I am not." He sighed and lowered his glass. "There is much money to be made by a wise lender."

"But Ranju was asking for a loan, wasn't he?" Anita was sure of what she had seen outside Jayan's hut.

"Ah, yes, both he and his brother have asked most passionately, but, alas, neither has anything to put up as surety. Collateral," he said, "is my most lucrative aspect."

"They don't own anything?"

"Ah, they say they do." He waved to the waiter, and counted out three rupees and fifty paisa.

"You don't believe them?"

"I cannot believe or disbelieve. I can only advance on the basis of surety." He recounted his payment. "There are no exceptions."

"What did they offer instead?"

"First I was to give an advance and then the surety would be supplied, as though I had to prove I was a reliable moneylender." He sniffed and straightened his shoulders. "Have I not loaned more money than anyone else here? Do shop owners not praise my name?"

"Actually, Bhaskaran, no, they don't."

He looked hard at her, frowned, then shrugged. "Hmm. No matter. No surety, no money." Then he leaned forward, sliding a shiny white business card toward her plate. "But if you ever need a consideration for any reason, for you . . ." He smiled, bobbed his head again, and rose. Anita watched him stroll across the dirt floor, pause at the lane as though deciding which way to go, and turn to the right. He patted his thick black wave of hair, as though adjusting it before making an important entrance, and walked away, his shoulders swinging back and forth.

"They own something but have no proof of it," Anita said to herself. "That can be the only explanation." She sat on for several minutes until the waiter, looking worried, bent over her and began to tug at the plate to gain her attention.

□ □ □

At the end of the afternoon, when tourists were abandoning the beach for a cool shower and a rest before setting out on the arduous task of choosing a restaurant, Anita closed up her gallery and took the lane leading up the hill past the Kali Temple; she emerged almost at the top of Lighthouse Road. She waved down an autorickshaw and gave him directions. Half an hour later the driver drew up in front of a house set in a small clearing, one of a number of small white-washed houses along the lane. Anita told the driver to wait.

Somehow, she reasoned, Jayan's hut and Ranju seemed to be at the heart of all this. Perhaps if Anita knew more about Ranju and his dispute with the foreigner, she would uncover something significant about the crime.

No one answered Anita's call at Ranju's family home, so she

walked around the side of the house. In the distance she could hear voices, but near at hand was only quiet. On the back veranda sat a rice-sifting basket, a pile of dirty laundry, and a stack of banana leaves. Anita poked at the pile of laundry, pulling out a large dirty t-shirt. She turned it over, then dropped it back onto the pile when she heard the squeak of bicycle brakes. She walked around to the front. A bicycle was now leaning against a pillar.

. Ranju met her on the veranda, his hands hanging down by his side, his eyes bleary from lack of sleep. He didn't seem alarmed to see her coming from the back of the house, only tired.

"I was looking for you out back when no one came to the front door," she said.

"Yes, of course, please, you must sit. Just there." He pointed to a rickety bamboo chair and looked around for one for himself; not seeing one, he settled on the parapet and stared morosely at the floor. Anita had to repeat herself before he looked up. "What? Oh, an argument?" Pain flickered across his face.

"I was outside," Anita said, "I couldn't help overhearing." He didn't look embarrassed, just sad, and she waited for him to continue. She glanced around the house and yard, a simple property and obviously, to her eye, a family home owned for several generations. Although there was electricity in the neighborhood, and a line ran into the house above her head, she didn't hear the telltale noise of a television running inside. "You grew up here, yes?"

He slowly looked up at her, nodded. "Yes, just here."

"It is good to live long in one place, isn't it? It gives a kind of identity and security not found in any other way." She smiled.

"Yes, I suppose that is so."

"I'm sorry about your mother. Is she recovering?"

"No."

"Oh. I'm sorry." She paused. "That must be very hard, having to be there every night, to assist with her care."

"My brother is helping."

"Your brother," Anita said. "I forgot you had a brother. Does he work at Kovalam?"

"He runs an auto during the season. His station is by the bus stop."

"I met Bhaskaran today." When Ranju didn't look up, she continued, "He told me you wanted to borrow more money but didn't have any surety."

Ranju shook his head, looking even sadder. "Do you own this house, you and your family?" He nodded, still staring at the stone floor. "I can arrange a loan for you, for medical care." Ranju's head jerked up, his eyes wide and wet. Anita explained the details and after giving in to a cup of tea and a long story about his family, she managed to get away.

An hour later Anita's autorickshaw pulled up in front of Natesan's Antiques Shop at Kovalam Junction; she paid the driver, and climbed out. She knew the number of Ranju's brother's auto, and walked slowly along the line looking for it. To her right the road ran down to Kovalam beach, and to her left, another, shorter but steeper lane ran down to another beach. Her driver trotted over to her and pointed to an auto just pulling into the drive for the Kovalam Hotel; she waited a few minutes, and then waved to the auto when it returned. She climbed in, directing the driver to Lighthouse Road.

"Are you Vidyut? Ranju's brother?" she said when he came to a halt at the end of the hill on Lighthouse Road. To her left was the lane to Hotel Delite. The driver turned around and studied her. "I saw him today, at your family house."

"He is at the hospital," the man said.

"He was just returning." Anita waited.

He glared at her.

"I have been trying to figure out why anyone would kill a foreigner like Kristen. She's certainly not rich enough to entice anyone—she's careful with her money, never flashy. All she has is a plane ticket, and that isn't very much. Others here are far richer and much easier to plunder." His eyes were fiery, like his name, but he rarely blinked, she noticed.

"What is that to us?"

"She had little money, but she did have some. And she could get money, like any foreigner. She had a credit card."

"What do you want?"

"I want you to tell me what happened. I think I know, but tell me."

"I have nothing to tell you," he said, turning around in his seat. He jerked his head toward the opening, ordering Anita out. She leaned forward.

"I saw a t-shirt, your size, at your home, spattered with blood. I think it will match the blood spattered on the compound wall near where Kristen's body was found." Again she waited. A blood vessel in his neck pulsed thick and large. "You killed her because she had something you wanted and wouldn't give you."

"What could such a woman have?"

"A deed."

His shoulders stiffened, his head turned, so she could see his profile and the jaw clenching and unclenching. She could hear his breath deepening.

"This is a guess, but I think it's a good one, and I think I can prove it. Ranju is a goodlooking young man, and the foreign women find him attractive, I'm sure. But he wasn't interested in them. He was desperate to help his mother, so when he found Kristen pursuing him, he saw his opportunity. He persuaded her to loan him a few thousand rupees for your mother's medical care, and as a show of good faith, he gave her the deed to your family home, just as he would give it to an Indian moneylender.

"But the loan wasn't enough. You and Ranju needed more

money, but Kristen wouldn't give the deed back unless you paid her, and you had no money to give her. Am I right so far?" She watched his back expand and contract as he breathed, the vein in his neck throb. "You tried to force her to give it back, but she refused. In anger, perhaps, you struck her and threw her body into the canal. Then you went to her lodging house and broke in, but you couldn't find the deed." She paused, waiting. "Because it isn't there."

He swung around, his hand shot out and clenched her neck. He squeezed, pressing her into the back of the seat; she could barely breathe. It was the middle of the day, on Lighthouse Road; surely someone was around to help her. She had sent the police to his home without a thought to her own safety. "Where is it?"

"I don't know. I have an idea." Her voice sounded alien to her ear—raspy, barely a whisper, as she pulled at his hand, as thick as a truncheon. "I can't breathe." He squeezed harder.

"You will give it to me."

"No," she said, still trying to pull his hand away. "It doesn't matter either, Vidyut. I have arranged a loan for Ranju—without surety." She struggled to breathe, her head pushed back on the seat back.

Wonder and doubt flickered across his face. "No surety?" His hand loosened, and he laughed, a coarse, harsh sound. He slumped in the seat, a look of despair mingling with relief.

□   □   □

"Why would an auto driver kill a foreigner?" Aunt Meena asked after Anita had finished her tale. "Did she refuse to pay?"

Anita burst out laughing. Perhaps it was the tension of the afternoon, perhaps the absurdity of the question, perhaps the affection she always felt for her aunt when Meena was at her most lovingly obtuse. "No, Auntie, it was very different." Anita raised her hand to her throat, unconsciously checking the bruises that ringed her neck.

"I do not understand these foreigners."

"Ranju gave her the deed to his family's home for a small loan, but since he couldn't repay it without getting a loan from someone else, Kristen wouldn't give it back; she was afraid of being cheated. So, in anger, Vidyut killed her."

"Oh, this is terrible!"

"After he killed her Vidyut went looking for the deed but he couldn't find it in her room either, and I think I know why." She moved to the back office, Meena at her heels. "Do you remember how nervous Kristen was when she first arrived, that someone would steal her ticket? I wondered why if she felt so unsafe she would leave our hotel and move to a lodging house. Well, she moved because she loaned Ranju most of her cash, but before she left, she put the deed into the safety deposit box with her ticket." Anita pulled the box from the shelf and opened it. There, on the top, sat a large folded document with lettering in Malayalam and Sanskrit, dotted with seals and notations in various colored inks.

"For this a young woman died." Anita tapped the paper.

"No, no, Anita, not for this," Auntie Meena said. "If what you say is true, she died for lack of trust."

Sibling Rivalry

Mike Wiecek

Tiffany Mallon's hospital bed was cranked to leave her half-sitting, woozy and pale. IV lines ran from one arm, and a monitor pinged quietly behind her. She stared at Detective Castle.

"I'm sorry," said Castle, politely removing his hat. "I know this must be a shock."

"It wasn't, like, an accident?" Fashionable blond hair kept falling across her eyes, and diamonds twinkled on her ears. Castle noticed a subtle, expensive perfume under the antiseptic and cleaning smells. "Someone tried to murder me?"

"Your brake lines were cut. No fluid left at all. You're lucky the car was going so slowly."

"Oh my God."

Castle knew he only had a few minutes before the family showed up. "May I ask some questions?"

"Oh my God," Tiffany said again. "But, yes, sure."

He already had the basic details from the responding patrol officers, so Castle skipped right to the interesting stuff. "Your husband died, let's see, nine months ago?"

"Dear Robert." A tear welled up. "So unexpected, his heart attack. We'd only been married a year!"

"He was seventy-nine." Castle knew this was about three times Tiffany's age. "But it's the will I'm interested in. He cut out all four

164

of his ex-wives—"

"Oh, no," said Tiffany, wide-eyed. "Robert told me they each got a nice alimony."

"Well, yes, but nothing more in the estate. And he locked up every remaining penny—about thirty-five million dollars?—giving you only the annual earnings on the principal."

Tiffany looked blank. "I get a big check every year, if that's what you mean."

"Right. But if you, ah, if you were to expire, only then would the principal be handed out, in three equal parts, to your husband's children."

"Sammy, Bob Junior, and Fiona." Tiffany nodded, winced in sudden pain, and then smiled bravely. "They're the greatest."

"Really?" Castle wondered if she could possibly be the total birdbrain she appeared.

"So friendly. Always asking how I'm doing. Letting me know they care."

Castle squinted. While Tiffany was alive, the children had zip. The day she died, they would each be worth twelve million dollars. "Yes, very thoughtful of them, I'm sure."

The door behind him banged open so hard the room's lights flickered. Two men and one woman elbowed in, all talking at once, loudly, and not to each other. Castle sighed.

"Oh, Tiffany!" The woman was about fifty, a few years younger than the other two, with jet-black hair and a power suit.

"Hi, Fiona."

The first man, bald and tanned and overweight, shoved an armful of flowers at her. "Got here soon as I could," he growled. He glanced at Castle and held out his hand. "Bob Junior. How ya doin?"

Before Castle could respond, the second man jumped in. "Do you mind? Our stepmother needs her privacy." To Tiffany, rather sourly: "Hi, Mom."

"You must be Sammy." Castle showed his badge. "How convenient. I was hoping to talk with all of you."

That slowed everyone down. Fiona and Sammy looked at each other and began backing for the door, until Castle closed it firmly. "Sit, please."

Musical chairs for a moment, which Fiona won by a nose, landing sharply in the room's only guest seat. Bob Junior crossed his meaty arms and glared at Castle. Sammy fussed at the foot of Tiffany's bed, frowning at her.

"I thought you said . . ." His voice trailed off.

"Her car was tampered with," said Castle. "It's a police matter now."

"Good heavens."

"But that's only the start. She was on her way to the doctor's office when she had the accident." Castle nodded to Tiffany. "You were feeling under the weather, is what you told the officers, I believe?"

"Oh yes." Tiffany pressed her forehead. "All feverish, like bird flu or something."

"I'm not surprised." Castle let his voice go grim. "Your orange juice this morning was spiked with Dalmane."

"What?"

"Sleeping pills. Probably an entire bottle or two—enough to kill an elephant. It's actually a good thing someone sabotaged your car, since the paramedics arrived just in time to give you a shot of flumazenil."

Fiona bounced in her chair and shrilled, "Poison? Sabotage? I don't believe this."

"There's more," Castle bored on. "When the patrolmen checked your house, they found a package on the front step."

"Oh, that's right!" Tiffany brightened, as much as someone in a hospital bed could. "I thought it might be my QVC order. But I felt so bad I just stepped over it and didn't even look."

"Just as well. The patrolman got suspicious and called the bomb squad." He glanced at the others. "Five pounds of C-4 and a contact detonator."

Tiffany looked confused, and the three others were finally stunned into silence.

"What do you . . . I mean, what?" Tiffany said.

"Attempted murder." Castle paused. "Times three."

Dead quiet at last.

Fiona recovered first, and turned to point a long, glossy nail at Sammy. "You." Her voice rose. "You were an explosives specialist in the army!"

Sammy threw up his hands. "I was in Vietnam thirty-five years ago. That doesn't mean anything." He swung to Bob Junior. "You're the auto mechanic, aren't you?"

Bob Junior sneered. "I sell cars, you halfwit, I don't work on them."

"Okay, settle down." Castle tried to step in, but Bob Junior over-rode him.

"Ask her," he said, directing his grimace at Fiona. "Look up her college record. Majored in pharmacy, she did. Got her certificate and everything."

"No, please," Tiffany interrupted weakly from the bed. "What is going on?"

Sammy gestured at his siblings. "One of them wants you dead," he said. "Sooner rather than later."

A sudden clamor as all three began shouting at each other. Castle wondered why the nurses hadn't arrived yet to throw them out. Just when he was about to arrest the lot, they finally ran out of steam.

"All right," said Castle. "Who'd like to tell me exactly where they've been for the last twenty-four hours?"

The three adult children looked at each other, and for the first time, their reaction surprised Castle. Bob Junior started to laugh, a deep rolling guffaw. After a moment Fiona joined in with a high-pitched giggle, and eventually even Sammy allowed a few nasty chuckles. Castle frowned at them.

"Someone better explain the joke," he said.

"We were all at Fiona's condo," said Bob Junior. "Had dinner, took care of some family matters. Sammy and I tipped a few too many, and we stayed the night instead of driving home."

"Neither one can afford any more points on their licenses." Fiona raised a meaningful eyebrow to Castle.

"I see." He felt a headache start. "So you're all going to alibi each other."

"Came straight here together when the hospital called," Bob Junior said cheerfully. "And Fiona's building has got someone in the lobby round the clock. We're ironclad."

Tiffany, no longer bubbly, narrowed her eyes. "Family business? What about?"

"You, dear, if you must know." Sammy shrugged. "And Dad's estate."

That set Tiffany off, and soon enough all four were shouting at each other again. But as Castle watched, he slowly came to realize that he was in that rarest of situations: listening to a roomful of suspects, and not a single one of them was lying. The wonderment eased his headache.

"All right, that's enough!" He waited, and the sniping and recriminations eventually dwindled away. "Fiona, Samuel, Robert— you three wait in the hall. I need to talk to Tiffany." When the door closed behind them, Castle pulled a chair up to the bed and sat down, close to her, so he could keep his voice low.

"I know what happened," he said. She just watched him, lips zipped shut. "And the only reason I'm not handcuffing you to the bedrail is that I can't figure out how to make a crime out of it. We can't even charge you with filing a false report, since you haven't actually made a complaint."

"I'm sure I don't know what you're talking about."

"They certainly would have stopped pestering you if they'd all gone to jail." Castle sighed. "But it seems like an extreme solution. Were you hoping to break the will if they were all convicted? Get the whole cookie jar at once, rather than just the interest?"

But Tiffany only shook her head, stubborn and silent, and Castle gave up.

"I recommend you talk to a lawyer," he said as he collected his hat. "I might come up with something later. You wasted a lot of people's time this morning." He left his card on the monitor, nodded goodbye, and went out to the corridor.

The three siblings stood against the wall, waiting for him. Bob Junior unfolded his arms and said, "Well?"

"Talk to Tiffany." Castle made a dismissive gesture. "No one's being charged."

"Why not?"

"But who—"

"That's ridicu—"

Castle's headache came creeping back.

"You're all just going to have to live with each other," he said. "I think that's punishment enough for everyone."

Wednesday's Child

Margaret Press

I am late picking up my son from school. Which means we'll be late for his doctor's appointment. I am perpetually late. And in my hurry I rear-end a car in the icy drop-off lane at the school. No damage to the other car, whose driver nevertheless manages a look that says not only am I an unfit driver, I'm an unfit mother.

Asa, for all of his seven years, reacts with adult-sized humiliation. He scrabbles his way into the back seat, crushed, rolled drawings in his fist, while I go around front to fish from the snow some plastic pieces that appear to belong to my Corolla. The good news is I didn't have a problem getting off work this afternoon. The bad news is, that's 'cause last week I was laid off.

Twenty stressful minutes later we land in the doctor's waiting room. I haul out one of my lists. Cross off the top. Add to the end:

> ~~doctors tues 3pm cars??~~
> Cap'nCrunch
> FIND APT
> milk
> call bank
> find a job
> fix headlight

When I first tumbled into single-motherhood the only neighborhood I could afford in Lynn, Massachusetts, was friendly enough by day, but caught in too many cross fires at night. Two weeks ago a teenager down the street was shot. I've finally made up my mind I have to get us out of there. A quiet little place by the seaside would do. In a good school district and a cheaper auto-incident rating zone. Getting laid off was not part of that plan.

So I need a new plan. Asa is my life. I would lie down in front of a truck for him. If I thought he could collect on the insurance, and get himself to school.

How about family? Family is everything, my mother used to say. However, I have scant few of them left. I've got a cantankerous old grandfather in a nursing home whom I adore to pieces. But during the last few visits Granddad's been begging me to help him find relief. He's at the painful end of a long, hard life. The hardest being outliving all his children. And most of their children. My cousins didn't have the brains to survive their wicked teens and reckless twenties. And frankly, not one of them is missed.

If truth be told, there has always been a rich vein of sociopaths in my family line. Most of my relatives have been nuts or cold-hearted. What they've lacked in empathy, they've compensated for in their survival instincts. Which would have worked better for them if they didn't keep killing each other off. Our family tree is choked with deadly nightshade. If we had a biographer it would be Charles Addams.

The only other survivor is my neglectful brother, who's got lots of time for a half-dozen women in his life, but none for us. Even though he and I are Granddad's only heirs my brother, Sheridan, hasn't managed to make it out to the nursing home in over a year.

So the warm bosom of our family is not likely to get me that place by the sea.

Later Tuesday, an hour after Asa's pediatrician writes out an expensive prescription for antibiotics, I stand hand in hand with my coughing, sniffling son at the foot of my grandfather's bed. Our boots leave four puddles of drippy, dirty snow on the linoleum.

Granddad looks at me with moist eyes, and wipes the corners of his mouth on a tissue. "How's Sheridan?" he asks barely audibly.

I raise my eyebrows, indicating it's no big deal my brother hasn't come around. "Oh, busy writing his reviews. You know. He's got one in some music magazine now. Hey—I think he's getting engaged, Granddad. That'll be nice, huh?"

Granddad looks doubtful. Clearly he doesn't expect to be around for any weddings. "Is it that teacher you told me about?"

"No, Granddad. Teacher's long gone, remember?" Replaced by a realtor, a yoga instructor, a housewife, a dancer, a grad student, an assistant clerk at Salem City Hall, and three or four who apparently do nothing. I know more about my brother's life than I care to. "I think this one's a nurse." I clear my throat. "Asa brought you a picture," I say cheerfully. My son unrolls his mashed drawing of a pig in a cape and lays it on the blanket.

"Oh. That's real good. Sheridan used to draw, remember? I don't know why he doesn't draw anymore."

My heart breaking, I slip my invisible son's arms into his jacket sleeves. "We gotta go, Asa. It's getting dark, and I have a broken headlight."

Granddad seems to notice him finally. This child whose pale shock of hair matches his own, and mine. The hair that through four generations still refuses to lie down. "Boy, come give your great-grandpa a big hug."

I protest. "Don't, Asa—you'll give Granddad your cold!"

"Rhode, that's the idea," he mutters. "It's called the old man's friend."

This is too ghoulish.

□   □   □

Wednesday afternoon I spend some time in Banking Hell. Now, I remember enough math that I can usually scrape by. But BankNorthShore has elevated simple arithmetic to a flesh-eating disease. No longer can you put money into your bank and watch it grow. Nowadays you can only watch it being nibbled away.

I had deposited my last paycheck hoping and praying my car insurance payment wouldn't hit till the paycheck cleared. But I missed by one day. So the insurance check bounced. I wrote a replacement, adding late fees. And by my careful calculations I still had enough to cover my phone bill, excise tax, and a check at the grocery store. With nine dollars to spare, even taking into consideration the twelve-dollar monthly maintenance fee. Plus the three they deduct from my non-existent savings account. But alas! The grocery store called: check returned—insufficient funds.

So I call BankNorthShore and wade through the menu system. It takes a full day to have a conversation with your bank. Not sure what tunnel I end up in, but after entering my full account number a couple of times along the way, I am on hold for someone in the wrong department for a very long time. Three calls later, and lots and lots of nice music, I am talking to someone who finally teaches me some new math. When the insurance check bounced, the bank deducted thirty dollars from my account. For bouncing it, not for covering it. Then when the next check hit, I was twenty-one dollars short. So they bounced that one, too. And deducted another thirty dollars. By then there was insufficient funds to cover the next check.

So another thirty dollars. The bank didn't honor any of my checks to other people. Just gobbled up my hard-earned, and final, wages for themselves.

"I had some problems a few months ago, and the supervisor I talked to then waived the fees. Due to hardship. She said I should just call . . ."

"I don't see any record of that activity on your account. Who did you talk to?"

"Mary, or Marion-someone?" It was worth a try.

I'd close out my account, but am terrified they'd just keep deducting fees for the rest of my life, sending me monthly bills for the negative balances. I often wonder why people go postal in post offices, but never banks. Or maybe that's actually why people rob banks. It's not about the easy cash—it's retaliation for the violence of the fees.

□   □   □

My brother and I used to get together on Wednesday nights—his only free slot when he was juggling six girlfriends. I'd cook us supper. We'd rent movies and watch them after Asa was in bed. Sheridan would talk throughout, expounding on his day, inflating his exploits and complaining about the oppression of his relationships.

Then he met a salsa instructor he couldn't resist, and with his dance card filled, he dropped us entirely. I get the occasional email from him, mostly when he needs something. Last week he was out of El Diablo Habañero Sauce. He can't get it at his local store and knows my corner grocer carries it. I tell him no way. But I add it to my list.

~~doctors tues 3pm ears??~~
    Cap'nCrunch
    FIND APT
    milk
rob call bank
    find a job
    fix headlight
    ~~pick up Rx~~
    win lottery!!!
    habañero sauce

"Granddad's dying," I email him Wednesday night.

Two hours later he responds. "It's unfortunate he's taking so long, Rhode. He's gone through most of what he meant to leave us, with what the lousy insurance won't cover. He never wanted this for us."

"No. What he wanted was to spend a little time with his grand-kids. His only family. He keeps asking for you, Sheridan."

"Don't forget that habañero sauce," Sheridan writes back.

I jab at the delete key. I was born on a Wednesday. And every Wednesday I reflect on the woe with which Wednesday's child is filled.

The next morning he emails me again. Goes on and on about his "troubles." His fight with his fiancé, Doreen. His opera DVDs lost in the mail. Broken printers. Never asks how I am, or Asa's ear infection. Or my being laid off. Just about how tired he is of Doreen's jealous tantrums. And poor him with a review deadline hanging over his head.

"For Chrissakes, Sheridan, who can blame her? You're cheating on her six nights a week!"

"She's just angry I haven't picked up a ring yet. I hate spending that kind of money, but I guess—I'll give her something Saturday night. That will buy some peace for awhile."

I think briefly about a future populated with Sheridan and Doreen's shock-haired offspring. Then I change the subject and ask if he'd consider coming to the nursing home with us tomorrow.

"Tomorrow? It's Friday. I've got a date."

I really don't like Sheridan very much. Takes after our dad. He has no male friends. He has a different woman for every night. But at the end of the day it's all about him.

Sheridan doesn't beat around bushes. He follows up his email with a phone call—the first I've heard his voice in weeks. "Speaking of Granddad. You know, Rhode, you should really consider putting him out of his misery. I've got something I can send you. Just mix some in his juice. A fraction of a teaspoon and he'll go peacefully in a couple hours. Grant him his last dying wish. His 'dying' wish, get it?"

I stare at the receiver.

□   □   □

Saturday morning Asa and I have no heat. Hawthorne Oil refuses to deliver because my account is overdue. I sit down at the kitchen table in my nightgown and parka, and paw through scraps of papers looking for numbers for emergency oil. We have probably used up all our discount sources this season. I dial Sheridan and hang up when I get his machine. I know what he'd say. Sheridan has never loaned me a dime in his life. "You made your choices" is his mantra. Around noontime a padded envelope arrives with no return address.

I can guess the sender. It contains a Ziplock bag with more than enough white powder for the current choice my brother is pressing me to make. I hide it out of Asa's reach.

After all the Boosts, Depends, and other indignities are subtracted, what's left of Granddad's estate will divide equally among his surviving heirs—my brother and me. My share would be just about half of what I need to get my baby out of harm's way—into a neighborhood where the statistics are in his favor. Warm, fed, safe. That's all we mama bears ask for.

There's a lot of folks out there with misery they could be put out of. Tired old men who breathe with pain and who will never feel the floor beneath their slippered feet again. Yoga teachers and assistant clerks facing broken hearts. Seven-year-old boys outgrowing thin winter jackets.

I duck out to the corner store to work on trimming my list. On the way home a neighbor stops me on the sidewalk, trying to rally some comfort for the family of the slain teenager. Would I bake something, she pleads? Every time I shorten my list, it expands again, like mold I can't eradicate.

> ~~doctors tues 3pm ears??~~
> ~~Cap'nCrunch~~
> FIND APT
> ~~milk~~
> rob ~~call~~ bank
> find a job
> fix headlight
> ~~pick up Rx~~
> win lottery!!!
> ~~habañero sauce~~
> EMERG OIL!!
> Leave faucets on tonite!
> bake something

Back at the apartment, I finally manage to get a local charity to help with my heating oil account. Hawthorne Oil comes through with an emergency delivery. Once again we're out of imminent danger. Asa tears into an afternoon bowl of Cap'n Crunch after enduring a week of denial. He moves his chair closer to the radiator and sits down across from me at the kitchen table. I'm staring at my list.

"Do we have to pay them back for the oil?" he asks, pulling the bowl toward his chest.

I nod.

"How're we gonna do that? Can we rob a bank?"

I shake my head. "We're not like that." I look at him with wonder. Asa was born on a Tuesday, full of grace and a thousand-watt smile. He sprang forth from the dark, primordial slime of our gene pool, defying the odds and filling me with hope, and the unfamiliar emotion of love.

"How then?" he sprays through a mouthful of milk.

I hand him a napkin. "We make the world a better place."

But the punches just keep coming. An hour later my burly land-lord pounds on my door. Looks like the rent check, too, was a victim of the termites at the bank.

"I told you last time that was the last time," he says.

I'm desperate. I put my hand on my stomach and puff it out a bit. "Mr. Tolman, I just need a little more time. Please! You can't throw us out on the street. I'm having a baby."

He snorts. "Well, it ain't my baby. I weren't there when you got it." But he gives me one more week. A lot can happen in a week.

Asa is upstairs packing for a sleepover at a friend's. The kitchen is quiet and dimly lit by the low afternoon sun. I unpack the rest of my groceries, retrieve the Ziplock bag from its hiding place, and I get to work.

Desperate times, desperate measures.

☐ ☐ ☐

Saturday evening I take Asa to his sleepover. On the way home I detour through Salem to drop off the habañero sauce at my brother's. Doreen is there, so I don't come in.

"Did you get my . . . letter?" he asks, too eagerly.

"I did." I look him in the eye. "I'll get back to you. That's six dollars for the El Diablo. Just in time for dinner. You're welcome."

Sheridan hands me the bills with his usual reluctance. "We already ate."

Perpetually late. The story of my life.

He adds: "Anyway, it's just for me. Doreen hates it. They all do. It's an acquired taste."

I know that. I'm counting on it.

☐ ☐ ☐

Sunday night the phone rings. My blood runs cold. For a moment I cannot move. Asa's in the other room watching TV. I pick up, finally.

It's the Salem Police. I'm not in Sheridan's Palm Pilot, apparently. But someone in there was able to direct them to me. I'm the next of kin. It seems my brother, Sheridan, is dead.

I muster shock. I blurt out questions.

"Your brother was shot," they reply.

The shock is now real. "Sometime around noon, we believe. Yes, we have someone in custody. Yes, we have a motive."

Apparently, the Friday girl had left her phone number on Sheridan's back. Doreen—the Saturday girl—flipped out and, well, made the world a better place. All too bizarre. I can't tell whether I'm annoyed I was too late, or relieved someone else spared me a homicide on my conscience.

□ □ □

Every week another Wednesday. While Asa's at school, I throw together a big batch of brownies and update my list, which has exploded mercilessly:

~~doctors tues 3pm ears??~~
~~Cap'n Crunch~~
FIND APT !!!
~~milk~~
~~rob call bank~~
find a job
~~fix headlight~~ shop for new car!!!
~~pick up Rx~~
win lottery!!!
~~habañero sauce~~
~~EMERG OIL!!~~
~~Leave faucets on tonite!~~
~~bake something~~
call funeral home
retrieve hab sauce
pallbearers

visit Granddad

Am I one of them, I wonder. I cannot be. Sociopaths are incapable of love, they say. And I love every flaxen hair on my son's tiny little head. And I love my grandfather. And look at me with the brownies, for God's sake.

□   □   □

I refill the vase from his water pitcher and shove in my carnations. I maneuver his rolling tray so he can see them without moving his head.

"How's Sheridan?"

Oh, fine, I say. Why break his heart now. The pallbearers were a problem, I muse. Since Sheridan had no male friends I had to press into service the brothers of three different girlfriends. One was Catholic and had four, bless her heart.

"He's getting married? To that teacher?"

"Sure is."

We sit in silence a good half hour while he dozes on and off, wheezing pitifully. Finally his eyes flutter open.

"Rhode, please help me."

I stroke his hand. I lean over and kiss his forehead.

"Goodbye, Granddad. Gotta go before it gets dark. No headlight."

I stand up and pull on my coat. "Granddad? Don't forget your juice."

Family is everything.

Mr. McGregor's Garden

Kate Flora

Alan McGregor was the first person I met in the neighborhood. Half an hour after the moving van had left me, an unwilling divorcee with a small boy, feeling rootless and dejected amidst the heaps of packing boxes, he was at the front door with a basket of produce straight out of *House Beautiful*. Ramrod straight and in impeccable trim, he reminded me of a British major, right down to the clipped and abbreviated phrases. To welcome you. Thought you might like. Friendly neighborhood. Right next door, y'know. Feel free to call, etc.

His whitening mustache lifted in a quick smile as he bent and shook hands with five-year-old Topher, who was clinging to my leg. "Got a dog. A cat. Some chickens. Come over and meet them some time." Topher nodded solemnly. He was at least as at sea as I. "Bring over that basket when it's empty," McGregor told me. "I'll refill it."

Somehow, those bright vegetables with their fresh greens, shiny reds, and vibrant oranges transformed the chaos into something more manageably homey. We dug out the stereo and played happy kid tunes while Topher crunched on carrots and I put the kitchen in order. Funny how little it takes sometimes.

McGregor was right. It was a friendly neighborhood. People up and down the street appeared with cookies and home-baked bread and invitations to pool parties and barbecues. Topher quickly joined

181

a small gang of five and six year olds who ran and tumbled, kicked balls and warred with sticks in the neighborhood's large yards. On the days I worked at home, those rampages were sometimes in our yard. Mr. McGregor was rarely at the parties, but as he'd told me one day while I'd begged his help to hang some heavy pictures, he was a man who liked his solitude.

Once a week, Mr. McGregor would come and get the basket and return it filled. Sometimes I'd let Topher take it over so he could see the chickens or the yippy little wiener dog, Toto. Mr. McGregor would take him out to the garden and they'd pick things together. It seemed like a perfect arrangement. Topher was more likely to eat vegetables if he'd picked them himself, and with his father out of the picture, it was nice for him to have a man in his life.

He'd return, dirty and grinning and clutching McGregor's hand, and give an excited rundown on all he had seen and done. Babbling about his gardening adventures and his plans for a garden of his own would carry him through dinner and bathtime and right up to the verge of sleep. Often he'd return from their expeditions with a strangely shaped vegetable, a cup of berries he'd picked, or a bug or worm in a paper cup for me to admire before squashing.

Some nights, by the time Topher was down and the laundry and dishes done, I was ready for bed myself. Barely able to read a chapter a night when once I'd read five books a week. I felt so drained I sometimes wondered if vampires were sucking my blood. But it wasn't likely. I rarely slept long enough for any kind of nocturnal visitation.

I'd left my ex-husband and the buxom secretary whose morals matched those of Stalker, Mr. McGregor's cat, sharing the spare blond wood bed where Topher was conceived. I'd bought a new bed, a warm cherry sleigh bed that made me feel safe and contained, and pushed the empty side against the wall. Between work, Topher, and tennis with my new neighbor, Glory, with her ruthless backhand, I didn't have much time to feel lonely.

It was only at night, when the world was black and still and the bed, lacking the intimate sounds of another's sleep, was too quiet, that I thought about my ex-husband, Rob, and his helpful secretary, Rona. How even nice-seeming people couldn't be trusted. How life could betray you in an instant. I would obsess about Rob's careless lies and betrayal, my own trusting stupidity and humiliation until I'd sweated through my gown. Then I'd pad through the silent house to the shower and eventually back to sleep. Moments later, it seemed, it would be dawn.

On those occasions when I threw off the hot covers and walked to the window, the whole neighborhood was as still as could be. No one coming in late, no one out taking a restless nocturnal walk. No one hunched over a glowing computer terminal or TV, no eerie blue lights in the darkness. A few times, though, there were lights at McGregor's house, and if the window was open, the faint sounds of music. Sinatra, Nat King Cole, Dean Martin. Once or twice, shadows crossed the shade. Otherwise, I was all alone in my nocturnal wanderings.

Topher slept like a child. After his story, his eyes would close and he'd fall into an amazingly deep, boneless sleep. Sometimes when I checked on him at night, he'd be draped awkwardly over a pile of stuffed animals, looking horribly uncomfortable and sleeping as soundly as if he'd just tumbled off a cloud.

It was hard to believe that he was mine. I'm dark haired, dark-eyed, and slight. Topher was a storybook angel child, with his fair, fly-away hair, innocent blue eyes, sturdy little frame, and sweet pink skin. Asleep, he looked far too much like his father.

Stalker, McGregor's cat, would come sometimes and camp on our porch. As I tallied my mistakes like beads through my weary brain, Stalker sang love songs to the ladies of the neighborhood, promising them, in his yowling, screeching, guttural aria, a night of

fun and whoopee, with not a nod, or caterwaul, toward the conse-
quences. And the female cats responded. Sometimes I'd lie in the
dark envying their foolish, hapless, unavoidable night of bliss.
Lately, cold showers and hard work weren't quite doing the trick. I
missed having a man in my bed.

In September, jarred by the fact that Topher was starting school
and pulling away from me, I did something embarrassingly reckless.

When Mr. McGregor appeared on the porch with his heaped-up
basket of produce, I asked if he'd like to come by later for a glass of
wine. He had stiffened, even half-turned, before turning back with a
slightly quizzical look. "Diana," he said, "how kind. I'd like that."

I suppose I'd been lonely too long. It was only Mr. McGregor
from next door, closer in age to my father than to me. He'd shown
no evidence of a social life unless I read something into those nocturnal shadows on the shades or the occasional purr of his Jaguar
going in or out while the neighborhood slumbered. Still, I straightened the already neat living room and whipped up a batch of my signature smoked trout paté. I set out flowers and put on a touch of
makeup.

Just moments before McGregor was due to arrive, Topher and
his band of renegades swarmed into the kitchen, seeking snacks and
drinks and begging for a movie. In our small house, the TV was in
the living room. I promised TV in an hour, stood firm in the face of
mob protest, and was just sending them back into the yard when Mr.
McGregor arrived carrying a plate heaped with scrubbed baby carrots, sugar pod peas, and tiny golden pear-shaped tomatoes.

Instead of irritation at the horde of boys many men might have
shown, he greeted them by name and bent to offer the plate. Small,
eager fingers flew at the food and before I'd gotten him to the sofa
or the plate onto the coffee table, it was empty. Hooting their thanks,
the ruffians departed, slamming the door behind them.

"Red or white?" I asked.

McGregor stroked his mustache thoughtfully. "Seems like a good day for white."

I poured us pale gold Pouilly Fuisse and offered the trout. "It's excellent with cucumbers," I said. "I haven't tried it with any other vegetables."

He looked ruefully at the empty plate. "Sadly, I guess we won't find out today. Still, can't say as I mind when youngsters willingly eat vegetables. Some of them act like it's a dirty word. Have you noticed?"

We talked about kids and vegetables, about how great the big lawns in the neighborhood were for playing. What a good street it was for raising children. It was pleasant, sitting with a kind man and sipping wine. But I had an agenda, so after a while I tried to make the conversation more personal.

"How long have you lived on the street?" I asked.

"Oh, a few years," he said. "I can't really remember. Seems like I've been here forever."

"But your gardens are so well established. That must have taken some time. All the rest of us suffer from garden envy," I said. Other topics, such as where he'd lived before, fell flat. I felt idiotic. Considered taking my wine glass into the kitchen and gulping it to see if it made me any smoother or more coherent.

"Anytime you want help starting a garden, call on me, please," he said. "Topher wants to plant a vegetable garden next summer. He's very keen on gardening, you know. And very careful around my plants. I appreciate that. Many children aren't."

We were sitting in my pretty living room, a room I'd worked hard to decorate. A room completely different from the living room I'd shared with Topher's dad, despite the presence of the same sofa and loveseat. I wore a pretty blue dress, and if my mirror could be believed, I looked really nice. But to Alan McGregor, it seemed I was invisible. He was as pleasantly formal as ever. He warmed only when we talked about children.

"I think we would like a garden," I said. "But something small. Something we could manage."

"You'll want to start with a lot of compost," he said. "In my opinion, it's the key."

He devoted a large area to composting, I knew. He'd proudly given me the tour. Three different bins in different stages of decomposition. Every bit as neat as the rest of his garden and his yard. I realized I'd never seen the inside of his house.

"We'll rely heavily on your advice, I'm sure." I set my empty glass on the coffee table and he courteously refilled it. "So, are you retired?"

"I like to think I've merely rearranged my priorities," he said. "From the office to the yard."

"What sort of work did you do?"

"Oh," he said, swooping down on the trout paté and loading up a cracker. "It's far too dull to talk about. I was a very orderly paper pusher, is all."

I couldn't ask what kind of paper pusher without seeming rude, so we talked about dahlias. About fall plants that might take the place of the ubiquitous chrysanthemum. Of the necessity for mulching beds in winter. Whether one needed to wrap shrubs in burlap.

I knew little about gardening. Rob and I had had a fairly traditional arrangement. He'd taken care of the outside, I the inside. Still, I managed, like any woman whose mother has taught her the basics of social conversation, to keep up my end. Despite his pleasant company, I felt startlingly sad and hoped I was keeping it off my face.

I guess I wasn't successful, for suddenly he set down his glass and took my hand. "I can see that you're disappointed," he said. "I hope I'm not being presumptuous in thinking I know what you were hoping."

He brushed his fingertips across his mustache. "I'm not what you should be looking for, Diana. You're a pretty young woman. A nice woman. You need someone closer to your age. Someone outgoing. Someone to complete your family. Not an old fellow like me in love with his gardens and his solitary life."

The fingers brushed the mustache again. "Please understand. I don't want to embarrass you. You're a good neighbor and, I like to think, a friend. . . ." He trailed off, his eyebrows raised. "I am upsetting you, aren't I?"

I shook my head. "It's not you, Mr. McGregor. Alan. It's . . ." But I couldn't go on. I was swamped with embarrassing tears.

"You'll find someone, Diana. You just need to get out more. It's easy for a young working mother, like you, to get stuck. You know, if you did want to get out and had trouble finding a sitter, Topher could come to me. We get on pretty well."

It was almost too funny. I boldly set out to find myself some male company and find a babysitter instead. Somehow, the humor of it, the unexpected silver lining to my cloud of mortification, made me smile.

Alan McGregor smiled, too. "That's better," he said. "Isn't it." Moments later we were overrun by Topher and his crew again, and yielded the room.

Topher, with an enthusiasm for life I envied, loved kindergarten. Loved his teacher and his classmates and his after-school program, happily recounting his days while he colored at the kitchen table. I tried to keep life orderly and manageable, doing my graphic design job, contemplating painting the kitchen apple green, and feeling like life had left me behind.

One night, after I had heard McGregor's Jag purr in around eleven, Sinatra was especially loud and I distinctly saw two silhouettes on the shade. Evidently, he liked slender, more androgynous women, rather than curvy ones like me. Feeling pathetic, I sobbed into my pillow and fell asleep before I heard the car go out again. In the morning, he was out, bright and early, working over one of his compost piles. I wondered if I should take up gardening. It seemed to do wonders for him. He was always content.

The weekend before Halloween, Topher was invited to a sleepover birthday party. They were going to wear their costumes and carve pumpkins and he was almost out of his skin with excitement. Topher was going as a NASCAR driver and it took us all of Saturday morning to get his costume together. It was so heartbreakingly funny to drop off a NASCAR guy carrying a stuffed bear that I had to take pictures. I wasn't alone. All the moms were snapping photos and exchanging the slightly abashed grins of the admittedly sentimental. But why not? What matters more than our children?

I had decided to treat myself to a spa night. Long soak with bath salts. Mask and pedicure. A bottle of good white wine. Chick flicks, two in case I couldn't sleep. At 1:00 A.M., I'd finished *Must Love Dogs*. I'm such a John Cusack fan I could probably be happy watching him peel potatoes for an hour. I poured a third glass of wine and was just slipping *Pretty Woman* into the machine when I heard a crash and a scream.

I shut off the light and rushed to the window, carefully raising the blinds. Lights were blazing next door at Mr. McGregor's. As I watched, I could dimly see two figures struggling, then another scream, and the light in the room went out. I held my breath, wondering if I should dial 911. Mr. McGregor wouldn't like it. He was a very private person. But suppose he was in danger?

For five minutes, everything was quiet. Then Sinatra got louder, and the rest of the lights went out. I watched a while longer, but the house stayed quiet. I went back to my sofa, curled up under a blanket, and started the movie.

I woke to a blue screen patterned with instructions and bright sunlight streaming in through gaps in the curtains. It was past nine—

later than I'd slept in years—and I was due to pick up Topher at 10:30. I'd barely kicked off the blanket and found the clip to pin up my hair when someone knocked at the door.

Alan McGregor was dirt-streaked and sweaty, a bruise on his face and scratches on his hands. The only time I'd ever seen him even slightly out of trim. He swiped a forearm across his forehead. "Diana, I've come to apologize. I hope we didn't disturb you last night?"

When I stared my incomprehension, he continued, "My nephew stopped in. My sister Anne's boy. He's . . . uh . . . not quite right. Schizophrenia. Fine if he takes his medicine, but he's been a little erratic about that lately. When he doesn't take it, he does impulsive things like deciding to visit relatives in the middle of the night. I'm afraid . . ."

He leaned forward, as if by getting closer he could read me more clearly. "I'm afraid we got into a bit of a tussle. He wanted to get into my liquor cabinet. I had to forcibly restrain him." McGregor rocked back on his heels. "Then he started yelling and trying to break things. I had to call my sister." His forearm swiped across his forehead again, streaking dirt across his pale skin. "In any case, I know he was noisy. I hope we didn't worry you."

Poor man. Families could be a trial, I knew. To spare him further embarrassment—for he looked absolutely terrible—I only shrugged and said, "I must have slept right through it."

"Amazing," he said. "That boy made enough noise to wake the d . . . uh, whole neighborhood. Anyway, please accept my apologies." He peered past me into the silent house. "Topher wasn't disturbed?"

"He had a sleepover."

"Ah. Good. Well then, I'll be getting back to my garden. Working in it calms me down. And it was a wretched night."

He turned and limped away, a different man from my neat, spry neighbor. I was glad Topher wasn't home. He would have been at me all the rest of the day with questions about what was wrong with Mr. McGregor.

Late that afternoon, McGregor rang my bell again. He wore a blue shirt and sports jacket, back in trim, if slightly distracted. "I apologize for disturbing you again, Diana. I have to go to my sister's. More nephew trouble, I'm afraid. I was hoping you might look after my menagerie? I'll be back by tomorrow night, and they pretty much care for themselves, except for Toto, who likes his early morning walk."

I nodded. It was easy enough to do. He handed over the keys and a list of what to feed when with a brusque, "Everything you need— cat food, dog food, chicken feed—is all on the back porch. Oh, and keep Toto in his fenced-in area, if you would. He's far too fond of digging in the compost."

He was backing down his drive almost before I had the door shut.

Topher was thrilled. Early the next morning, he led me through the ritual of morning pet care with scrupulous attention to detail. We fed the chickens, put out smelly high-end food for Stalker, and walked Toto briskly around the block. In the midst of Topher's ecstatic clamoring for a dog of his own, I was the one who carelessly failed to put Toto back in his yard.

When I pulled back into the drive in time to meet Topher's bus, Toto's excited barking drew me next door, and to the site of a small disaster. I'd left the gate open, and, just as McGregor had warned, the dog had been at the compost pile. Bits of rotting vegetation were strewn about and the dog was rolling in it happily.

Sighing, I got a rake and a shovel and made things neat again, carefully reburying the torn old shirt Toto had been wrestling with, then hosed off the dog. From a distance, the garden seemed neat and orderly. Up close, the compost stank and buzzed with flies. I left less certain that I wanted a garden of my own.

At the end of the day, I gladly handed back the keys, hoping Toto had done no other damage that I'd missed.

The following week, a colleague at work asked if I'd come to a dinner party she was giving. I warned her I wasn't much good at dinner parties, but she insisted it would be informal and that her friends were eager to meet me. I did need to get out more. I was having far too many dates with late evening glasses of wine, so I agreed.

After exhausting every teenager on the block, I turned to Mr. McGregor, unsure if his offer had been sincere, or if he still felt neighborly after the night of the howling nephew. He hadn't seemed himself lately. But he seemed happy to do it.

Filled with trepidation, I walked Topher, clutching a storybook and bear, to McGregor's door, and handed him over. By the time I was a few blocks away, my nerves about leaving Topher had become nerves about being in a room full of strangers. Rob used to call me the Ice Princess because I always froze at parties. But Rob had said lots of unkind things. In most ways, I wasn't sorry he was gone.

I hoped tonight might be different. My colleague had assured me it would be low key. Nice people. No pressure. But in social situations, pressure generally comes from within. If the trouble I'd had getting dressed and putting makeup on was any barometer, I'd spill my drink, drop my plate, or fall face first into the soup.

As it turned out, none of those things happened. The company was great. People made me feel comfortable. They loved the salad I'd brought and I loved the adventure of eating potluck instead of my own cooking. I was seated at dinner next to the best-looking man in the room, a bright-eyed, quick-witted man named Gary who seemed amazingly easy to talk to. Without meaning to, I told far more than I should have about my divorce and Topher, the pressure of being our sole support. About the pain of having Rob gone.

Lubricated by wine and company, I'd rather boldly said, "You're awfully easy to talk to. What do you do?"

"You can't guess?" he said.

"Therapist?"

His grin was mischievous. "You got me."

We talked on. Family. He was divorced with a daughter, Miranda. Schools. Topher was going to the best one. And neighborhoods. It turned out he lived only a few blocks away. "You live near that odd old pedophile, don't you?" he asked.

"I haven't heard of anyone like that in my neighborhood." Oh, I said it lightly. Lightly. "What's his name?"

"Mcsomething. Or Mac. McTavish. MacIntosh. McIntyre. No. Wait. McGregor. That's it. Alan McGregor."

His response nearly stopped my heart. Suddenly the food didn't agree with me and I'd gone cold. I shoved back my chair and practically ran from the room.

When I came out of the powder room, he was waiting. "What's wrong?" he asked, his look making it clear a brisk "nothing" wouldn't fly. "Are you all right?"

I was clutching my bag like it was a safety device that might keep me afloat. I still wasn't sure about my ability to breathe. "He lives . . ." Could I be having a heart attack? ". . . next door."

"Hey," he said, taking me firmly by the arm and leading me to a chair. "Hey. It's probably not a big deal. I haven't heard about any problems with him. And I'm pretty attuned to those things because of Miranda."

"But he's . . ." The words wouldn't come. How could I admit that I was so dim and trusting I'd just left my only child with a pedophile?

He pulled up a chair facing me, our knees nearly touching, and took my hand. "Breathe, Diana. Breathe." He held on, repeating "breathe" until I'd begun to unfreeze.

"He's taking care of my son tonight. Alan McGregor is looking after Topher." I could barely squeeze out the words. "How could I be so stupid? I thought he was a nice man. A good neighbor."

"That's why they don't get caught," he said, an angry edge in his voice. "Because they are nice. Charming. Because they're good, quiet neighbors and they love kids."

"Does everyone else know? Do they know and didn't tell me?" I was horrified at the possibility that my seemingly kind neighbors had failed to warn me of this awful thing. Suddenly my mind was a jumble of suspicion. Had they been willing to sacrifice Topher to keep their own kids safe? What about my realtor? Had she known? Was that why the house was affordable? But everyone let their kids roam freely. Maybe they didn't know.

"I heard from a friend who's a cop," he said.

"I have to go," I said.

Our hostess stuck her head around the corner. "Hey, you two," she said, "I'm serving dessert."

My first dinner party and I was about to make an abrupt, and rude, departure. I couldn't summon the grace to respond.

He put a friendly arm around my shoulders, winking at our hostess. "Got something cooking here, Bev," he said. "Would you mind if we just slipped out?"

Her satisfied smile said she'd planned this. "Let me just wrap up some cake."

I needed to rescue Topher right now. He squeezed my shoulder. "Easy," he said. "Easy."

I stumbled on the walk, tripped on the curb. Couldn't find the ignition. Finally, we were under way, Gary following in his car. When I pulled into the drive, he parked at the curb, beside me before I could run over and pound on McGregor's door.

"Easy," he said again, his voice low, resonant. "You've got to live with this, Diana, and it's unlikely anything has happened. From what I remember, McGregor's fond of older boys. Be yourself, get

Topher home, then worry about what to do next."

"But I . . . but he . . . but what do I . . . ?" My wits were scattered like buckshot. "But what if?"

"It's unlikely," he repeated. "If something's happened, we deal with it. But you don't help Topher by going in all wild and hysterical."

"I'm not . . ."

"You are. Now breathe, Diana. Slow and regular, until you feel normal enough to knock on that door without wanting to punch his lights out."

I liked it that he understood my impulse toward violence.

I breathed until I could paste on a shaky smile, then walked to McGregor's door. Topher whined that I'd come too soon. They were having fun and he wanted to stay longer. Alan McGregor was charm itself, handing over bear, storybook, and my son with a reluctance that matched Topher's. I smiled politely, suppressing my urge to pick up the nearest weapon and bash McGregor over the head. I wanted to stuff Topher in the car and drive until we were as far from here as my energy would take us.

I couldn't run, though. We didn't have the money. I would just have to be very vigilant.

On Mondays, one of the two days I worked at home, McGregor made his weekly pilgrimage to the garden center. As soon as I heard the Jag purr down his driveway, I was out the door and into his back yard, carrying my shovel. Toto hurled his tiny body against the fence, yapping wildly, as I began to dig in the freshest and smelliest of McGregor's compost heaps, the one that swarmed with flies. Past the carrot tops and vegetable peelings, the shriveling tomatoes, grass clippings, and fallen leaves, down to the shirt Toto had gnawed and I'd reburied.

A white t-shirt for a music group I'd never heard of, dotted with rusty stains more the color of blood than dirt. Down into the pile I dug, hearing Alan McGregor's clipped tones. "Must turn the pile from time to time. Aeration. Keep the process going. And Diana, never, ever even think of adding any meat or bones or even fish skin. The results are ghastly."

Flies swarmed around my head as I went deeper and the smell got worse. A foot. A leg. McGregor was right. The results were ghastly.

He should have been gone at least two hours. He was always gone at least two hours. His car was so quiet and the flies and Toto so noisy that I didn't know he was there until I heard his shocked, "Good gracious, Diana. What are you up to?"

Then silence, only the rasp of breath, as he understood. Toto barked. The flies were as noisy as a buzz saw. I stared at the rotting foot and leg. At Alan McGregor's shocked face. Another glib and charming liar who thought me a sweet fool. "This is not your nephew," I said.

I looked at the row of neat compost piles. Three, in various stages of decomposition, structure in place for a fourth. Wondered if the other two housed difficult "nephews" as well. Silhouettes on McGregor's shades who had gotten out of control.

Then, while he was still deciding what to do, I swung my shovel at Alan McGregor's head.

I debated putting him under the third compost pile, the neatest and most deliciously earthy, burying him deep under all the rich, soil-enhancing compost. It was where he'd like to be. Instead, I buried him in the newest pile. The one he'd prepared for his next victim. It was a good way to make a new start.

Then I neatened up the yard, washed my shovel and put it away, and got ready to meet Topher's bus.

Tit for Tat

Leslie Schultz

For Jackson, the future is simple: He has to get even. But Baxter is in rehab, has been for almost two months, so Jackson must be patient.

A lot has been lost in those two months. First Jackson's son, then his wife's affection, then his job. His life has become a parable of pain, as if God had gone out looking for a modern-day Job and had settled on Jackson. But Jackson is no Job. He'll wait for Baxter to get out of rehab, and then he'll get even.

□ □ □

After his shower, Jackson walks down the hall to his son's room to check on Katie. He opens the door to find her still sleeping in a mound of bedding she's assembled by the makeshift shrine on Timothy's bureau. Jackson crosses the room to open a window. The sliding of the sash makes Katie stir. Jackson kneels down and strokes his wife's cheek. "Do you want me to stay while you wash?" he asks. She nods and rises.

When Timothy died, Katie set up residence in his room, surrounded by his toys, and took to burning candles, saying novenas, mumbling incessantly to God. At first, Jackson thought, Of course the boy's things would comfort her, as he waited for her to come out. But she never came out. Days became weeks and finally one night he pleaded, "Come to bed, Katie. Please. This is too much."

"I can't leave," she said as she sat in the rocker by Timothy's bed and absently twisted her wedding ring. "If I leave, what do I do?"

"It's all right," Jackson coaxed. "There are plenty of people in heaven to help him."

"None of them is his mother," she said, and went back to her mumbling.

Now, if Katie needs to leave the boy's room, Jackson must stay to keep Timmy company. Humoring her makes him weary, but he's grown used to the weight of it. As Katie disappears down the hall to shower, Jackson turns to Timothy's shrine and begins to scrape the wax hardened on the bureau's surface, silently scolding himself for forgetting to snuff the candles last night after his wife fell asleep.

Katie has stacked supplies on the bureau, things she thinks their son needs: his Pat the Bunny book, a baby bottle shaped like a football, his blanket, a stuffed toy duck Timothy mistakenly called Chicken. Chicken was Timmy's near-constant companion, tucked under his arm daily in a chokehold of love. Some nights before bedtime, Timothy would lose sight of Chicken, and Katie would send Jackson off to search for it, under the wing chair, in the laundry, behind the couch pillows, on the back porch. Jackson would finally find it, calling out "I've got him!" which sent Timmy fleeing playfully from room to room, refusing sleep. Jackson would chase him down, tuck Chicken under Timothy's arm again, wrap his hand around his son's, and palm-to-palm they'd head down the hall and off to bed. Jackson can still feel his son's small hand in his own, like the tingle of an amputated limb.

Jackson doesn't know how long he stands there scraping wax before Katie returns, wrapped in a robe, her dark hair wet, her skin pale as ice. She places a cup of tea on the windowsill and begins to sift through a shoebox of photographs. For the past week, she has been pasting pictures of Timothy on the walls. She says she is making a "Timothy quilt." The quilt now covers all of one bedroom wall and half of another, making it impossible for Jackson to stay in the room for long. Reminders are snipers lying in wait. The night after they buried Timmy, Jackson came home from work and caught a glimpse of something white hidden under a hedge by the front stoop. He bent over and fished it out only to realize it was one of Timothy's sneakers. It occurred to Jackson that it must have flown off the boy's foot with the impact. The thought brought Jackson to his knees, where he sobbed so long and loud his neighbor Martha finally came over and helped him inside to mourn privately.

"What are you doing today?" Katie asks as she stacks photographs on the floor beside her.

"The garage," Jackson answers.

"That's good," she says. "It needs it."

"I know," he says as he turns to go. After Jackson lost his job he woke every day with an urgent compulsion to clear away clutter. He has been clearing for over a week, now—first the basement, then the closets, now the garage.

Outside, the morning air is cool and Jackson is aggravated by the change of season, the way the world continues to shift and turn, obstinate and unaware of its new cargo, his boy buried deep in a box. Jackson flings open the garage door and stands back to survey his task. As he catalogues the contents of the space, Martha appears on her front lawn and hollers, "I've got muffins! What do you say?"

"Sounds good," Jackson answers, and steps into the garage to inspect his workbench.

Martha soon appears, clears a space on the workbench, puts her plate of muffins down and smiles. She stops by daily with food in the only gesture of help she can conjure. Jackson knows Martha worries that Katie has given up all custodial care, so she packs her offerings with nutrients—wheat germ in the muffins, tofu in the casseroles—to boost the household's health. Jackson samples everything she brings to reward her care.

"How's Katie today?" she asks.

"The same," says Jackson as he pinches off a piece of muffin.

"I'm going grocery shopping. Can I get you anything?"

"No, thanks. We're fine," he says, certain that she'll bring them something anyway. At times this constant feeding seems futile to Jackson, until he remembers Baxter. "Maybe some eggs," he concedes. Martha squeezes his arm and leaves.

Jackson puts the piece of muffin back on the plate, turns back to his workbench, and rifles through his tools to weed out the rusted or broken ones. He makes two piles—good stuff, bad stuff—pulls over a large plastic garbage can, sweeps the bad pile into it. He carefully arranges the remaining tools, hanging the hammer and saw on the two hooks on the side of the bench, placing the rest in rows in the drawer. He tows the garbage can a few feet over to a jumble of lawn tools, where he sights what he is really there for. Timothy's scooter pokes out from a cobwebbed corner, anchoring a stack of colorful plastics: a beach bag full of shovels and pails, a child's rake, a deflated wading pool, a nylon tent covered with Winnie-the-Poohs. He cloaks them with a musty tarp to smother their power until collection day. A slippery blue ball pushes out from under the tarp and rolls toward the toe of Jackson's shoe. He kicks it hard, watches it ricochet against a wall and lodge in a stack of flowerpots. "Fuck you," Jackson says, and returns to his collection of rakes, weed-whackers, hoes, and shovels. He sorts, he tosses, he arranges. He moves around the garage for over an hour, putting disarray to order, until Martha returns from shopping. Jackson helps Martha carry in the groceries, first her bags to her house, then his bags to home. Martha follows him in to visit Katie.

Jackson puts the groceries away, noting that the kitchen cabinets will need his attention when he finishes the garage. He walks back outside to take up his work again, but stops short when he sees a car pull up to the curb across the street in front of Baxter's house. Baxter emerges from the passenger side, slams shut the car door, waves as the car leaves, then turns and walks up the path to his door. He fishes through his jacket pockets and pulls out a set of keys.

Martha appears on Jackson's front stoop and calls to him, urging him to come in. At the sound of her voice, Baxter turns briefly, catches sight of his two neighbors, appears about to speak, then turns, fumbles with his front door lock and disappears inside.

At first, Jackson is rankled by Martha's interruption, thinking his time is limited, not wanting to miss his opportunity. But the thought of the waiting weapon calms him, so he lets Martha lead him into the house.

"Sit," says Martha as they enter the kitchen. "I'll make lunch."

"I'm not hungry," says Jackson. "You should go feed your kids."

"The kids are with Ben. He took them bowling," she says, pulling supplies from the refrigerator. "What's going on in that head of yours, Jack?"

"Nothing but cobwebs in there," he says, smiling to disarm her suspicions.

"It's not too late to press charges," she says. "You could get him in civil court."

"Not exactly an eye for an eye, Martha."

"Maybe. But it's better than nothing."

Jackson only shrugs and watches her as she moves about the kitchen, his hands folded on the table in front of him, his future gaining shape.

After Baxter has been back for two days, a realtor pulls up to his house and plants a For Sale sign on his lawn. Jackson watches from the living room window, remembering the morning a year ago when he looked out from this same vantage point to see Baxter passed out on his overgrown grass, every one of his wife's prized roses torn from their roots and scattered around him. His wife had left him the week before, fed up with his drinking. Jackson wanted to leave Baxter there, splayed out ridiculously like a toppled yard ornament.

But Katie took pity and asked him to help guide Baxter inside and to bed while she brewed coffee and straightened his kitchen. The rank smell of whiskey on Baxter's breath reminded Jackson of his father, reason enough to leave him displayed on his lawn.

Jackson tells Katie about Baxter's sign when he brings her breakfast.

"It's for the best," says Katie, as she dusts around the shrine's artifacts with one of Jackson's old t-shirts.

"What's for the best?" he snaps, tired of her complacency. When they met four years ago, he took her acceptance as compassion, all the sad causes she championed, the relentless volunteering for women's shelters and animal rights groups and hospice programs. Now he thinks she's never angry enough, should be furious such programs are needed, outraged at the proliferating misery.

Katie stops her dusting, walks over to Jackson and wraps her long fingers around his wrist. "He hurts too, Jack. You know he does."

"Not like I hurt, not like you."

Katie sits on the bed, squeezes her eyes shut and massages her forehead with the heel of her hand. "Just leave it alone, okay?" she says. "He'll be gone soon."

But Baxter isn't gone soon. He quickly takes up his usual patterns, appearing on his porch every morning to retrieve his paper, sweeping the front walk every evening, trimming his lawn on Saturday, golfing on Sunday.

For three weeks Jackson cleans and preps as he carefully notes Baxter's comings and goings, driven in and out of the neighborhood by his daughter or Red Morton, Baxter's best buddy on the force before Baxter retired as chief of police. Red was the first to arrive on the scene the day Baxter drove his big boat of a car over Jackson's curb, sailing across the lawn and tossing Timmy and his toy mower as if they were so much flotsam, killing the boy instantly while Katie watched. No charges were filed against Baxter, despite his previous DUIs.

Tonight is Friday, Baxter's poker night. Red Morton will pick him up at eight and return him near midnight. The thought makes Jackson restless. He is unable to eat, but he remembers to bring Katie Martha's casserole for supper. He leans against one of the quilted walls in Timothy's room and watches his wife prod her plate of food with a fork. Katie coaxes her husband to sit in the rocker while she discusses the contents of the casserole.

"There's something weird in here, Jack," she says, fishing around in her plate while she perches on Timothy's airplane bed. "Something stringy." She pulls up an oddity with her fork and wrinkles her nose at what dangles in front of her.

"I think it's a rice noodle," says Jackson, rocking ferociously.

"You try it, then," she says, offering the fork to him.

Jackson reaches out, plucks the noodle from the tines and pops it in his mouth. "It's fine," he says. "Go ahead and eat. Martha made it. It's not poison." He stands to leave.

"Don't go, Jack. Stay and talk."

"About what?" he says. He presses his forehead against the doorjamb, his hands stuffed in his pants pockets. "I'm kind of busy, Kate."

Katie puts her plate aside, reaches out and grabs her husband's shirtsleeve as if clinging to his reason. "There's a purpose to this. Something God wants us to learn by taking Timmy."

"God didn't take him. Baxter did."

"It was an accident, Jack."

"No, Kate. It was homicide. Vehicular homicide." Jackson pulls away from his wife and leaves the room, flouting her rationales, her forgiveness, her mercy. He walks down the hall to the linen closet, opens the door and fishes around on the top shelf until he finds the box he needs and carries it to his bedroom. It's nearing nine o'clock and though he knows it's early for Baxter's return, he feels he needs the time to arrange and organize. He pulls the .38 from the box, a relic of his father's army days. Jackson checks the cylinder for the full count of bullets, and places it on the windowsill. He opens the window wide and pushes up the screen, pulls the armchair over to face the street, sits and surveys the angle of his vision. From this spot, he can easily see across to Baxter's front yard, the pale line of the walk that leads to his front door, the small pool of light from the street lamp at the edge of the curb.

Jackson is finally hungry, and decides to bring up a tray of provisions for the long wait. He creeps quietly down the stairs, flips on the kitchen's overhead light, and searches around for portable food—a jar of pistachio nuts, two cans of Coke, a box of animal crackers. He loads up a small tray and heads back to his bedroom, catching the low drone of Katie's prayers as he passes Timmy's room.

He sets the tray on the floor by the chair, sits, then lines up the Coke cans, jar of nuts and box of cookies on the sill next to the gun. He opens the pistachios and methodically begins to shell them until he has assembled a pile of nuts the size of his fist on the tray beside him. Jackson eats them one at a time, as his eyes patrol the dark street in search of his target.

Jackson holds vigil for over two hours, barely moving. The Cokes, nuts, and cookies have made noxious soup in his stomach, and the waiting has brought on a headache that threatens his vision. He decides to hazard a trip to the bathroom for aspirin. On the way, he peeks in on Katie, notes that she is sleeping and blows out the candles on the bureau.

He brings the bottle of aspirin back to his room, chews two

tablets without the aid of water, and checks his watch for the time. If Baxter keeps to his usual pattern, he should be home in half an hour. Jackson leans forward, elbows on the windowsill, gun set before him. He cocks his head to listen for the sound of a motor, hears a low rumble, scans the street and sees Red Morton's car nose around a curve in the road and pull up in front of Baxter's house. Jackson picks up the gun and sights the car. Baxter emerges, leans in to say something to Red before closing the passenger door, and watches as the car pulls away. Baxter slowly weaves his way up the ribbon of his walkway. When he reaches his front porch, Jackson leans out the window and yells, "Hey, Baxter!"

Baxter turns, bewildered, and looks around for the origin of the voice.

"Up here, you sorry bastard!" says Jackson, steadying the pistol and sighting Baxter's chest. Baxter peers up at his neighbor's open window as Jackson releases the hammer of the gun. The recoil knocks Jackson back against the frame of his chair. The bullet skins the tree at the edge of Baxter's lawn. Baxter hollers something as Jackson quickly takes aim again and fires. The second bullet takes a chip out of Baxter's sidewalk. Jackson curses as Baxter stumbles back, scrambles off the porch and disappears behind the hedges at the side of his house. Jackson jumps up, knocking over the chair, stuffs some extra bullets in his pocket and turns toward the door, only to find Katie standing there, her robe wrapped tightly around her, her hair disheveled by sleep.

"What are you doing, Jack?" she asks.

"Nothing, Kate. Go back to sleep."

"It's not nothing," she says as she moves slowly toward him. She stops next to the overturned chair, surveys the windowsill, then holds out her hand. "Give me the gun, Jack."

Jackson finds he is confused by her sudden interest. He has wanted her attention for months, but now it's inconvenient. He sets the safety on the gun, shoves it in his waistband, rights the chair, begins to clear the sill of debris, brushing the pistachio shells into the palm of his hand and dumping them onto the tray.

"Look at me," says Katie. Jackson looks at her but doesn't know what he sees. He stares into her eyes trying to remember where he first met her, if he still loves her.

"Give me the gun," Katie says again. "You know this isn't right."

Jackson doesn't know any such thing. In fact, he's certain he knows nothing she knows, not her God or her visions, not her purpose or grief, but he pulls the gun from his waistband, empties the cylinder, and places the revolver in Katie's palm.

"Stay with me tonight, Kate."

Katie sighs, sits on the edge of the bed, stares at the gun in her hands. "Soon," she says.

"When, Kate?" Jackson asks.

Katie shrugs. "When I find the courage." She stands, plunges the gun in the pocket of her robe, brushes her cheek against Jackson's, turns and leaves the room. Jackson watches her go, the gun swaying in her pocket, knocking against her thigh.

Jackson walks back to his chair, sits and rubs his sweating palms against the upholstered arms. A light goes on in Baxter's living room window and Jackson thinks he sees the curtain move. As the faint sound of a police siren grows louder, Jackson raises his hands, wraps them together in the shape of a gun and leans forward, one eye shut to help the other gain focus. "Blam," whispers Jackson. He leans back in the chair, closes his eyes and imagines the bullet ripping a trail in the nighttime air, shattering the lit window, finding its target and slamming through the bones of his neighbor's chest, displacing every molecule in Baxter's heart.

Growing Up Is for Losers

Rosemary Harris

Somewhere in CT, 1985

W anda Sugarman lifted one slim leather-clad leg in the air and unzipped her boot. Next time, Doc Martens, she thought. Her fishnets had runs. They always did after a long night on the job. She massaged her toes, then made little circles with her ankle before peeling off the other stiletto-heeled boot and flinging it into the corner of the room.

No matter how many scented candles she lit, Wanda's room smelled of Lysol and old mop. She'd draped a peach-colored scarf over the cheap lamp, but it hadn't softened the harsh glare, or helped her forget she was camped out in a fleabag motel. And it wasn't the first time.

She made her way to the wall sink and a two-by-three-foot rectangle of tile, which passed for a bathroom, then took a long look in the mirror, and scraped off her eye makeup. When she finished, she took the room's one scratched glass out of its white paper bag and poured herself three fingers of Jack from a silver flask—a gift from an admirer in Burlington. Wanda never drank on the job. Too many things could happen. She only let herself drink when the night was over and she was safely in her room, alone, and with the chain lock on the door. At twenty-six, she was already too old for this line of work.

She pulled off her tank top and was wriggling out of her leather miniskirt when an earsplitting scream ripped through the night. She tiptoed to the window and peeked through the grimy blinds. Just then someone pounded on her door.

"Wanda, you gotta come. Please." It was Katie, one of the other girls. Wanda left the chain lock on, and opened the door just a crack.

"It's Nina. Something's wrong with her. She fell."

When did I get named den mother, Wanda thought. True, she was the oldest, but this wasn't *Little Women* and she wasn't the motherly type. These kids came and went. A few cheap thrills, and they're on the next bus back to Dubuque or wherever they came from. Still, she grabbed her silk kimono from the back of the door, tied it tightly around her waist, and unlocked the door.

"Hurry," Katie said, pulling on Wanda's arm, and dragging her down the hall to the room she shared with Nina.

That was one good thing about being senior girl, getting her own room. At least Wanda could bolt the door and lock out the noise, the booze, the gropers, and be blissfully alone. She padded behind Katie barefoot, getting God-knows-what sticky stuff on the soles of her feet, and sidestepping beer cans, cigarette butts, and what looked like week-old pizza in the hallway.

Two other girls, in various states of undress, stood in the door-way, too afraid to go in. They stepped aside for Wanda. Inside, clad only in her panties, and sprawled face-down on the cold bathroom tile, was Nina MacFarland.

"Jeez. Did anyone call 911?" Wanda asked, running over to the girl. "Call 911. Now!"

Only Katie had the nerve to speak up. "We didn't want to get her in trouble. We thought you could help."

"Me? Who do I look like, Dr. Quinn, Medicine Woman? Get on the phone," Wanda said, disgusted. "She's already in trouble."

As Katie dialed, Wanda put her fingers on Nina's neck, and did her best to find a pulse. The girl was breathing, but just barely.

"What did she take?" Wanda asked. The girls looked at each other but said nothing.

"Listen, with any luck, an ambulance—if they have one in this hick town—is going to be here soon, and they have a better chance of saving her if you tell them what she took."

"Nina doesn't take drugs," one of them answered. "Ever. She's a vegetarian."

Oh, brother. As if Wanda hadn't seen vegetarians who smoked, and drank, and OD'ed.

"Let's get her on her feet." Wanda and Katie had no trouble lifting the girl, who must have been all of ninety pounds. Apart from the tile's faint imprint on the side of her face, Nina looked like a sleeping angel, sylph-like, hair the color of cornsilk, her nearly naked body heartbreakingly vulnerable and exposed. With one hand, Wanda untied her own kimono, shook it off, and wrapped it around the narrow shoulders of the girl who'd be dead if EMTs didn't get there fast.

□   □   □

The ambulance lights threw garish, funhouse shadows on their faces. Wanda sat on the edge of the bed, absent-mindedly fingering the cheap bedspread. She hadn't been able to watch while EMTs tried resuscitating the girl, but the sound of a bag being zipped shut told her they'd failed.

If they'd called 911 first, if she'd sprinted down the hall instead of stepping gingerly over the crud, if Nina MacFarland had stayed in Mystic . . . who knew? She might be dead anyway.

An EMT technician put his hand on her shoulder. "Sorry, miss. No one seems to know much about her except her name."

"That's all I know. We just worked together." She heard one of the other techs snort. In her black lace bra, half-zipped miniskirt, and torn fishnets, Wanda knew what the creep thought, and gave him a look that froze blood in lesser men. "We're backup singers, asshole. The Jimmy Collins Band?" Then she uttered four magic words, "We're with the band."

It was a dream gig for lots of young girls—starry-eyed, Madonna wannabes. You got to travel around the country, sometimes even Europe. And in every town, guys fell in love with you, and girls wanted to be you. Sometimes Wanda got to sing lead. Jimmy liked her and let her take the mike when the band needed a break. But it was a guy band; their fans didn't want to hear some skinny chick whining about lost love. Three years ago, she'd cut a demo, but it went nowhere, and Wanda was back in the line, showing a steady stream of new girls the hand motions that went with Jimmy's one big hit, "Growing Up Is for Losers."

Now, past the age of twenty-five, the long nights, crap food, and secondhand smoke were taking their toll. To say nothing of the drugs. It took all of her resolve to say no, but with every tour it got harder to resist the bright eyes and instant energy a little blow seemed to promise. Apparently, Nina hadn't resisted.

Squeaky Jackson finally showed up. He was the band's manager. Wanda had never seen him in anything other than jeans and tour t-shirt, and he stank of alcohol, even early in the morning. He stood in the doorway, his arms around the other girls, and gave Wanda a useless look that said, Whaddya gonna do?

Two of the EMT guys strapped Nina's body to a gurney. The third, who'd thought they were hookers, scooped up a handful of orange pill containers scattered on top of the girls' dresser. He dumped the pills into Nina's suede shoulder bag, then pawed through the rest of the stuff on the dresser. Katie started to protest, but thought better of it.

One of the nicer ones asked if anyone wanted to ride in the ambulance. When no one answered, Wanda just stared at them—the sleazy manager who'd hired (and probably slept with) the girl, her pals in the band, the roommate who'd bunked with her for three months.

"You guys are really something," she said, standing up. "I'll come. Let me get my shoes." She brushed past them, giving Squeaky a shove, then jogged down the hall to her room.

She quickly pulled on a t-shirt and jeans, and stepped into her Doc Martens, but by the time she got outside, the ambulance was gone.

"Sonofabitch. I can't believe they left without me." Squeaky and the girls were gone, too, and Wanda was left alone in the yellowish light of the motel's Exit sign.

At the top of the outside stairs she saw a shadow wave just behind the railing. "Show's over, perv. Just go back to your room."

The person stepped into the light. "It's me, Pete. I heard what happened. You okay?"

Pete Chinnery was not a perv. And not your average roadie. For one thing, he wore a cross. Before it was fashionable. For another, he wasn't always screwing the backup singers and groupies. Maybe he was gay. Or maybe he was just a decent guy who loved rock and roll, and didn't mind working behind the scenes. He took the stairs slowly. "Can I take you to the hospital?"

"Yeah, that'd be great."

Wanda ran inside to get a jacket while Pete brought his Harley around.

"You know where you're going?" she asked, straddling the bike and leaning back on the sissy bar. He nodded. They took the back roads and the combination of the bike's rhythm and the wind on her face almost blew away the memory of the ugly scene Wanda had just witnessed. Almost, but not quite.

At the hospital, with just a sheet covering her tiny body, Nina looked about twelve years old. The Indian doctor had been quiet, and sympathetic. "We tried to reach a next of kin, but, no luck," he'd said. "Is there any chance her ID is counterfeit?"

"Beats me," Wanda said. He handed her the black plastic garbage bag that held Nina's personal effects and her own kimono.

"In a case like this, we're required to hold onto the body; there's a mandatory autopsy in the state of Connecticut for any death that appears to be drug-related."

"Her roommate says she didn't do drugs." Even as the words came out, Wanda knew they were lame, but the doctor just nodded and pretended to believe her. She scribbled the motel's number on a slip of paper, and he agreed to call if the autopsy results came back while the band was still in town.

Outside, in the cool evening air, Pete suggested they go for coffee before heading back. Wanda squashed down the plastic bag that contained most of Nina's worldly possessions, wedged it between Pete and herself, and climbed back on the bike.

Pete Chinnery had been with the band almost as long as Wanda, and this was the first time they'd been alone for more than a few minutes. She was conscious of how tightly her arms were wrapped around him, but couldn't seem to relax her grip. It was almost 3:00 A.M. when they pulled into a rundown joint with the unlikely name of Paradise.

"That's wishful thinking," Wanda said, swinging her left leg over the padded seat and hopping off.

The Paradise was a little bit of the Caribbean inexplicably dropped in the middle of New England—turquoise and pink, with Christmas lights in the window despite the fact that it was April. There were a few jocks in the last booth, and two drunken commuters at the counter trying to sober up before they went home and lied to their wives about where they'd been.

Wanda tossed the plastic bag into a booth before sliding in and ordering coffee and donuts. Suddenly ravenous, she wolfed down the two stale donuts and Pete signaled for more.

"I don't get it with these kids," Wanda said, warming her hands on the cup. "Don't they see the burnouts at every show?"

"They don't. They only see the fun, the glamor, the rush of being 'with the band.'" They talked for hours. Pete, about his ex-wife, and the guy she left him for. And Wanda, about her younger sister, who'd fallen in with a rough crowd and died of an overdose while Wanda was shaking a tambourine somewhere in Michigan. By the time the sun came up, they knew everything they needed to know about each other, and when they got back to the motel, for the first time in ages, Wanda was happy to share her room.

□   □   □

Next afternoon, Jimmy Collins and Squeaky called a band meeting. Only half of the crew made it, and most of them were nodding.

"Anyone wanna say anything?" he asked. A few embarrassed faces, then a deadly silence, which Jimmy broke.

"Hey, man, I know this is some heavy shit, but we've got a show tonight. Two more before we blow this 'burg, then New Haven, then Boston, then, for some of us, merry old Ireland. So try to chill. Get some extra rest today. Katie, you take over Nina's spot with the tambourine." She beamed, apparently forgetting the reason for her promotion was her dead roommate. "Okay, people, setup at 6:30."

From the other end of the room, Pete caught Wanda's eye, and knew what she was thinking: *That was it?* The girl's life and death had been reduced to "some heavy shit?"

That night the show went off without a hitch. If anyone missed Nina you wouldn't know it. To the crowd they were the singer, the blonde, the redhead, the black one, and the one with the boobs. There'd be a new blonde on the next tour.

After the encores, Wanda was in no mood to hang out, so she went straight back to the motel. A note had been shoved under her door. "Autopsy results inconclusive. No signs of any known drug in Nina MacFarland's body. Official cause of death is cardiac arrest.

Have you had any luck finding a relative?"

Not a relative, and not a soul who seemed to care that the girl was dead. She poured herself a drink, then shuffled through the papers on her night table for her contact sheet. She dialed a number.

"Squeaky, you busy?"

"Not yet. What is it, Wanda? You gonna make me a happy man after all these years?" She could almost hear him scratching himself over the phone.

"Dream on. I want to talk about Nina. Do you think that could have been a fake ID she gave you?"

"It's been known to happen." She heard him fumble around, then strike a match and suck in air. "Look," he said, breathing out hard, "are *you* really *you*? I'd be pretty paranoid if I started thinking people weren't who they said they were." She hated to admit it, but he had a point.

"She ever say anything to you about her family?"

"C'mon, Wanda. Do you and I sit around and chat about Grandma Sugarman? She was over eighteen. We had the standard interview, and then nothing, zip. Not even a return match. I give her a shot at fame and glory and that's the thanks I get. Now, I gotta get pretty and see if I can't get lucky tonight. Unless you wanna come down here and save me the cost of a few Sam Adamses . . ." Wanda hung up.

Despite the hour, she couldn't sleep. Somewhere Nina's parents would be waiting for her to come home, or to call. Maybe not tonight, but maybe at Christmas, or her birthday, or whenever she got over whatever rift with them sent her out of Mystic with just the clothes on her back.

Mystic. A small Connecticut town just like her own. When Wanda left home, she snuck out her bedroom window in the dead of night, her clothes in a pillow case, chasing after a drummer. His band had done five nights in town and after the fourth he'd asked her to leave with them. One semester at UConn hadn't made her any smarter, so she went. She called home once, then not for another three months. By that time her sister was dead, buried for two months before Wanda even knew.

She opened the black plastic bag they'd given her at the hospital, took out Nina's shoulderbag, and spilled the contents on her bed. The prescriptions were Katie's—probably the reason they were given back. A pack of American Spirit cigarettes, a Bic lighter, and some chewing gum. The bonded leather wallet held a few dollars, her birth certificate, and two pictures, one of the band at a party best forgotten, and the other, a snapshot of Nina and another girl flanking a litter of border collies. Not much else in the bag, a tin of Tiger balm, a broken Walkman, and a rabbit's foot that clearly didn't work.

Just then there was a knock at her door, more gentle than last night's, but startling just the same. This time she guessed who it was. She unfolded her legs and walked to the door, with a quick look in the mirror to check her hair.

Pete Chinnery stood in the doorway with a Dunkin' Donuts bag in one hand and a cardboard tray of coffee in the other.

"I couldn't sleep."

"Me neither. Come on in."

The two of them sat on Wanda's bed, on either side of Nina's possessions.

"Not much to go on," Pete said. "We leave for New Haven tomorrow. Mystic's not far from there." Wanda thought she might be falling in love. They shoveled everything back into Nina's bag, and put aside the coffee and donuts for breakfast.

The next night, on the tour bus, Wanda pestered everyone who wasn't sleeping about Nina, until Jimmy begged her to stop.

"You're screwing up our karma. You gotta let it go. Life is impermanence, man. Nina would have been the first to tell you that."

"Why? Was she a Buddhist?"

"She had some crazy notions. Remember that guy in Providence she hung out with, the Brown Guru? He was out there." The guru was a Brown dropout with no spiritual training as far as Wanda could tell, but he had a good line, and a few of the younger girls fell for him.

"Ask Katie about him. She and Nina seemed to buy a lot of his crap. Literally and figuratively."

She climbed back over the outstretched legs of sleeping band members and into her double seat. Katie was curled up two rows behind her.

"Are you really sleeping?" Wanda whispered, kneeling over the back of the seat. Two other people on the bus grumbled yes but there was no answer from Katie. Wanda sank into her seat, and looked out the window for Pete, who was following the bus on his Sportster. Sometimes they towed it, but tonight he wanted to ride. It was just as well. They'd been moving pretty fast. For the rest of the drive, she flipped through the new Springsteen bio but kept putting it down to ask herself how she might find Nina's family. Before two months passed without them knowing their daughter was dead.

The bus pulled into Palmer's Motel at 4:30 A.M., and they stumbled off like extras from *Night of the Living Dead*. Two hours later, Wanda was in the lobby drinking watered-down coffee from a cup so small it could have been used for a urine sample. Pete flopped down next to her on the flowered sofa.

"Couldn't sleep?"

"You know why."

"Look, get some rest. Meet me back here at 10:00 A.M. No one but farmers are up at this hour anyway. I'll get directions to Mystic."

She kissed him on the check and dragged her butt back to her room. By the time she woke up it was after eleven. She ran her fingers through her hair, grabbed her bag, and Nina's, and sprinted down the hall to the lobby.

Pete smiled as if she was right on time. "While you were catching up on your beauty sleep, I did some research. Mystic doesn't have its own phone book; the county one lists four MacFarlands but none within a hundred miles. Sorry, Babe." She couldn't believe they'd reached a dead end so soon.

Once again she rooted around in Nina's bag for a clue. She opened the wallet and stared at the picture of Nina and the puppies.

"Who has five border collies?" Even before she finished the sentence, she reached for the phone book and flipped to the business pages. "Howling Moon Border Collies," she said. "And guess where they're located."

When Pete and Wanda got to Mystic, they stopped at Helen's Burger Barn to refuel and start asking questions.

"Sure I know Howling Moon. It's right across the road from Merritt High," the waitress said, topping off their coffees. Wanda took a chance and showed her the picture of Nina and the collies. She shrugged. "Lots of girls around here look like that—scrawny, dishwater blondes with long hair. When you're my age everyone under twenty looks the same." She laughed.

"What about the name Nina MacFarland?" Wanda pressed. "That sound familiar?" Another head shake. "Bobby, you know anyone around here named MacFarland?" the waitress yelled.

A kitchen helper came out from behind the swinging chrome doors. "Who wants to know?" he asked, wiping his hands on his grease-splattered apron. Wanda was glad they hadn't ordered food. They told him as much as they could without revealing the girl was dead.

"I went to school with a girl named MacFarland."

Wanda showed him the picture.

"Yeah, that's her. She used to work at the dog breeder's. What'd she do? Rob a bank?" He had a laugh like a donkey, and something in the way he asked made Wanda want to hit him with a nearby ketchup bottle, but good sense prevailed.

"I owe her money. Just trying to pay her back," Wanda said. "Any idea where her family is?"

"You kidding?" he brayed. Wanda wasn't surprised; she got up to leave. Pete peeled off a few bucks, including a nice tip for the waitress. On their way out they heard Bobby yelling, "Hell, you can always leave the money with me. I'll get it to her."

"Nice town," Wanda muttered.

"Who knows, maybe she wouldn't go bowling with him."

"How did you get to be so reasonable?" she said, as if it were an extraordinary trait.

"I'm in love."

"Save the sweet talk for later. We're going dog shopping, and we've gotta do it and get back to New Haven before the curtain goes up." She checked her watch. Two hours until showtime.

One small, barracks-like building was opposite the high school. There was no sign, but the bike sputtering into the driveway caused a riot of barking, and they knew they were in the right place. A young, very pregnant girl came out, holding her lower back with one hand and a black and white puppy with the other.

"How you gonna take her on a bike?" she asked. "Oh, you're not the Frasers." She put the puppy down, and heaved herself onto a dirty white plastic chair. They told her why they'd come.

"I haven't been here long. Lots of kids from Merritt work here part time." As if on cue, a lanky boy crossed the road toward them, still carrying his schoolbag.

"These folks were asking about a girl who used to work here," she told him. "What was her name?"

"Nina MacFarland." Wanda showed him the picture.

"I remember that litter," he said, smiling and tapping the photo. "I love the red ones. Yeah, that's Nina. She and her family moved to

Storrs so she could go to school without living in a dorm. I don't think her parents trusted her to live away from home."

"Maybe you're mistaken. The girl we're talking about has been traveling with a band for the last year."

He was emphatic. "My older cousin went out with her. That's her, I'm sure. The redhead."

An hour later, in Storrs, a redhaired Nina MacFarland stared at them through a screen door. "Can I help you?"

"I believe you can," Wanda said. "We were looking for Nina MacFarland's family. Seems we found the genuine article. Maybe you can tell us who the blonde in this picture is?"

"Why?"

"Because she's dead," Wanda snapped.

"What happened?" Nina asked, hanging on to the door, to steady herself.

"We're not sure," Pete said, gently. "Can we come in?"

The real Nina let them in and motioned for Pete and Wanda to sit down in the parlor. "I can't believe she kept that picture," she said, handing it back to them. "She was Caroline Geraci."

"Any idea why Caroline would tell people she was you?"

Nina said no, but she was a lousy liar.

"She's past protecting now," Pete said. "And the authorities in another part of Connecticut think you're dead. You're gonna have to tell someone. Why not start with us?"

"Caroline borrowed my birth certificate once. She never returned it. I probably wouldn't even have remembered if I hadn't needed it when I registered for school."

"Why did she need it?"

"Who knows? Some party, some club she wanted to get into. She liked to party. She wasn't bad, just a little wild. Caroline and I lost touch the summer we moved here. My parents were glad; they thought she was a bad influence."

"Drugs?"

"No way. Caroline was a juicehead. But she tried a lot of herbal stuff. My mom's a nurse. She said it wasn't safe. Anyway, I didn't hear from her for over a year, then I got a postcard. From Atlanta."

Where she joined the Jimmy Collins tour.

"She sounded happy. She thanked me for being her friend." And, silently, for the birth certificate and new life, Wanda guessed.

"Do you know where her parents are?"

Nina shook her head. "They divorced. I think her mom remarried, but we'd moved by then. I don't know what her new name is."

The girl nervously checked the clock. "Um, I gotta get to class now. I don't know what else to say. Can you just tell them I'm not dead so my folks don't have to know about this?"

"We'll do what we can. We should be heading back, anyway," Wanda said, "we have a show tonight."

"Cool. Um, are you gonna keep that picture? I don't have many of me with the litters."

Wanda handed over the photo.

"It's a good one," Nina said. "I bet Katie posed us for twenty minutes."

□ □ □

They raced back to New Haven. By the time they got there, it was close to seven and everyone else was at the theater. Wanda ran to her room, grabbed an outfit, and they took off again. Backstage, people were practicing their moves, and psyching themselves up for the performance.

"Jeez, where have you two been?" Squeaky asked, taking a swig and screwing the top back on a bottle. "It's a little late for a nooner. Never mind. Just get your asses in gear."

"Where's Katie?"

"Inspiring our fearless leader."

Wanda marched to Jimmy's dressing room, Pete trailing behind.

"Hey, I don't think you want to interrupt them," Squeaky yelled. She banged on the door.

They heard grunting and heavy breathing. She banged again.

"We got fifteen minutes, man. Take a walk."

"It's Wanda and Pete. We want to talk to Katie. About Caroline."

Jimmy opened the door slowly. In the mirror, Wanda could see Katie buttoning her shirt.

"Wanda, I love you, but unless Caroline is here to make it a threesome she's not needed," Jimmy said, running his hands through his hair.

"I think Caroline's already been here. Not tonight, though. Isn't that right, Katie?"

"What the hell is she talking about?"

All eyes were on Katie. Hers were fixed on Wanda. She held Wanda's gaze for a few minutes, then dropped her head in her hands.

"You couldn't just drop it. In five days we would have been in Ireland. We're gonna open for the Spice Girls. I could have been out of here." Katie looked around helplessly, knowing it was over.

"Tell us what happened," Wanda said.

"She followed us everywhere in high school. Every concert, every party, there was Caroline. At first it was fun, having this little kid look up to us. Then she got to be a pain. She was a slut; I caught her making out with my boyfriend." She said it as if that explained something.

"Two summers ago, Nina moved, and another friend and I hitch-hiked cross-country. I wrote to Nina but not Caroline. The bitch tracked me down. How psycho is that? She found me in Atlanta, and pleaded with me to talk to Squeaky about hiring her. I wouldn't do it. I didn't want her around, so I lied. I told her they'd never hire her because she was too young.

"So she went to Squeaky on her own, told him she was eighteen, and proved it by whipping out Nina's birth certificate," Wanda said.

Katie nodded. "What happened the night she died?"

"I knew Caroline had slept with Squeaky, who hasn't? But, she was working her way through the rest of the band, and it was only a matter of time before she got to Jimmy. I thought if she was out of the way, he'd notice me." She broke down. "I didn't mean to poison her. I just wanted her out of commission that night." Jimmy Collins took a few steps back; he looked like he was in shock. Katie rambled on. "It was going to be so good."

"What did you give her?"

"Pennyroyal. I got it from the Brown Guru. I mixed some in her tea, but I must have put in too much." Katie was sobbing now.

Just then Squeaky knocked on Jimmy's door. "I hate to break up your orgy, but you guys have five minutes to get your asses on stage."

Pete Chinnery took charge. "Stall for time. Jimmy, zip up and get out there. Wanda, you round up the rest of the girls. I'll stay with Katie until the cops come. You guys have a show to do."

A Work of Art

Janice Law

Of course, he came the minute he got the news; it could not have been otherwise. If there has been one constant in my life, it has been my regular visits and calls from Stig Mellanson. How I remember the first one, the very first. We were living in a fifth-floor cold-water walk-up, toilet down the hall; kitchen, tub, and bed squeezed around the work bench and the easel. I was still painting seriously at the time, and the smell of last night's beans and rice mingled with the acrid perfume of turpentine and pigments. I saw at once that he was rich despite the countrified down jacket, thick corduroy pants and hiking boots—among Stig's many affectations was his habit of dressing in Manhattan as if he had just left the woods, the ski slopes, or the shooting range.

Which showed imagination of a sort. I sometimes think his air of living elsewhere, of having in hand a score of roles and residences, must have been what attracted . . . but no, too soon. I've promised myself that all will be in order. Nothing will be explicable if my story lacks order. Start at the end, and the result is monstrous. But start right, start from the beginning, and you will see the logic, the artful, the inevitable, logic of the whole.

So, back to my fifth-floor studio with Stig Mellanson's feet ringing on the metal treads, the sound of money, hope, prosperity. I had just begun making the jewel boxes then. The first ones were crude, admittedly crude, wood with smoked and painted glass, not at all as elegant as the later, post-Stig ones, when I could afford onyx and special plastics and custom tiles, black as ebony. Just the same I put my heart into them, literally and figuratively. As soon as I completed the first one, I knew I had something, because my paintings—Pop with a touch of surrealism—suddenly looked anemic and derivative. The little black box in my hand was the real thing, new and mysterious, heavy with suggestion.

"What do you call them?" he asked.

"I call them madelines."

"Of course, of course," he said with a laugh, "for your beautiful wife." A glance at Madeline; I remember that glance in retrospect. "But maybe for Proust, too?"

He was educated, you see, and perceptive. A dream patron, really.

"And do they open?" he asked.

"For my heart," I said. How honest and naïve I was. People with patrons and customers soon lose such openness.

He examined them all. The one he chose surprised me. It was the one with the little black heart, anatomically correct, embedded in strips of paper with letters, words, and astrological signs like an egg in a nest. A curious choice; perhaps unconsciously prescient. That a man is a rascal doesn't mean he is obtuse. "This one," he said. "I must have this one."

He didn't ask the price; I named a figure three times my usual and saw Madeline blanch: the rent was due, our phone was gone, and we daily anticipated darkness and a dead stove.

Stig smiled slyly as if he'd gotten a bargain and took out his checkbook.

That night we had steak and a bottle of red wine at a decent restaurant; I toasted Madeline and she threw her head back and said, "To the madelines," her black hair whipping against her face with the violence of her gesture. She was a little drunk. I was, too, drunk on hope and success and the promise of better things, which, against all odds, artistic and economic, arrived.

I entered my happiest period, the period of the madelines, which evolved into ever more beautiful, subtle, and luxurious items. They are famous now. Connoisseurs speak of Armond's madelines as they speak of Cornell's boxes.

But I did not repeat myself for long. The coffins came next, receptacles for dead things, dead styles, dead ideas. I used a great deal of ebonized wood and violet stained glass and, later, lead. By then we had left the fifth-floor walk-up, and I had hired a proper studio with jacks and trolleys that would accommodate large and heavy creations.

These works proved to be even more celebrated—and lucrative—than the madelines. There are articles, a book even, on the meaning of Armond's coffins. My patron, my friend, Stig, was there every step of the way, admiring, suggesting, purchasing. He dropped into the studio at least once a week, immersing himself in all the technical details. And if I was working out a problem, if the studio door was not only closed but locked, he got into the habit of visiting with Madeline.

Stig was kindness itself, wheedling from her information about whatever was needed. Was the studio cold in the winter? He could provide a better heater. Was she concerned with a build-up of fumes? He contacted a ventilation expert. Had I been working too hard? A trip to the sun was in order—tickets for an interesting cruise would be forthcoming. When I won my first big prize for the madelines, he insisted on contributing first-class tickets to Rome for the ceremony. He was a friend, indeed. And if I protested, he always said that my work was appreciating every year, that I was making him money, which was the truth.

But there are truths and truths, aren't there? Increasingly I felt trapped by his friendship, his obsession with my work. I cultivated other patrons, found a dealer, urged Madeline, who knew well how to make herself charming, to attend openings with the famous and the influential. To no avail. No sooner would an idea take shape than I would hear Stig's feet on the steps, see his square, red, handsome face appear in the doorway, hear him say, "A little bird tells me you are up to something good."

It was at this time that I began to make my coffins of lead. They grew so heavy that we had to find yet another studio, one on ground level with a cement floor. I wanted to make a coffin too big and heavy for Stig to buy, a mausoleum of lead, a sarcophagus with a lid too massive to lift, a box he could not peer into, a secret he could not uncover.

"It is your finest work yet," he said and made immediate arrangements with Madeline for it to be transported to his country house.

I began to avoid him and became secretive; I refused to share, as I had hitherto done, my hopes and plans.

"You've hurt Stig's feelings," said Madeline one day. She'd had her hair styled for an opening, and she was wearing something dark from Prada with high, elaborate heels. I might have asked where she had acquired such taste, but she looked so beautiful that I decided to make casts of her long, delicate feet and create sculptures for them in the form of high-heeled shoes. Perhaps you've seen one of the Objects for Madeline, because they were later featured in an advertising campaign and became famous, like everything else I touched. It was my Midas time for sure.

The cast feet were realized in white porcelain or fine crystal; the shoes, red, black, gray or silver, evolved from wood to silver to cement to lead, my darkest, my most favorite material. Madeline hated them, which didn't surprise me, but hurt all the same. She'd always had such faith in my work—and in me. "You've cut off my feet," she cried.

"To keep you from running away," I said. Of course, I was joking. Madeline did not laugh.

Neither did Stig. "These are strange fetishes," he said.

"You have made me a witch doctor, a juju man."

He frowned and looked doubtful, but it was too much to expect that he would blame himself or even fully understand the Objects. Nonetheless, he opened his checkbook after the show, and I saw that there would be no easy escape. My course of action remained in doubt for some time, because, cowardly and much in love—have you understood that I loved Madeline?—I preferred doubt and ignorance to certainty. I arranged a holiday in Southern France. Madeline and I lay in the sun, drank good wine, bought flowers at the outdoor markets and antiques at the boutiques. I came back determined to put coffins and fetishes behind me.

I thought about flowers and my suntanned, blooming wife and the preservation of happiness—just as I sensed that my own was slipping away. As so often, Stig was the catalyst that gave me the direction I needed. One day I noticed a paperweight on Madeline's desk: a chunk of plastic with a shell enclosed.

"Nice," I said. "Did you get this in France?"

"I don't know where I got it."

I looked more closely. "Block Island it says on the back."

I thought she colored slightly.

"Stig must have brought it back," she said. "I think he did. He likes to bring souvenirs."

I closed my fingers around the paperweight. Had I the strength, I would have squashed the plastic and crushed the shell to bits. I could see, as clearly as if I had been looking over their shoulders, my Madeline and Stig, wandering along a pretty street, stopping for a souvenir at some small seaside shop. Stig's taste ran to high-end objets d'art; Madeline's was altogether simpler and more sentimental. That they had bought this together I hadn't the slightest doubt.

I now entered a curious period in my personal, and my artistic, life. I watched with intense absorption the progress of their affair— that there was an affair I was virtually convinced, because a multitude of previously troubling details, from Madeline's soigné wardrobe to the days when she just "needed to get away," to her indifference, even hostility, to my newer works, to Stig's arrival on precisely the days when he knew I would be busiest, dropped into place. I fell into despair.

You can see the results, the Couples. Unless you follow the art world, you will not know them; they're too new: little cast-lead figures of embracing couples who sink slowly down into what looks like sand. Getting the composition of the "pit" material was a challenge, I can assure you. They were a true cri de coeur and a warning, but it was a warning not taken. Stig bought one with a smile on his face, and though I had long disliked him, I now began to hate him.

But such is human nature that even while I was working on the Couples, I conceived a different project. One goes so far into misery that to keep working at all something different must be done. Mozart warbled though sick and broke; poor tormented Van Gogh put all the radiance of the south on canvas. Not that I share their genius, but there were days when I looked at Madeline and remembered happiness. I recalled the flower market in Nice, and with the example of the fatal paperweight in mind, I considered the possibility of a perpetual garden. After considerable research, I ordered a stainless steel refrigerator unit sufficient to keep a faceted glass container at below minus 292 degrees Fahrenheit and made arrangements for the proper quantity of silicone oil to fill it.

I will spare you the scientific complexities involved in setting up even a small container, the difficulties with suppliers and technicians, the timing of deliveries, and skip to the happier memory of the day when Madeline and I visited the city florists and wholesalers, buying roses, anemones, orchids, violets, and ranunculus, some coleus with their neon colors, succulents with wonderful thick leaves, and a carpet of Spanish moss and peat.

That was the last day we were ever to work together. I remember my joy when she helped me set up our garden, our immortal Magic Terrarium. When it was complete, a garden of earthly delights such as there never was, we pumped in the silicone and froze the lot at their very peak of beauty, color, and perfection.

"So long as the oil is kept properly chilled, they will last forever." I looked at her to see if she understood that this perpetual garden was the image of our happiness and of my hopes for its continuance.

"I don't like it," she said. "It is unnatural."

As all art is unnatural, you can see how far apart we had become. "Stig will like it," I said. "I made it for him."

"What if the power goes off? The terrarium would be ruined in a matter of hours."

"Stig will have a generator. The piece will be expensive and difficult to keep up, and he will like that, too."

You can see that I had become cynical about the ways of wealthy collectors. And I was right. I'd studied Stig as he had studied my work, but I proved the better student. I knew that he had collected my wife, that he had lured her away with his beach cottage, his country house, his ski lodge, his wealth and luxury—including his art—for by this time, the Mellanson Collection was becoming famous. He purchased widely, but everyone knowledgeable agreed that the Armonds were the heart and glory of the collection. Madeline might, if she chose, have the best of both worlds.

I found that notion intolerable. The winter I finished the Couples and made the Magic Terrarium, I put in orders for larger glass containers and more powerful refrigeration units. I did not reveal their purpose to anyone, not even to myself. As far as I knew, the equipment might linger in my studio as an expensive folly, an artistic dead end, and I honestly did not understand their utility until spring, the season when Madeline lost her caution.

I weep now to think of it, because her carelessness was a token of our alienation. She no longer possessed that extra sense which says "too far," "go back." She no longer understood me—or perhaps cared to understand me—she, who once perceived every shade of meaning, was now blind to my work with all its warnings.

One evening I came up early from the studio. Could there be any more banal denouement? We had a fine townhouse then with a work area in the basement and a smaller studio and showroom on the first floor. I had been working at the easel, something I had not done for years, and I had gotten paint on my shoes, which I took off to spare the polished floors. Do you see how coincidence, not to mention the smallest detail, the smallest decision, can be crucial? I went silently up the stair.

Madeline was above, in the office, talking on the phone. I could tell at once from her tone that this was serious business but not artistic business, not my business: she was talking to Stig. I stopped on the stair to listen.

". . . frightened," she said. "Those last works . . ."

So she had understood after all. Understanding is the beginning of wisdom. I strained my ears, but there was silence, as Stig, the rat, was no doubt enticing her to leave.

"I can't just go; you know I can't . . ."

I could almost have forgiven her for that hesitation.

"How can you think that!" A cry of alarm—but for him, not for me. "As soon as I can. No, no, of course not. I'll say nothing until . . . Yes, yes, when everything is ready. He is entitled . . . some warning."

I did not wait to hear any more. I slipped back downstairs to the studio and commenced preparations that very night. You may be curious: was I secretive? Yes and no. Certainly the container sat in the studio, where Madeline rarely now ventured and Stig was not invited. Invoices for the refrigeration units and the container work went through the office. Several bales of moss were delivered to the back door. I put in an extensive order with one of the big flower wholesalers. Madeline handled all of these. But she was listening to Stig; she was not listening to me. So I don't think I am to blame if she missed my warnings.

How did I do it? Ask me rather how I had the heart to do it— therein lies the story, the secret. The occasion itself was quite ordinary: a big sale came through and we celebrated with a bottle of champagne. I laced hers with sleeping pills. When she went up to bed early, feeling dizzy, I followed her and, like Othello, covered her face with a pillow. I don't believe she suffered; I hope she did not have a consciousness of what was happening for even a second. I hope not.

And then, as you can guess, downstairs at all speed to where the container, filled with blooms, was waiting. People aren't flowers; they do not do well when plucked. There were difficulties and sorrows and Madeline was wet with my tears before she lay in blossoms like a goddess of the spring, asleep. I sealed the container, set the refrigeration unit going and pumped in the oil. When everything was finished, the hose detached and the temperature right, the box was a masterpiece, at once modern and classical, gorgeous and macabre, the last and greatest of the madelines.

Back upstairs, I slept. There was no hurry. It was afternoon, late afternoon, before I woke up, still exhausted. A gray, overcast day was breaking up into a spotty orange sunset. I felt like Lazarus, brought back untimely, even impertinently, from the dead, because my own life was already posthumous with only one thing of importance to be done.

I made a cup of coffee, then called Stig to ask if he knew where Madeline was. Not an hour later, I heard his footsteps ringing on metal treads, on that first stair, although, in reality, he walked up the brownstone stoop and rang the bell. I was waiting for him.

Stig was full of questions and anxieties. He hadn't seen Madeline for two days. Lunch, they'd had lunch. He named a popular restaurant. And she had called. Yes, a call yesterday. Around four. He started toward our living quarters, but I opened the studio door.

"I have something to show you," I said.

"Not now, not now. We need to find Madeline," he said.

"She left something curious," I said. "You'd better see."

He came down to the landing, and, in spite of my grief and the fatigue of the grave, my heart beat faster. I could hear it even over the sound of the refrigeration unit and the exhaust fan.

"Where is the light switch?"

I reached past him to turn on the lights. The last madeline glowed like a jewel with the splendid, unfading colors of the flowers. Stig took a step forward and screamed: my wife lay on a carpet of moss, her nightgown draped over her long legs, her beautiful face staring out in wonder, with the faintest look of surprise.

"Oh my God!" cried Stig and clutched his chest. "Oh, my . . ." He began gasping for breath and dropped to his knees. "I need, I need . . ." He waved his arm.

I had not expected this. I had expected rage leading to a homicidal assault, and I was disappointed in him, and insulted that Madeline should have left me for such weakness. "You need another artist," I said. I picked up one of my mallets and cracked him on the head, ending breath and complaints in one. All unexpected, but maybe not entirely, for I have another container and a lot more oil. I am thinking now of a companion piece, what the old artists called a pendant.

I'll have to work quickly, because Stig can't be kept fresh for a few days in a florist's vase. And he's heavy. But I'll make the effort for him. As Madeline is Persephone, whose loss ended spring and joy and life as I knew it, he will be Pluto, the god of the underworld and her kidnapper, who will watch her lustfully for as long as the cooling units work.

No matter what our technology or aesthetic, we all become classicists in the end, and every story is an old one.

Stagnant

Stephen D. Rogers

The tide comes in. The tide goes out. Nothing else moves. Sure, rocks and shells and pieces of driftwood are pushed here and dragged there but they don't matter worth a damn.

Once you get Cape Cod beach in your sneakers, you're never really free of the place.

I should know.

I once killed a man along this stretch of shoreline.

He haunts me still.

My mother could never understand why her darling daughter wanted to become a cop. Mom could never understand her darling daughter at all. I wasn't what she expected, what she'd been conditioned to expect. My favorite dolls didn't form off into families. They asked each other for license and registration.

Looking back, I realize how that must have embarrassed her whenever she heard me at play, considering she'd only been pulled over the one time.

If it was any consolation, my son was no less the personal reminder.

And the man I'd killed. He never let me forget either.

I hugged my knees tighter against my chest.

Stared down a gull that had started to run closer.

Screeched at him for good measure.

The bird took to the air but I knew his escape was only illusionary. He'd simply circle and climb until he rose too high to be seen, soaring until he coasted down to earth, trapped within the borders of what had happened here.

The Atlantic was gray, the wind sharp.

Time, meaningless.

"I have your husband and son."

"What do you want?"

Out of the corner of my eye, I noticed a jogger headed my way, far enough in the distance that I couldn't even begin to identify the person.

The department's psychologist suggested I take up running. Or swimming. Or kickboxing. Any activity that would give my body something to fight, my mind something to focus upon besides the job. The good doctor said I needed to learn how to relax, to unwind before going home each day.

Face down an armed drug dealer. Transition. Make cupcakes with Jason while running a load of laundry.

I could see now that the jogger was probably male. And blessed with a fluid pace, his movements seemingly effortless.

That was not me by any stretch of the imagination.

I ran as though I carried the weight of a patrol officer's belt. Comic, jerky strides. Determined to catch the perp. Ready to dive for safety if someone opened fire.

The psychologist wasn't a bad guy. He was another one who just didn't understand.

"I have your husband and son."

How many missing children had I located over the years, first as a uniform and then as a detective? How many parents had I tried to reassure? How many words had I mouthed?

". . . and son." I could still hear the slight drawl in his voice. Whoever the monster was, he hadn't always been a local.

Of course I knew that now for a fact. Back then, I knew simply because I knew. Cops had that privilege. Moms, too. Being a member of both groups, I must have known everything.

And yet, I received the telephone call out of the blue. My son and husband went through hell because I'd been taken by surprise.

"What do you want?"

The gull was back, darting at me and then racing away, his beady little eyes probing for food.

I had nothing to give him unless I wanted to peel back some layers of skin to offer up the tasty morsels inside. I'd originated worse ideas.

Such as meeting the kidnapper along this stretch of beach to make a trade.

Tired of the gull's company, I threw a fistful of sand in his general direction.

My son and husband stood six feet apart, shackled and gagged, their hands bound behind their backs. I didn't recognize the kidnapper standing behind them but the evidence he wanted me to bring told me enough.

How could he think I would comply?

The jogger had halved the distance between us and now the rhythm of his feet pounding the packed sand reached my ears.

Why is it that we're never haunted by our good decisions? We're not any more free to take them back. But then I suppose we're not rushing to do so.

"I have your husband and son."

"What do you want?"

I'll tell you what I want: I want not to have sprayed some stranger's blood all over my son.

And yet—bottom line—the alternative was worse.

The jogger was close enough for me to find him familiar, which always raised interesting questions.

Did I once give him a ticket for doing five miles an hour over the limit? Book him for being drunk and disorderly? Slam him against the side of the vehicle before kicking his legs apart in order to take some of the attitude out of his sails?

Or did we make pleasant conversation while holding plastic cups filled with apple cider at one of the meet-and-greets favored by Jason's pre-school?

Either way, would he recognize me?

Stop to chat?

Or, in this case, dig down to put on a sudden burst of speed?

I lowered my face into my knees, the cold fabric stiff and gritty from the wind coming off the water. Some people actually enjoyed going to the beach but I'd never been one of them.

Now I couldn't seem to stay away.

The jogger sent vibrations through me.

I hugged my knees tighter still. Buried my face in them.

"I have your husband and son."

"What do you want?"

And then, very distinctly, as my ears placed the jogger in front of me, "Run with me, Dana."

The footsteps passed and slowly receded.

Past. Once again, I'd resisted the urge that pulled at me with the grip of an undertow that carried strong swimmers out to sea.

Why did he have to jog along this stretch of beach when he had the whole of the Cape Cod shoreline to choose from?

A foolish question, I know.

I let go of my knees and lay back, staring up at the open sky.

How could sand be any worse for my hair than the salt and spray? In fact, the fragments of mica might add highlights if they could gather enough sunlight to sparkle.

I'd met the kidnapper on a day not unlike today. Not unlike now. Just before sunset, a sunset we east-coasters took on faith.

He picked the place. I picked the time.

Now.

Why did he think he could get away with grabbing my family? My son?

I don't care how badly he wanted that evidence.

Did he imagine I was just going to let him go?

Cops weren't so much forgive-and-forget as tail 'em, nail 'em, and jail 'em.

Assuming the kidnapper knew that, he never intended for me or my family to leave this beach alive. He should have given me more credit. I was good at my job.

My husband could never understand why I wanted to stay in law enforcement. Sure, I'd worn the badge when we met, but then I became a wife. A mother. When was I going to back-burner the whole cop thing and get on with my real life?

"I have your husband and son."

The kidnapper thought he could have everything.

He was wrong and I left him with nothing.

I closed my eyes.

Carried on the wind that moaned across the sand: "Run with me, Dana."

I jumped to my feet.

The jogger was no longer visible in the distance.

For that matter, there was no trace of him at all. No footprints in the sand. Nothing.

The jogger—"Run with me, Dana"—might never have existed.

Of course, if that was true, how could I have shot and killed him?

He bared his teeth. "Did you bring it?"

I nodded as I studied Jason (scared) and my husband (furious). He'd never forgive me for allowing my work to invade our home this way. I could see the accusation in his eyes: "Look what you've done to your son. This changes everything."

My husband thought no further than I'd placed my family in jeopardy. He didn't recognize that the gun I carried was our only hope for salvation.

"Lay your weapon on the sand." The kidnapper was thin and wiry, accustomed to being obeyed.

"No."

"What?" The kidnapper blinked twice and then laughed. He could afford to. He held all the cards and he always would, especially when dealing with a woman. "Have it your way. Did you come alone?"

"I did." There hadn't been time to request backup, to sweep the shoreline and determine if the kidnapper had posted accomplices. "Just you and me."

His smile bordered on a leer. "Maybe later, somewhere a little more private. But for now, where is it?"

"Where's what?"

"Don't play with me." He stepped forward, stopping just behind Jason, trying to intimidate me.

"You made a mistake. Or was it bad luck?"

"All part of my plan. You didn't know that, did you?" His grin hardened. "And now I'd like my property returned."

"Oops."

He frowned. "That's not funny."

"Let my family go."

"I don't see that happening. Not if you didn't bring anything to trade."

By moving so close to Jason, the kidnapper had made himself an easier target. He'd also hampered his ability to move quickly. I didn't have much else.

"You can turn and walk away. That's what I can trade."

The kidnapper pointed his gun at the nearest seagull and fired.

The bird exploded.

The gun swung toward my husband and then me.

Jason sobbed, clamped in place by one long arm.

"I don't think you understand. I want what's mine." The kidnapper spat. "I'm going to count to five. And then I'm going to kill somebody."

"That isn't going to change anything. The evidence will still be back in the station locker."

"Why didn't you bring it like I told you?"

"Because I'm going to nail you. I'm going to do everything within my power to ensure that you spend the rest of your life in prison."

"I don't think so. Did you forget your family here?"

"Kill us all. You won't stop the investigation. People like you? We don't rest until we close the case."

The kidnapper laughed. "You don't understand. We're the same, you and I."

"We are nothing alike." Bonding was how I usually convinced them to surrender, to turn themselves in, to confess their crimes. I couldn't do that with this guy, couldn't find a common ground.

The kidnapper gripped Jason tighter. "Believe what you want. You're not fooling me. When I point this gun at you, I'm aiming at myself."

"I don't think so." I drew my weapon. "Release the boy and lay your gun on the sand."

He grunted and then tensed before pulling the trigger.

My shot blew out his throat.

Blood sprayed.

Jason screamed through the gag.

My husband finally moving.

The sand soft and cool.

My father's palm, cupping my face.

The roar of the ocean.

My son, stretching his mouth.

Nightfall.

The screech of the gull brought me back and I turned to see the jogger coming this way again, effortlessly. Preparing to ask me to run with him.

How could he think I would comply?

I'd visited the crime scenes. Examined the bodies. Read the forensic reports. Interviewed the families of his victims. Tried my best to enter his mind and look through his eyes.

The press dubbed him "The Wolf" and I put him down.

Waves slapping the shore.

The endless expanse of the beach, the ocean disappearing into the horizon, the big sky: all were illusion.

We were trapped here, him and I. Confined within this space and time. Our only chance at escape a seagull no more free to leave than either of us.

His mouth, forming the words over and over, "Run with me, Dana."

My husband had been right that day. Everything did change.

And now nothing would, ever again.

Nuisance Call

Mo Walsh

Somewhere in Plumdale a serial killer could be planning his next strike. A master thief might be in the midst of a major heist. Surely some Boston drug lord had sent a minion or two to infiltrate their little town. And for dead certain the Markle sisters were working the aisles of the new MegaMed, slipping anything smaller than a bedpan into their voluminous purses.

So why, fumed Officer Beth Frobish, were she and her partner wasting their time on these nuisance calls? Didn't these people know there was real police work to be done?

It was just that comment, uttered in the hearing of her captain a week earlier, that earned Frobish and Lon DiAngelo a straight week of following up the kinds of calls that usually were handled by the desk officer or spread among the patrols on each shift.

"Officer, every call tells us something about what's going on in this community," the captain reproved her. "Names, patterns of activity, contacts with citizens, a chance to contain a minor situation before it blows up into something bigger. This should be an instructive week for you, Frobish."

Lesson for today, thought Beth: the infinite variety of objects that were never meant to be spray-painted purple. She and Lon had already pacified the owners of a lamp post, a basketball hoop, a whole block of mailboxes, a stockade fence, and a lawn deer. For

Plumdale—a town of modest homes in cozy neighborhoods where the work ethic didn't take the weekend off, but just moved outdoors—this Homecoming prank gone wild amounted to a major crime spree.

Beth aimed her best cop frown at the pair of sullen seniors slouched in folding chairs against the wall of the Plumdale High football coach's office. It was easy to see why the Purple Paint Perps had been riding the bench for three years. After this, she figured, they'd be lucky to sub for the last play in the fourth quarter of the last home game, and only then if it was a blow-out victory.

The one called Larry had actually posted a picture of himself astride the purple lawn deer on the Pep Club website. She'd bet there was a pair of jeans with a purple streaked crotch stuffed under his bed at home. The other one, Pete, had tucked his left foot back under his chair, as if they hadn't already noticed the mist of purple paint covering the toe of his sneaker.

"So whaddya got to say, guys?" Lon nodded toward the desk, where a purple spray can cap was displayed in his sandwich bag, as if it were evidence of capital murder. "Picked that up next to a big smiley face sprayed on a nice old gentleman's garage door. We gonna find your prints on that?"

"Coach said he would fix it with you guys about the paint and stuff." Pete scowled.

"Coach promised you guys would do the fixing. You're gonna paint like professionals by the time you're done." Lon tapped the corner of the baggie. "You gotta learn not to leave your materials lying around. That's sloppy work habits."

"That's evidence of trespassing," snapped Beth.

"But we're not interested in that—for now." Lon picked up the sandwich bag with deliberate care and swung open the office door. "You clean and paint everything you tagged or we'll be back. Now get to class."

Outside the high school, a crisp fall breeze tossed leaves and yesterday's returned test papers around the parking lot, and the sun glared off the windshields of the largest collection of used cars outside the Drive Buy lot.

"Maybe their moms will send them to bed without dessert tonight," grumbled Beth as she slipped behind the wheel of the cruiser and radioed their status to Dispatch. "Another blow struck for truth, justice, and the American way."

"You're the one ticked off the captain, got us stuck with this duty," Lon reminded her. "You want the Purple Paint Perps behind bars?"

"What I want is to get some real bad guys off the street. Is that such a crime?" she snapped. "What else have we got?"

"Kids skate-boarding outside the stores at Patriot Plaza, where some doofus put the new arcade next to a coffee shop. No fatal collisions so far, but a couple of near-misses. Known casualties: one Jumbo Java, a glazed cruller, and a Boston creme."

"Which, coincidentally, is my preferred end-of-shift pick-me-up. And it's your turn to buy."

"Deal. In the meantime, we've got plant pilfering from the cemetery—"

"The Green Bandit making off with granny's mums?"

"Filching funeral wreaths, would you believe? And the witness says the cheapskate drives an SUV."

"That makes it a felony, right?" Beth snorted. "Tell me there's something like a real crime on that list."

"This last one's a career-maker, maybe a movie of the week." Lon paused for dramatic effect. "A neighbor who rakes his leaves too loud."

"Hard time with no parole."

"Assaulting leaves with a deadly?"

"Not the raker." Beth rattled the handcuffs clipped to her belt.

"Let's get the loony with the sensitive hearing."

"That would be Mrs. Esther Goodbird, Nimrock Circle, two blocks over."

"And the industrious and unsuspecting neighbor would be—?"

"Lymon, Derek. Hey, I think my brother Mack went to high school with him."

"Mack the Truck?" Beth shook her head. "I'm not hassling any friend of his!"

"Actually, I think Mack broke the guy's nose for peeping in the girls' locker room. Blood everywhere, Lymon squealing like a little chauvinist piglet," Lon recalled with relish. "You woulda loved it."

"Obviously a born felon."

"Maybe he's turning over a new leaf?"

"Hah."

Lon whistled the *Dragnet* theme as Beth eased the cruiser away from the curb. "Let's go get the facts, ma'am."

□   □   □

The Purple Paint Perps seemed to have bypassed Nimrock Circle, though Beth spotted a cluster of grape-colored stepping stones and a number 1 painted on the sidewalk of the cross-street. The Goodbird and Lymon homes were tucked at the end of a small cul-de-sac framed by the town's oldest surviving grove of maple trees.

The foliage had passed its peak, but the stately maples still provided a red and gold screen between the neighborhood and the rear parking lot of Plumdale's old-fashioned strip mall. A dense seven-foot hedge separated the Lymon property from Mrs. Goodbird's and completely surrounded the back yard.

"Five bucks says the lady on the lawn casting nervous glances our way is Mrs. Goodbird," said Lon.

"Ten bucks says she tells us to forget the whole thing," answered Beth, "especially if Officer Hardnose here takes the report while you pat her hand."

"Anything to keep the cuffs off her."

Lon stepped out onto the curb and flashed his most benevolent smile at the elderly lady fluttering toward them across the lawn. "Good afternoon, ma'am. I'm Officer DiAngelo and this is Officer Frobish. We're looking for Mrs. Goodbird?"

"Oh, yes, I'm Esther Goodbird. Good afternoon," she said, bobbing and twittering like one of her avian namesakes. "How can I help you, officers?"

"You called the station about your neighbor, Mr. Lymon," Beth stated briskly. "We're investigating your complaint."

"I don't want any trouble!" Mrs. Goodbird darted an anxious look at the ragged hedge that separated her yard from her neighbors. "I believe in cordiality between neighbors. You can't like everybody, but you can be cordial, don't you think?"

"Yes, ma'am," agreed Lon, sounding like Sergeant Joe Friday's jollier brother.

"Why don't you like Derek Lymon?" demanded Beth.

"Oh! I didn't mean—it's just that we never really speak, since his Aunt Edith passed on—not so that I'd feel comfortable." Tears brimmed in Mrs. Goodbird's gray eyes and her voice was a tremulous whisper. "If you could just have a word about the noise, that awful raking sound . . . don't even mention my name."

"The man has a right to rake leaves. Ma'am," Beth added as Lon grimaced at her over Mrs. Goodbird's shoulder.

"If he could just do it some other time, when the sound wouldn't disturb me." The old lady shuddered. "Scrich-scrich, scrich-scrich! It's worse than chalk on a blackboard."

"With me it's squeaky sneakers." Lon nodded sympathetically.

"Then you don't think I'm being ridiculous?"

"Many people are sensitive to certain noises. Perhaps you could play music or wear ear plugs," Lon suggested.

"Get out of the house," Beth snapped. "Run some errands."

"Errands?" Mrs. Goodbird looked bewildered. "In the middle of the night?"

Beth was certain the surprise on Lon's face was mirrored on her own. "Your neighbor rakes leaves at night?" she asked.

"Why, yes, that's the problem, you see. My bedroom window faces his yard. I haven't had a good night's sleep in three days!"

The two officers turned toward the Lymon property. From the street, they could just see a narrow driveway on the other side of the dividing hedge, leading up to the solid door of an attached garage.

"How late is 'middle of the night,' ma'am?" asked Lon. "Midnight? Or is it more like nine o'clock?"

"You do think I'm being ridiculous!" Mrs. Goodbird bristled. "Well, let me tell you, Officer, last night that awful scriching sound woke me up at two o'clock in the morning. Two o'clock in the pitch dark and the man is raking leaves! I didn't sleep a wink the rest of the night."

"Maybe it was something else that woke you, ma'am," said Lon. "We had some kids pulling pranks around here last night."

"Well, I did have to get up in the night. I sometimes do, you know." The old lady blushed. "But no one could go back to sleep with that awful noise. I could see him from my window, wearing that funny light on his head and thrashing about with that rake. He doesn't even do the job properly, just moves the piles around—scrich-scrich, scrich-scrich, till I'm going crazy!"

"I suppose he could be sensitive to sunlight," said Beth. "Does he do other chores at night, do you know?"

"Oh, my, no!" trilled Mrs. Goodbird. "He begrudged every penny poor Edith paid her odd job men, but he never so much as picked a dandelion till she died. Oh, that sounded unkind!" Her eyes widened in distress. "It's just that Edith lived for her garden and he's let all her lovely flower beds go to weeds, but she truly thought the world of Derek!"

"But she never said anything about a sun allergy or anything like that?" prompted Beth.

"I believe she mentioned asthma. It kept him out of West Point, I remember she said that." Mrs. Goodbird beamed at Lon. "A perfectly healthy young man, she said, such a shame to turn down a perfectly healthy young man."

"So why is he raking leaves at night?" Beth scowled.

"Exactly!" The old lady smiled hopefully at the officers. "I saw him drive off a little while ago, but you will come back and talk to him? And not mention my name?"

"Yes, ma'am." Lon tucked his thumbs in his belt, aiming for classic John Wayne, Beth figured, but hitting Columbo, the early years, instead. "We'll just take a look around first."

The two officers followed the hedge to the back property line without finding a spot thin enough to yield more than a ground level view of the Lymon yard.

"West Point!" Lon snorted. "If this is the clod I'm thinking of, he couldn't give an order for a cheese pizza."

"So auntie made excuses for him." Beth started back toward the street. "Was he weird in high school?"

"Kind of a geek, as I remember—a dumb geek, if there is such a thing. He set fire to the chem lab once trying some kind of mad scientist experiment."

"What about after high school?" Beth crouched down to check the view at the base of the shrubs as the two officers worked their way back toward the street.

"Lymon's cousin runs a charter out of a marina near Marblehead. The kid did odd jobs for him in the summer. As far as I know, he just slid on into doing it full time. I had no idea he was back in town."

"We could check if he's got a sheet. Take a peek through Mrs. Goodbird's window."

"Guess it couldn't hurt." Lon shrugged. "But let's not try too hard to find a crime here."

"You heard the captain: 'names, patterns of activity, contacts with citizens,' not to mention containing a minor situation before it blows up. Something about this makes me twitchy."

"You think Mrs. Goodbird's gonna go after him with a garden hoe?"

"Hard to be cordial when you're short on sleep." Beth glanced at the elderly woman hovering by her front door. "Maybe she should sleep in another room tonight."

◻ ◻ ◻

"You know, we're gonna feel pretty stupid if the guy is making compost or harvesting night-crawlers."

"Stop chewing in my ear." Beth nudged aside the plate of homemade cookies Lon was holding out to her and peered through Mrs. Goodbird's bedroom window into Lymon's back yard. "If the guy's harmless, no harm done except you and me lose a night's sleep."

"As long as the captain doesn't find out."

"So take your snickerdoodles and go home."

"Can't." Lon leaned closer and whispered. "Mrs. G. is afraid of 'Officer Hardnose.' I promised I wouldn't leave her alone in the house with you. Besides," he dodged away from Beth's fist, "there's that dropped assault charge on Lymon's sheet. Better if we do the peeping."

"At least she gets a good night's sleep. I think she wants to adopt you." Beth had to admit Lon had done an excellent job handling Mrs. Goodbird.

"If we can hear the raking noise ourselves, ma'am, then we can talk to him without bringing in your name," he'd explained. Though initially flustered at the thought of police officers posted in her bedroom, she'd been willing enough to move down the hall for a night. She'd even baked them cookies.

Beth hefted her police issue Mag-lite from the piecrust table by the window. "Thanks for backing me up on this, partner."

"Yeah, well, I see the House of Hardware is hiring again, so why not?"

"You take the chair. I'll call you when it's showtime."

"We'll switch every hour." Lon settled into an antique side chair and set the silent alarm on the kind of watch that could reprogram satellites. "Help yourself to the snickerdoodles."

Beth turned back to the window and her view of Derek Lymon's property. Aunt Edith was some gardener, all right. Earlier, Beth had been able to make out a dozen flower beds bordered in brick and covered with leaves. Every other foot of space was occupied by concrete birdbaths and plaster fairies, a cobblestone wishing well, wrought iron benches and a shed decked out like a miniature windmill. Now shadows shifted across the yard as the half moon dodged in and out of the clouds.

By 1:00 A.M., there was still no sign of Lymon or the black Bronco registered in his name. Beth took her turn in the chair while Lon kept watch, and they switched again at 2:00 A.M. All remained dark and silent on the Lymon property, but soft sounds from the hallway and a faint light outside the bedroom sent Lon gliding to the door to investigate. He rejoined Beth at the window. "Mrs. G.'s in the bathroom. Any sign of Mr. Scrich?"

Beth shook her head, then rolled her shoulders to loosen the muscles. She shouldn't really have expected much. This was Plumdale, after all. Even the sound of the toilet flushing in this solid colonial house seemed somehow genteel. The soft pad of Mrs. Goodbird's footsteps stopped for a second as she switched off the hall light.

"Awmff!"

At the muffled shriek from the hallway and sounds of a struggle, the partners spun away from the window and reached the doorway already in covering position.

"Police!" Lon's flashlight picked out Derek Lymon at the far end of the hallway trying to wrestle a wriggling Mrs. Goodbird toward the head of the stairs.

"Let her go or I will shoot!" warned Beth, knowing she wouldn't dare risk a shot that had as good a chance of hitting the old woman as her target.

"Awmff!" shrieked Mrs. Goodbird as Lymon thrust her toward Lon and escaped down the stairs.

Beth hurtled down the stairs in pursuit. She heard Lon calling for backup, then his heavy footsteps bounding after her as she checked at the open front door. Lymon hadn't pulled a weapon in the house, but that was no guarantee he wasn't armed.

"Stop! This is the police!" she yelled, and swept the front yard with her flashlight.

"Give it up, Lymon!" shouted Lon, and a shadow shifted near the end of the hedge. "Got him. Cover me."

"Go."

As Lon exploded through the doorway, their quarry bolted from hiding and streaked around the end of the hedge. Beth caught up with Lon just as Lymon disappeared through the front door of his house.

"Locked!" Lon pounded on the door. "Open up, Lymon. This is the police!"

Over the sound of their heavy breathing and her own pounding heart, Beth thought she heard the sound of a stiff door opening at the back of the house.

Blue lights flashed and a cruiser swept into the cul-de-sac. "Cover the front!" Beth shouted to the backup team and jumped for the edge of the garage roof. "Lon, give me a boost!"

He tossed her up and shouted for one of the backup cops to do the same for him. Beth scuttled across the roof and dropped into the yard. Lon lay flat at the edge and swept the yard with his light. The powerful beam caught Lymon zig-zagging around the garden clutter, heading for the garden shed. He dodged away into the shadows.

"Keep the light on him!" Beth picked her way as fast as she could through the maze of plaster fairies and bordered flower beds. She detected movement near the wishing well, and Lon's light caught Lymon crouching in its shadow. He ducked and twisted away, but Beth countered his moves till he plunged wildly back toward the house.

Beth intercepted him from the side and tackled him around the knees. They hit the ground and rolled up against a stone birdbath. Lymon kicked free and scrambled away into the shadows. Beth sprang to her feet and started after him, following the sweep of the flashlight beam.

A harsh scream brought her up short, just as Lon yelled a warning. Beth dropped to the ground.

"Stay down, Beth!" Lon called, then another cop took control of the flashlight and her partner carefully crossed the yard to give her a hand up.

Ten feet away in the spotlight, the middle of a leaf-covered flower bed had disappeared. Five feet down, Derek Lymon lay curled at the edge of a tarp that had covered the pit. Leaves cloaked his head and shoulders, and under his feet a dirt-encrusted skull grinned up at them through a wreath of funeral flowers.

□ □ □

"I swear I will never so much as think the words *nuisance call* again." Beth looked up at the window where they'd kept their vigil two nights before.

"Just be grateful we can still think the word *pension*." Lon squared his shoulders as they started up the driveway.

"It would've been worth it, for Mrs. Goodbird's sake."

"That's the problem with cordiality between neighbors." Lon

shook his head. "You start collecting each other's mail, feeding the cat. You forget who's got a key. Nobody woulda suspected a thing if Mrs. G. was found on the stairs with her neck broke and the house all locked up."

"Must have been a shock for old Derek to see her bathroom light go on and him standing out there with a light on his head clearing out an old grave." And a bigger shock, Beth figured, to find cops in the house the next night when he came to get rid of a possible witness.

The search warrants had cleared yesterday, and the crime scene team was turning up one surprise after another on the Lymon property. The police officers' presence may have been unofficial, but it wasn't illegal, the judge determined, and their subsequent actions were justified by Lymon's assault on Mrs. Goodbird. It was a huge relief when the captain stopped calling her Miss Frobish, and she and Lon were ordered to meet the detectives at the crime scene.

"Some cops we are," Beth snorted as, by unspoken agreement, they stopped short of the back-yard hedge. "I can't believe we walked that thing and never saw the pot planted all along the other side."

"When you think about it, this scraggly hedge is great camouflage," said Lon. "And who woulda figured Aunt Edith as the Cannabis Queen of Plumdale? With her loving nephew raking in his share of the profits, of course."

"Ha." Beth tried to peer through the thick shrubbery and shook her head. "It took the crime scene guys long enough to spot it. Hard to focus on anything besides that skeleton in the grave." She was still seeing that picture every time she closed her eyes.

They entered the house through the garage and logged in with the cop at the back door. Beth looked around the yard, stunned by the number of scattered markers.

"Those can't all be the odd job men," she said past the

lump in her throat.

"Aunt Edith's favorite fertilizer, if you believe Derek," said Lon. "Claims she got them to dig their own graves, the first few feet anyway, turning the soil for new flower beds. Then mixed a little oleander or some deadly nightshade in their personal stash. Neat way to dispose of seasonal help you can't trust to keep their mouths shut."

"And Derek never knew a thing till she confessed on her death bed? Right. And he was just digging up graves to say a prayer and toss in a few flowers." Beth shivered at the thought of Lymon's macabre sense of humor. "Well, Aunt Edith didn't plant the fresh corpses in those two old graves or those drug caches in the others, and she didn't dig that tunnel from the garden shed to the mall parking lot either."

The pieces were still coming together, but already Plumdale PD was buzzing about what looked to be serial murder and a multimillion-dollar narcotics operation. The feds were sending one team to look at the drug-refining set-up in the basement lab and another to check out the "charter boats" run by Lymon's cousin. Prints on the two fresh bodies unearthed so far matched a couple of DEA snitches who'd dropped out of sight.

"And they say the family-run business is dying off." Lon snapped a salute in the direction of the house next door. "Mrs. G. better get a reward and a medal for this. Do you think she'll sleep tonight?"

"I hope so." Beth turned away as the crime scene techs sifted through the leaves covering another burial site in Derek Lymon's back yard. "I know I won't."

Dog Sees God in the Mirror
A Jack Russell Mystery

Kevin Carey

It's a dog's life. At least it was until I came here to Provincetown, where a guy can be anything he wants to be. Here, a guy can be a dame or a dame can be flame or a he-she strutting can-can girl and a dog can be something more than somebody's pet paper chaser. I gave up the leash-and-bone trick and the braided rug by the fireplace for a chance to be myself, a sports-page reading, cigarette-smoking, blues-loving snoop dog trapped inside the body of a Jack Russell terrier.

Sure I may still squirt on a fire hydrant now and then, but I'm not the only one pissing in public on a Friday night in July after the bars close.

What I liked best about P-town was that people didn't even turn their heads when I walked in and hopped up on a stool, set my deck of butts on the bar and yelled, "Three fingers of Bourbon, Bubba." I made friends fast, here in the land of the tolerably different, here where a guy can be . . . whatever. Truth is, some cats like to talk, and this dog is one of those cats, dig. I can bark with the best of the boys in the bar, talking sports, I'm an ESPN encyclopedia, I'm a walking talking book of facts, try me.

You'd think it would be tough for a pure-bred hound to get work, attitudes on animals in general being what they are, but not in a place like this. I wormed my way into the P-town sports scene—a few columns a week in the local rag, the softball league, the road races, a beach volleyball report. One team sponsored by Howard's End had me playing second base on account of my range, three errorless seasons, thank you very much. Word around the league was, don't hit the ball up the two hole, or the three hole, hell I even chased 'em down into the outfield.

The fact that I'm a dog still follows me like my tail though. That's why you might see me wagging it at someone with a camera around their neck scratching my chin, "a Jack Russell, isn't he cute?" and you might think I'd meet this kind of comment with disdain, seeing how by now you've figured out that cute isn't something I'm after. But I don't. I play both sides of the street. I have my reasons. All you need to know is this: I may look like a dog, but don't make the mistake of thinking I'm only a dog. When I'm trotting my way up the sidewalk, letting people pat me and throw me snacks (most of which I deposit in a trash can, as you would, I'm sure. I mean, why pressed cornmeal when my friend Sal will burn me up a tenderloin on request? I wrote the menu boards for his eatery), don't think I'm not on top of it, whatever it is.

I hang at Grendel's, an armrest on the commercial street strip. I'm part of the local flavor. You might say I am the local flavor here.

"Hey dog, sing a song." Why not? It's not like karaoke is a dirty word. Some nights it's Sinatra, or my own crooner version of a Beatles song, but what really gets them wild is when I sing the blues, when I get my teeth into a Billy Holiday tune or something courtesy of Paul Butterfield or Howling Wolf. It's easy for me to sing the blues—I'm a four-legged beast named Jack Russell. I got the blues in my soul.

I didn't set out to be in the investigative biz; it just came to me, the way the P-town tide rolls to the dunes, naturally and repeatedly. People were always asking me stuff. "Hey, Jack, do you know this and where is that and you ever heard of him?" That, combined with being generally nosey and always eavesdropping and poking my snout into other folks' business anyhow, got me thinking it was only natural to be a sleuth. Instead of writing bad sports copy and hanging in the gin mills spouting off four nights a week, I figured why not put this calling to work, why not get on with it and take home a dollar or two?

So the legend grows. Jack Russell, private eye. "I can find what's lost at half the cost." I even embossed it on a business card with that stereotypical snoop dog likeness of Sherlock Holmes—you know the one with the dog looking into a magnifying glass wearing some kind of tweed getup and a hat with two lids.

Much to my surprise, however, business was not booming. Seems I was better at selling fun facts to the other booze hounds than I was at selling myself. Ain't it just like a dog to have a good idea that doesn't pan out, like chasing a car or sniffing the wrong butt. I was sitting in Grendel's having second thoughts and third thoughts and fourth thoughts alongside each accompanying Bourbon shooter when a date with destiny parked it on the stool beside me, a tall blonde drink of water who called herself Nikki, but I knew to be Nick, the local letter carrier dressed in drag. Nice drag, too, a long red number with side slits and a push-up bra.

"What's up, Nick?" I asked

"Nikki."

"Right, Nikki, sorry."

"I've lost somebody," she said, holding out a card of mine. "Can you help me?"

"Can I? Of course I can. You've come to the right dog."

Nikki's cousin Sid was vacationing in Provincetown and had been sharing space with her, him, since the day of the Fourth of July parade. He had some dough and apparently spent it on Nick now and then, which made for a comfortable summer. Come last week, first week of September, they had a little falling-out and he took a room downtown and did his best to avoid Nick.

"We'd see each other on the street and he'd cross over and walk fast away from me." He looked down into his brandy snifter, swirled the Hennessy up around the rim. "And I'm not a fast walker by any means."

I knew this to be true. Nick had the last seat on our bench two seasons ago. He was content to just watch over the water cooler and keep the bats neat and lined up in the dugout, but one game we needed him to pinch hit. He hit a slow roller by the second baseman and proceeded to get thrown out at first by the right fielder. He was slower than frozen molasses.

"What was the fight about? The one that made him leave."

"I asked him to buy me a new rug."

"Braided?"

"No. Oriental"

"Ouch."

"Machine made would have been fine."

"So he took a rug burn."

"Kind of. Told me to never ever look him in the eye again."

I called for more brain juice, "Bourbon," then said, "Excuse me, Nikki, for not sounding so deep-hearted but where in the name of drag racing is this going?"

Then she lay full tilt into the drama—two more weeks of seeing this cousin by proxy, asking friends about his whereabouts, and doing a little snooping of her own, keeping tabs on where he was keeping tabs, running all the tricks of the trade, a real snoop job. I asked her, "So you were following him?"

"Not really, just making sure he was okay."

"Any idea where he is now?"

"No, and I'm worried."

"Why?"

"Why? He's my cousin."

"What's the last you heard?"

"I heard he was planning a barbecue, some pals down the surf, a twilight thing. They set up the grill and all, but he never showed. So they called me, looking."

"How long now?"

"A few days."

"Not exactly a lifetime, but it is strange to miss your own barbecue."

"Straight up, brother."

"Got a list of names?"

She scribbled onto a damp bar napkin. Stopped to ponder three or four times, then let me have it.

"Can you read my writing?"

Sure I could read it and I didn't like what I saw.

The first name on the list was a guy named Brain Peachio, a New York real estate developer come to P-town three summers ago in search of beach-front property and a little New England tail, fortunately not mine. He managed to find a home, which he bought and immediately redid in glorious gaudy fashion, which leads me to a pet peeve of mine: why is it people with a lot of dough find a need to remake everything as if they conquered the territory? I digress. Peachio, or rotten Peach, as many of the locals called him in not-so-hushed whispers, tried his best to make the scene, to blend in, and after a while folks got used to him waltzing into the bar in bright pink sweaters and a scarlet ascot. Not really Mister Popularity.

The rest of the list were locals, people you'd expect at the party: Pablo the piano mover, Abbey, everyone's favorite bartender, Little Joe, Barney, Kate and Rita (they always came as a pair), and Donovan (his father actually named him that because he fell so in love with the "Atlantis" song. You remember, "way down below the ocean . . ." Well P-town in some ways is way down below the ocean and in some ways it is Atlantis).

As much as I hated to do it, I had to start with Peachio.

"Greetings and Salutations," he said, a smart white-wool sweater wrapped around his generous belly. The living room behind him looked like the love den, hooked up with every conceivable lover's stereotype—a big bear rug, black leather couches, a candelabra, and a mammoth fireplace. This was where he got to his business.

"I'd ask you take your shoes off," he said, "but . . ." He laughed at his own observation.

I wiped all fours and scurried onto the corner of the black leather loveseat.

"Sid invited you to a party?" I asked.

"Yes and he's lucky I went. A guy with my social calendar can't usually make it on two days' notice."

"Bullshit," I coughed.

"Bless you," he said.

"Any idea why he never showed?"

"Beats me," he said, picking something between his teeth and making a sucking sound. That, combined with the large moose head I'd seen hanging in a nearby study on the way in, made me want to beat him. I felt an uncontrollable urge to bare my teeth.

"It's odd to throw a bash and not show, don't you think?" I asked.

"I suppose," he said. "I get so many invites these days. It's hard to keep track."

"Right," I said.

When I left I tripped down the cobblestone walkway feeling like a snoop feels, often disgusted having to talk to people you don't like, never satisfied with ninety percent of the answers you get, and never sure you're going to get any closer toward figuring out what it is you need to know.

Peachio may be an asshole, I considered, but I don't think he even cared if Sid was on the face of the earth, never mind still in P-town.

The next name on the list was Pablo Singer. Pablo was the strongest man I knew. The strongest man anyone I knew knew. The "go to" guy of strong men. Just under six feet tall, he weighed about 280 pounds, all shoulders and stomach. He was a white guy, a real pale white guy, almost albino. He was bald with a long scar across his forehead where a hook from an ocean trawler caught him as a kid and dragged him three knots before he managed to snap the line with his teeth.

But Pablo was a gentle soul, soft spoken and introverted, a contrast to the stories that surrounded his strength. The first time I heard about him I was nursing a brandy on a stool at Grendel's and his name came up in a conversation between two Cape Cod home boys.

"Pablo shows up alone to a three-family walkup, a saloon upright to move," the first guy says.

"He moved it down three flights himself?"

"No," the first man says. "This was a delivery. Three flights up."

Pablo lived on Pilgrim's Point in the basement of a two-family. He lived by himself, except for his cat of fifteen years named Martha. He answered the door in an Italian undershirt, his fifty-five-year-old pumps showing off his two tattoos, one a red canary, the other a two-fingered peace sign.

"Jack," he said, "Que passo?"

"Nada, P, you?"

"Same old. Coffee?"

Pablo had the best coffee on the beach, mild roasted macadamia. Ground his own beans.

"Black," I said.

We sat on a puckered green couch, our thick white mugs steaming from the glass-covered lobster-trap table.

"I got the invite all right," he said, "a couple of days before the bash. Even went for a couple dogs, dragged through the yard with sauerkraut. Kosher Kayems if I remember right." Pablo knew his dogs.

"But he never showed," he continued. "At least not while I was there. Nikki manned the grill."

"Nikki's worried," I said. "His cousin throws a bash, never shows, and goes missing."

"Nikki's always worried," Pablo said.

"Yeah, but this time it's more than the hem line."

"Let's see the list," Pablo said. His forehead furrowed and he squinted a little in the low light.

"I never saw Barney when I was there. Come to think of it, I haven't seen him since."

Pablo wasn't the only one who hadn't seen Barney. Barney was as absent from P-town as the Republican party. I asked around most of the afternoon and couldn't find anyone who had recalled seeing him since before the barbecue bash, including Rita and Katie.

They lived in the small beach house on the end of the strip, red shingles and a sidewalk porch. They cooked every afternoon, lunched like Europeans. I picked the right time to stop by and quiz them on the missing Barney. It was shrimp over linguine and I said yes to a second plate.

I was sucking a long piece of spaghetti when Katie started laughing. "Jesus, Jack, you look like the dog in the Disney movie, *Lady and the Tramp*." I stopped in mid suck, let the remaining pasta hang from my frown.

"But you and Disney don't belong in the same sentence," Rita said, pouring extra garlic and shrimp into a bowl on the table.

"No," said Katie, "there's nothing cartoon about you."

I sucked the rest of the spaghetti in with a loud snap. "So you were saying—Barney?"

"Yes," Katie said, wide-eyed, "he's freaky, Jack, he snaps unconsciously."

"It's true," Rita said, " I saw him kicking a volleyball down the beach a half-mile once. He just kept kicking it and walking after it, kicking it again, until he was almost out of sight."

"Was it a bad call?" I asked

"I think so," Rita said. "A back line out."

A cup of mint tea and a piece of squash pie later and I was starting to think it was more than a coincidence that Barney and Nikki's cousin went AWOL at the same time. The girls were as suspicious as I was, but if there's one thing about life that I knew, it's that nothing is ever quite what it seems. I wasn't ready to tie a knot around this package, not yet.

I walked back along the beach, had a smoke, and stopped to pee on the No Dogs sign" in the public parking lot. I was back at Grendel's by nightfall, trying to sort a day's worth of information into something I could sink my teeth into.

Abbey was telling a joke to a crowd of eager tourists when I walked in. He held his hand up as if he were waving to someone, "so the Bear says, 'I'm looking for the man who shot my paw.' "

I snuck past the guffaws and the polo shirts and the beach hats and sat at a table in the back where I could still see the Red Sox's game but from a comfortable bleacher seat. I couldn't deal with any tourists today.

After a few minutes Abbey wandered over with an Old Fashioned neat, set it on a white napkin and smiled.

"You need new jokes," I said.

"Why," he said, "the old ones are still working. Besides, what do you know about bear jokes, you're a dog."

"Funny," I said.

Ortiz went deep off the monster for a stand-up double, then the bums stranded him with two consecutive pop-ups. That's how I felt, stuck on base with useless information and no one around to help me home, no real leads to the missing cousin. I was swinging at air, I was entertaining a whole litany of baseball clichés, then in a heart-beat, it all changed.

Nikki came running in from the sidewalk, in leather hip boots and a plaid mini. "They found him," she said, "he's dead."

Nikki had piled a small mountain of crumpled napkins in front of her, sobbing out blobs of incoherent information and the occa-sional relevant factoid. I got that her cousin was found under the pier on front beach (not far from the barbecue sight) by two kids who were drop-lining for crabs. Seems a line got snagged on his belt buckle, a Johnny Cash silver dollar from a trip to Nashville three summers ago.

She said the cop told her he'd been there a few days, which would make for not a pretty sight, which is "why," she explained, "I need you to come with me."

The cops had put him in a zip-up body bag and set him on a table in the back room of the station. A young cop donned a mask before unzipping for us. Like I figured, not a pretty sight. Nikki's cousin looked like the back of your hand looks after sitting in the tub for three hours—white and wrinkled and like hardened petroleum jelly.

"That's him," Nikki said. "It looks like closed casket city." She picked me up and hugged me. Not something I let happen very often, and not something I wanted to happen at this moment, but things being what they were, I sighed and got hugged, and Nikki wept a bucket of tears on my pretty white coat.

Later, I spoke with Frank Cadre, the handy man who lives with the girl who works at the coroner's office. He owed me for a four-line jingle I'd written for the business.

> *Anything busted*
> *big or small*
> *I work all night*

I fix it all.

He revealed what little he knew, that the cousin had whacked his head, probably on the rocks below, and drowned from being unconscious. There was also a fair amount of booze left in his sea-soaked body. They had not totally ruled out that he was pushed from the pier to his salty grave or whacked on the head with a rock and tossed over the side, but it seemed more likely to those involved that he simply fell on his own from being drunk.

Barney turned up the next day and got dragged into the precinct and had to answer a bunch of wheres and whens. Turns out he was visiting some friends in Ohio, had the plane tickets and the alibis to prove it, so even though he was a temperamental volleyball sore loser, he wasn't likely to be someone who would leave the cousin for dead under the pier.

The remaining names on the list shed no new light either; most of them didn't even know Nikki had a cousin. It was looking more and more as if no one in P-town had a reason for wanting him dead and there seemed to be nothing on the horizon that might alter that opinion. That was until it hit me right between the eyes, like chasing a rear fender and having it stop short. It hit me the way most things hit me, after one more drink.

I was nursing a nightcap at Grendel's, at the behest of Abbey, who had glasses to wash and needed someone to chat with until he was done, when Nikki knocked on the door.

I sat with her and listened to another round of sob stories, all somehow related to the death of her cousin if you had the experience to decipher what she was saying. When she got blabbering it was hard to tell. Abbey took his time with the cleanup and let us have another round, which I insisted was my last. Nikki cried some, laughed a little at some old childhood memories of her cousin riding his bike into the lake at their grandmother's summer cottage in Concord. We even finished a plate of leftover jalapeno poppers when Abbey was ready to kick us out.

"Let me put a bottle on my slip, will you, Ab?" she asked.

He slid over a house bottle of vodka and Nikki signed the slip, making a big looping *N* before the rest of her name.

I stared at the slip before she pushed it back. She cradled the bottle under her arm and walked out the door.

That *N*. I'd seen it before.

"What's eating you?" Abbey said, holding the door open for me before he locked up.

"I should have been a cat," I said. "At least curious would be cute."

At home I pulled out the list she'd written from the party. Nothing there. But later I woke from a sound sleep and realized where I'd seen it. The invitations to the beach party. "N"ice day for a barbecue, it had said, the same pompous swirling N. The cousin hadn't written those invitations, Nikki had, and I'd bet an acre of puppy chow she'd written them after he was dead.

Nick was on his route the next morning, not exactly whistling, but a little more pleased with the sunny morning ocean breeze than a grieving cousin had a right to be. I sat on the corner a few houses away and waited for him to finish the few boxes he had left on the street. If I had timed it right, his bag would be close to empty. One thing I didn't want to do was interrupt the delivery of the mail. Some things are sacred.

He saw me after he closed the last box. "Jack," he said. "Que passa?"

"Nada, Nikki. Got a minute?"

We sat on the curb. Nikki in dress blues, a little unshaven for his usual meticulous self.

"Want to tell me what really happened?" I asked.

"What do you mean?"

"You wrote those invites, Nick. You wrote them after he was

dead, hand-delivered them." I held up an envelope. "No postmark."

His face dropped and he looked to the ground. "Just a few that were unfinished."

"Shame on you," I said. "All mail goes through the P.O. You know that."

"He had a thing for me, Jack. He told me it didn't matter. 'It's not like we're going to have children,' he said."

"Really? He said that?"

"And just that way."

"Freaky."

"I'll say. And you know me, Jack, I'm no straight line, but kissing cousins. No thanks."

"What happened?"

"He moved out, got drunk all the time, started following me."

"You ended up on the pier arguing?"

"Yes. But I left him there yelling after me. 'I'm going to jump,' he was saying. But I kept walking. The next day I went to his apartment, saw all these invites on the table. There were a few envelopes that needed to be filled. You know me, Jack, I'm efficient. When I saw the date I thought I was doing him a favor. I wrote the few that were missing, scooped them up and delivered them myself. I still didn't know he had actually jumped."

I listened to his teary tale and another thing hit me. Nick might be many things, but a guy who could kill his cousin for coming on too strong was not one of them.

"If I'm guilty of anything," he said, his eyes glazed over, "it's of not using proper postage."

Bernie Nat set up the karaoke machine in the right-rear corner of Grendel's low-light back room, the portable disco ball reflecting off his long silver hair. Folks were already filing in, couples and groups of four or better, pushing tables together and staking out space. Once a week Grendel's became the P-town equivalent of

American Idol.

I was at the bar nursing a brandy when Nikki walked over. She was wearing a smart blue pantsuit, white shirt, and blue tie. Her hair was cut short and dyed bleach blonde.

"Annie Lennox is in the house," I said.

She threw down a roll of stamps. "It's all I have for now, Jack. I'll catch up," she said. "For all that leg work, you know."

That's what I do. Leg work. I'm a dog, right? If I'm not walking, I'm sleeping or scratching fleas.

Nikki brushed my coat with her hand and kissed the top of my head. "Thanks," she said, and walked away, her black heels clicking out the door.

I looked down at the roll of stamps. They were thirty-sevens. "Ain't it just like a letter carrier," I said to myself, a tad bit louder than a whisper, "bringing me yesterday's mail."

"Hey, Jack," Bernie yelled from under the disco-balled lights, "want to start us off?"

"Why not?" I hopped off the stool and did a slow trot to the stage. A few people clapped, someone yelled, "Go dog," as Bernie lowered the mike for me.

"What will it be, Maestro?" he asked me.

"Make it Sinatra," I told him. "I'm feeling velvety."

Contributors' Notes

Mark Ammons is a Medford, MA, based former stage director, producer, and sometime screenwriter/script doctor. He is currently trolling for a publisher for his comic self-help book "Secrets of the Smart Baboon: Workplace Survival Strategies for Alleged Higher Primates" (with co-author J. R. Rivera) while he completes his first full-length mystery, which one early reader describes as an "existential-slapstick tough-guy novel." "The Catch" is his first short story.

Glenda Baker is a lifelong New Englander living in Hudson, MA. She's a graduate of the Famous Writers School, Clark University, and the 2001 Maui Writer's Retreat, and has won awards for her poetry, personal essays, and non-criminous short fiction. A member of SinC NE and the International Women's Writing Guild, Glenda has been owner/editor-in-chief of *NEWN* magazine since 1994.

Kevin Carey teaches Writing and Literature at Salem State College and coaches seventh-grade basketball at the Glen Urquhart School. Recent work appears in *The Literary Review, The Paterson Literary Review, Tiferet: Journal of Spiritual Literature,* and *The White Pelican Review,* where his poem, "Shredding Me," was nominated for a Pushcart Prize.

Louy Castonguay holds a BS in Community Nutrition and a BFA in Creative Writing. She's been published in *Timber Creek Review,* had Honorable Mention in *Writer's Digest,* and is currently looking for an agent to help place her novels and a short story collection. Currently, she does volunteer driving for MaineCare patients and DHHS clients besides writing and reading voraciously.

S. A. Daynard has crossed paths with a serial killer/rapist, testified before grand juries, and taken lie-detector tests. She's been offered the services of professional hit men, been scrutinized in county retirement fund corruption and bank fraud scandals, and been labeled "a person of interest" in a major illegal drug find. In her spare time, she writes mysteries.

Kate Flora is the author of ten books. Thea Kozak returns in *Stalking Death* (Crum Creek Press, 2007). *Finding Amy: A True Story of Murder in Maine*, co-written with a career police officer, was a 2007 Edgar nominee. *Playing God*, a gritty police procedural appeared in 2006. Flora's stories have appeared in the Level Best anthologies, *Sisters on the Case*, edited by Sara Paretsky, and *Per Se*, an anthology of fiction. Flora teaches writing for Grub Street in Boston. She is an MFA candidate at Vermont College.

Judith Green is a sixth-generation resident of a village in Maine's western mountains, with the fifth, seventh, and eighth generations living nearby, where she was director of adult education for her eleven-town school district. She has twenty-five high-interest/low-level books for adult new readers in print, and is currently working on a novel starring her Maine high-school English teacher and sleuth.

Woody Hanstein has been a trial lawyer for over twenty-five years. He also teaches at the University of Maine at Farmington and coaches that college's rugby team. He is the author of four mysteries: *Not Proven, Cold Snap, State's Witness,* and *Mistrial.* His fifth mystery is *Sucker's Bet* (December 2007).

Rosemary Harris is a former bookstore manager, video producer, and media executive. "Growing Up Is for Losers" introduces

Wanda, a colorful secondary character from Rosemary's debut novel, *Pushing Up Daisies* (St. Martin's, 2008), the first in a new series featuring amateur sleuth/master gardener Paula Holliday. www.rosemaryharris.com

Janice Law's recent books are *The Night Bus, The Lost Diaries of Iris Weed,* and *Voices*, novels with strong mystery elements from Forge. She has also published a mystery series featuring Anna Peters, including the Edgar nominated *The Big Payoff*. Her short stories have appeared in *Ellery Queen* and *Alfred Hitchcock* mystery magazines. She teaches part time at the University of Connecticut, and paints for pleasure.

Stephen Liskow left teaching English to return to writing, and "Running on Empty" is his first published story. He is also working on a PI series and has a novel currently seeking a home. In his spare time, he leads a playwriting workshop and has acted in, directed, or designed for over ninety productions throughout central Connecticut.

Ruth M. McCarty is an editor and partner in Level Best Books. Her short mysteries have appeared in *Undertow, Riptide, Windchill,* and *Seasmoke*. Ruth has received honorable mentions in *Alfred Hitchcock Mystery Magazine* and *NEWN* for her flash fiction. wwww.ruthmccarty.com

Susan Oleksiw is the author of the Mellingham series featuring Chief of Police Joe Silva; the fifth and most recent entry in the series is *A Murderous Innocence* (2006). Stories featuring Hindu-American sleuth Anita Ray have appeared in a number of anthologies and *Alfred Hitchcock Mystery Magazine*. She has published non-criminous stories and her *Reader's Guide to the Classic British*

Mystery is well known and, well, a classic. www.susanoleksiw.com

Ang (Angelo) Pompano retired in 2006 after thirty-five years of teaching. Ang has written many academic pieces for the Yale-New Haven Teacher's Institute, including one on teaching detective fiction. He is a recent contributor to the New England Sisters in Crime newsletter, and his recently completed novel "Killer View," featuring Quincy Lazzaro, won the 2006 Helen McCloy/Mystery Writers of America Scholarship.

Margaret Press publishes mystery fiction and true crime. Her essay "Salem as Crime Scene" appeared in the award-winning anthology *Salem: Place, Myth and Memory.* "Feral" (*Windchill*) launched a collection of concurrent stories viewing one murder from different points of view. "Wednesday's Child" is the second in that collection. Press and her feral cat can be reached at www.margaretpress.com and www.whokilledscottrogo.com.

Pat Remick has co-authored two professional development books, including *21 Things Every Future Engineer Should Know* (Kaplan, 2006). She has written for UPI, CNN, and Discovery.com, and various newspapers. Pat is a member of the Mystery Writers of America and Sisters in Crime. She lives in Portsmouth, NH, with her husband, Frank Cook, and their two sons. "Mercy 101" is the first short story Pat ever entered in a contest.

Stephen D. Rogers has published over five hundred stories and poems in more than a hundred publications. His website, www.stephendrogers.com, includes a list of new and upcoming titles as well as other timely information.

Leslie Schultz has been a financial journalist and copywriter for more years than she cares to reveal. She is also the host of WMFO's "Words & Music," a weekly community radio program that features the work of Boston-area writers. She just completed her first novel, and is now merrily collecting rejection slips.

James T. Shannon, after retiring from teaching high-school English, has had three stories published in *Alfred Hitchcock*. He won the 2006 Al Blanchard short story contest. His current story, inspired by too many formative years misspent watching westerns, is dedicated to movie cowboy Gene Autry, a gifted rider, fighter, and marksman, and to Jim's wife, Kathy, who, fortunately, has other gifts.

Maureen "Mo" Walsh is a National Novel Writing Month "winner" with three 50,000-word manuscripts of "impressively adequate fiction" to show for it. She is editing a fourth novel (not a winner, since she finished it on December 1st) to submit to agents. Mo's stories have appeared in *Family Circle-Mary Higgins Clark Mystery Magazine, Woman's World, Windchill* and *Gator Springs Gazette*. The former advertising copywriter and news writer lives in Weymouth, MA, with her husband, Kevin, and three teenage sons.

Leslie Wheeler writes the Miranda Lewis "living history" mystery series. This is her third story to appear in a Level Best Books anthology; previous stories appeared in *Windchill* and *Seasmoke*. Leslie currently serves as the Speakers' Bureau Coordinator for Sisters in Crime, New England. www.lesliewheeler..com

Mike Wiecek lives outside Boston, at home with the kids. He has traveled widely in Asia and worked many different jobs, mostly in finance. His stories have won a Shamus and two Derringers; he was a finalist for the PWA's Best First PI Novel. *Exit Strategy*

(Penguin/Berkley, 2005) was short-listed for the ITW Thriller Award. www.mwiecek.com.

Leslie Woods attended the NYU School of Journalism, published nonfiction for years, then studied fiction in workshops and classes, notably with Steve Almond. Over the past few years, she has published fiction in several journals, including *The Macguffin* and in the Level Best anthology *Windchill*. After years of farming in Maine, she works harder at writing.

Still Waters
Crime Stories by New England Writers

edited by
Kate Flora, Ruth McCarty
& Susan Oleksiw

Please send me _____ copies @ $15 per copy _____

postage & handling ($2 per book) _____

Total $_____

_____ check (payable to Level Best Books)

_____ credit card

Name on card _____

Card No. _____

Expiration date _____

Send book(s) to:

Name _____

Address _____

City/Town _____